MAVERICK Key

HEARTS ON THE LINE

MAVERICK *Key*

MARGOT KEENE

Published by Gulf Stream Fiction, an imprint of
Margot Keene Publishing LLC

Edited by Jennifer Herrington
Cover Design and Book Formatting by Ashley Santoro

eBook ISBN: 978-1-967133-00-0
Paperback ISBN: 978-1-967133-01-7
Hardback ISBN: 978-1-967133-02-4

Library of Congress Control Number: 2025912800

For permissions, inquiries, or more information:
contact@margotkeene.com

Printed and bound in the United States of America

AUTHOR'S NOTE

Maverick Key and Carter's Drop are fictional locations at the heart of the *Maverick Key Series*. Nestled off South Florida's Gulf Coast, these settings serve as vibrant and immersive backdrops, blending some of the best of Florida's coastal beauty, charm, and mystery.

While the diving sequences are based on the author's research of actual practices, aspects have been fictionalized for storytelling.

To all the men and women who explore our earth, ocean, and beyond—you have my deepest admiration.

DEDICATION

To my cow without a tail,
and to every small story that begins with a dream
and ends in a reader's heart.

PROLOGUE

DR. NATHAN CARTER

The Atlantic's dark tide laps against the dive platform with a pulse too calm to be trusted. Although the waters surrounding Maverick Key appear harmless and inviting, I know better.

Twenty feet below the surface lies an underwater cave system—a blue hole. I discovered it seven months ago, igniting a surge of interest from academic communities eager to capitalize on its potential for significant scientific contribution. It could take years to secure university funding to map and study the caves, but private investors have wasted no time jumping in to fill the financial gaps. I accepted one of their offers, stepping into the role of lead marine archaeologist.

Against the boat railing, I take a deep breath, savoring the fresh scents of ozone mixed with brine and aquatic life, allowing my thoughts to wander. Our research team has mapped the main cavern, but deeper penetration into the caves remains unexplored. I've started those treks on my own, and today, I'll venture further than what is safe.

The weight of this decision settles deep in my chest. I've broken the rules before, sure, but this? A solo dive into unmapped overhead cave passages defies every safety protocol. Always dive with a partner. Always take a support team. The rules exist for good reason. But some people aligned with this project have an agenda, and they're starting to ask the wrong questions. My trust has been misplaced, and if I don't keep my progress secret, I may lose control of the discovery altogether.

So here I am. Alone.

Maddie's voice echoes in my thoughts—sharp with frustration after I'd told her I was planning to dive solo. It was a mistake to do so since I couldn't explain all the reasons why.

"Nathan, why are you pushing boundaries? It's reckless. One day, you might go too far. You're smarter than that."

"You're right. I'm sorry for bringing you into this."

"Mom and I need you. Whatever's driving you to do this just isn't worth it. Please don't do it." She struggled with her words, her voice shaky, a sure sign she was holding back her tears. Once they started, she couldn't stop them. Each of her whimpers was a dagger to my heart.

"Sssh. It's okay. Please don't worry. I promise I'll be careful, and I'll find another way." I tried to walk it back—to ease some of the anxiety I'd caused.

"Promise?"

"Yes. I promise."

Her sobs subsided into a soft, wet sniffle. "Thank you. We love you."

"You and Mom are everything to me. Get some sleep."

I imagine her face—eyes focused, mouth set with determination, gripping the phone in her hand. I lied to her on our call, and the guilt is eating me alive. She's sacrificed too much already—finishing medical school and caring for Mom as early-onset dementia claims more of the woman who raised us. Soon, I may be the only one Maddie has left.

After I complete this project, I'll ask them to live with me on the island. I have more than enough space at the inn, and Ms. Connor will help with Mom. Maddie and I just get each other, and there's so much more that I can teach her. I think of our childhood in Sarasota. Playing, growing up, and diving. My little sidekick until she became her own woman. Now, I picture her swimming in the ocean again, happy and carefree like she used to be.

She's going to love Maverick Key.

Sorry, Mads.

I tighten the straps of my rebreather.

One day, I know you'll understand.

Now, I picture another's face, and my heart beats faster. Her gentle smile disarms me in ways I never expected. I'd rested my hand on her stomach after we made love last night, trying to memorize the softness of her skin and the measure of her breaths. Every risk I take now isn't mine. It's ours. The promise of our future is heavier than the gear on my back. It's not fear making it heavier—it's hope.

I shake off my memories and check the readings on my dive monitor. There isn't any room for mistakes or distractions on this dive.

The rebreather will recycle my exhaled air, scrubbing out carbon dioxide and replenishing oxygen. The closed circuit allows much deeper, longer dives than traditional open circuit scuba diving but demands vigilance. Malfunctions are often deadly.

I signal to the captain and roll backward off the dive platform.

Cold water hugs me in an icy embrace. At ten feet, sunlight still filters through the water. Parrot fish dart around me, flashing blue and yellow at the edge of my vision. At fifteen feet, I approach the outcropping of coral and an oasis of life. At twenty feet, the world darkens, and the coral fades into a center of barren sand and jagged rock.

The blue hole.

My pulse quickens. Eels, sponges, starfish, and barnacles circle the entrance's edges, opening like a portal into another world. I swim in, cutting through the cobalt-blue water as the temperature drops. My flashlight illuminates the limestone walls peppered with striations and veins of quartz. The waters inside the hole are beautiful but empty, as if life doesn't dare linger here long.

Stalactites hang from the ceiling, formed over thousands of years by dripping water, above ground, then flooded into giant sinkholes under the sea. My dive light reflects off their surfaces, casting an eerie menagerie of dancing shadows.

But the real mystery lies deeper.

There are seven tunnels of various shapes and sizes that branch from the main entrance. One of the narrower passages looms ahead, a jagged throat carved into the limestone wall. I find the nylon permanent dive line I'd laid during my prior dives. Tightly tucking in my arms, I adjust my position and angle my body, gliding forward with small, controlled kicks.

My fins don't stir the water. One kicked-up cloud of silt could blind me.

The passage narrows, walls of rock grazing my suit. I exhale slowly, deflating my chest to slip through a pinch point barely wider than my shoulders. The tightness of the space presses in from all sides. Each breath I take is deliberate and loud in the silence. I take a left and push my limits even further, navigating through an unbelievably narrow vertical shaft. The tunnel shifts abruptly, its narrow clutch forcing me to inch through sideways. The loud grating of my tanks against the rock echoes against the walls. Entering another cavern pocked with over a dozen more tunnels, I follow the path I charted on my last dive, entering the corridor. When I reach the end of the existing line, I unspool more, carefully securing and tightening it every few feet. I'm now in unexplored territory. Unsure if this path will close off, I push forward.

Then, the passage opens.

I float into a massive open chamber and adjust my light. Sweeping the beam over the floor, I catch my breath.

Half-buried in the silt is a ceramic shard. I pick it up and gently wipe it clean. Intricate patterns emerge, delicate carvings untouched by time. My breath fogs my mask as I scan more of the chamber. Another object, this one with a beautiful patina. Platinum? A tool or weapon?

My chest tightens as recognition of the objects sinks in.

After years of research and fighting my skeptics, and now, here it is. Proof.

Excitement surges through my body as I catalog each item, keeping my movements steady. But this is more than a breakthrough—it's now a target. He will try to take this discovery and twist it into greed. This is just the beginning of a larger journey. I have to keep it safe.

The red glow from my monitor pulls my attention back to the dive. I've stayed too long. The rule of thirds dictates using a third of your gas to go in and a third to get back, leaving what's left as a reserve to account for the unexpected. My gauge reads 40 percent.

I pack my tools. I'll need a proper team to procure these artifacts once I'm sure I can keep them safe. I begin my return, following the line with steady movements. The moment I prepare to enter the transition chamber, the rebreather hisses, followed by the terrible vibration of the alarm.

My stomach drops as I check the system. Every muscle in my body tenses. The scrubber canister has stopped working. Switching to the bailout, I take a slow breath.

Nothing.

This isn't an accident. Panic claws at my heart, but I push it away. I only have enough air left for a few more deep breaths. I keep my tanks, but drop all the other gear. Kicking harder, my lungs burn as I push through the pinch points to reach the exit. I take my last breath as I enter the main cavern. When I emerge from the exit, the faint glow of the surface is in sight. But there's no air left, and it's too far away.

She smiles, her soft voice whispering in my mind—a siren's call. Stay with me. Don't leave me. It's beautiful here. The call to stay, to embrace the peace of the deep, is strong.

But I've made promises to those I love, and I won't let myself give up.

With every ounce of strength I have left, I push upward—toward the light. Darkness closes in, and my vision tunnels. I exhale.

Forgive me.

CHAPTER 1

MADDIE

As I step out of my rental car, a sea breeze hits me. The air is warm, salty, and tinged with the smell of green growth and wild coast. Maverick Key isn't like anywhere else I've ever been. It's earthy, untamed, and alive.

The gravity of returning to this place and breathing the same air Nathan once did presses down on me. Memories pull me back to my visit here seven years ago, just before graduation. It was the last time I saw him in his element. After my trip, he visited us in Sarasota when he could. Those days in the Key keep circling in my mind, a carousel of lost dreams.

But he's not completely gone. When I need him most, his voice still rings out from my heart, and it feels like he's still here.

Our last phone call replays through my thoughts—the one not long before he died—five years ago. I'd begged him not to go into the caves alone. But he did.

Why did you lie to me?

Now, here I am, only twenty-eight and already so damn old.

Ding, my shaggy Polish Lowland Sheepdog, leaps from behind me, barking as his paws hit the sandy gravel.

I met Ding, when he was a stray pup, during my veterinary internship. A teenage boy begged me to keep Ding so his parents wouldn't take him to a shelter. Given my responsibilities to Mom, I couldn't afford to care for a dog, but I'd never listened to logic where my heart was concerned.

Ding saved me. I wouldn't have made it without him after losing Nathan.

There's so much to do. I used all the money I received from selling Mom's home to buy a small, abandoned building on the outskirts of town near the marina. It needs a lot of work, but it will soon be Maverick Key's first animal clinic. This will help the townsfolk, since the only way to get pet care now is a twenty-minute drive over the Castle Light Bridge to Naples. There's no set date for the grand opening, but I expect to finish the work in a few months.

If I stay focused. Contractors begin renovations in a few weeks.

Ding and I walk up the gravel path toward the historic inn, a thriving bed-and-breakfast. The wide front porch is dotted with swaying flower baskets, and weathered wooden shingles shimmer under the late afternoon sun. A sign carved in elegant script, Driftwood Inn & Cottages—Your Island Escape, swings from iron chains.

For a moment, I freeze. I'm intruding on a memory which doesn't belong to me. Nathan's memory.

Beyond the inn, the island stretches out in a lush mix of tropical charm and untouched wilderness. We pass blooming hibiscus, the air sweetened by their fragrance and mingled with the sharp tang of saltwater. A pair of white egrets fly across the road, disappearing into a swaying palm canopy.

Farther up, two old men lean against a weathered fence, chatting in low, good-natured tones.

As Ding and I near the front porch, a Welcome Home sign hangs from the edge of the railing. The uneven letters are in Nathan's handwriting. He painted it during my last visit.

"Don't worry, sis," he'd said back then, hammering it into place with a smile I'll never forget. Handsome and quirky, wearing his *Protect the Seas* T-shirt, ripped jeans, and glasses—all quintessential Nathan. "This place will always be here for you."

My heart aches.

I'd postponed dealing with my inheritance, as I cared for our ailing mother. And after she passed away last year, Sarasota held nothing for me.

Now, the inn is mine.

The weight of ownership is heavier than the South Florida humidity pressing against my skin. Standing on the porch, my gaze sweeps across the grounds, taking it all in. I'll try to make a life here. Moving to Maverick Key opens a world of possibilities—a chance to start over and reclaim Nathan's legacy. There's so much I'm missing from the last years of my brother's life. Never one to talk about himself, it was still clear he was a rising star in the scientific community. But the details of his life and death are shrouded. I need to know more. I want to understand what he was looking for and do everything in my power to be sure his work is remembered.

The inn's double doors open, and a small woman steps out, waving enthusiastically like she's been waiting for me. She's in her sixties, gray hair pinned back in a simple bun. Her expression is warm and friendly.

"You must be Maddie." She strides toward me with arms outstretched, squeezing me into a big hug. "I'm Ms. Connor, the innkeeper. Who's this handsome guy?"

"This is Ding."

He jumps up at the sound of his name and flops onto his back, shamelessly asking Ms. Connor for a belly rub.

"He's not shy about introductions."

"Well, then. He's going to fit right in here." She kneels and obliges him with a few rubs before straightening back up. "Come on inside, honey. I've got some refreshments waiting for you." She looks down. "And there's something meaty and delicious for you, too, Ding." He wags his tail, following her inside like he owns the place.

The cool air inside the inn is a relief. A pitcher of lemonade, glistening with condensation, sits on the kitchen counter beside two tall glasses. I pour myself a drink and take a slow sip. It's tart, sweet, and laced with a hint of mint.

"This is delicious." I lick my lips. "Did you make it yourself?"

She beams. "It's an old island recipe. Keeps the heat at bay." She's buzzing around the kitchen, wiping down the counters as she chats. "Why don't you put your bags down and take a look around? Later on, I'll show you the cottage."

While she works on dinner, I wander through the inn. The living area's dark wood and leather furnishings are cozy, though dust covers some surfaces. Ms. Connor has been caring for this place all by herself. It's amazing she keeps it as clean as she does. Behind the kitchen, there's a staircase leading to the inn's guest suites. I start up the stairs.

Ding's bark from the porch brings my attention back to the door.

To find out what's alarmed him, I step outside. The steady crash of waves, a distant hum of voices, and birdcalls wash over me. I look back at the ocean. Somewhere out there, past the endless blue horizon, lies *Carter's Drop*.

Nathan's lifework.

His final resting place.

The blue hole my brother discovered now bears his name. I blink back my sadness.

"Hey there. I hope I'm not intruding." A cheerful voice calls out.

I turn to see a young woman with bright red hair pulled into a messy ponytail, strands escaping in every direction. She's wearing flip-flops and a vibrant sunflower-print dress, her smile as bright as the fabric.

"I'm sorry for just showing up." She catches her breath. "You're Maddie, right? I figured I'd come by and say hello."

"That's me. And you are?"

"Hannah Rodriguez. I live a few blocks down." She crouches down to greet Ding, who sniffs her hands and jumps around her legs, tongue wagging. I laugh when he earns yet another belly rub.

"Seems like he's making friends quicker than I am."

She straightens, brushing sand from her knees. "Well, you've got me now. And I'll give you all the local scoop so you don't have to hear it through the island's grapevine."

We chat for a while and then head back inside. After grabbing a few of Ms. Connor's freshly baked cookies, we sit on the living room couch, the television humming in the background.

I learn she frequently visits the inn and has been helping with its advertising for years.

"Were you and Nathan close?"

"Your brother was the best. He was so nice, a friend to everyone. But personally, nah. He was just too busy and rarely around. It was hard to get to know him on that level. That said, he used to talk about you all the time."

"He did?"

"Oh yeah. He was so proud of you." With her napkin, she cleans off some of the dust from the coffee table. "He was always bragging about his smart little sister, the veterinarian, and musician. The whole town knows who you are."

"Oh Geesh." The idea of being infamous before meeting anyone alarms me.

"Don't worry. Everyone's looking forward to meeting you."

Hannah and I lose track of time as we gossip about all the juicy things happening in Maverick Key. There's an instant connection with her. Even though we've just met, her fun, open nature is infectious. She's the pretty brown-eyed, red-headed, sassy bestie I always wanted to have in school.

"You're going to open a veterinarian practice here on the island?"

"Yeah. I've been interning for a few years. The animal clinic will be my first business venture. Something of my own."

"You'll crush it." She straightens and tilts her head, eyes shining. "So, tell me about this musical talent of yours. Didn't you attend Juilliard?"

"I was accepted for Piano." I pause, averting my gaze. "My plans had to change because of Mom."

The corners of her mouth dip. She reaches out and touches my arm, giving me a gentle squeeze. "Another thing he talked about all the time was Carter's Drop. He was obsessed. He's our local small-town hero. It was Carter's Drop that put Maverick Key on the map." She picks up another cookie. "It's not surprising someone's finally picking up where he left off. What's surprising is that they waited so long."

"What do you mean?"

"You've heard about the project to explore Carter's Drop, right?"

"No. What's going on?"

Hannah leans closer. "They're calling it An Interdisciplinary Exploration of the Carter's Drop Blue Hole. Dr. Garrett Harlow—a big-shot marine archaeologist—is leading it. I think he and Nathan were colleagues. Now, he's taking over where your brother left off. He's hired a cave diver, Scott Rickter, and his dive team to explore and map the caves. They've been out there for weeks already, surveying the caverns and looking for—" she shrugs. "I don't know. Old bones, maybe? Nobody outside of the project knows. Scott hasn't said much, and Garrett doesn't talk to anyone unless he has to."

"Why didn't anyone tell me about this?" My face flushes.

"I'm sorry. They should have. Scott's a straight shooter. You can ask him anything you want to know."

I make a mental note to talk to this Scott Rickter. I want to be sure Nathan gets credit for his work and no opportunists are planning to bury his contribution.

Hannah tilts her head with a wry grin. "And then there's the treasure hunters."

"Treasure hunters?"

"Oh, that's right. One high-profile news story isn't enough for Maverick Key." She shifts in her seat, drawn into her own story. "Harrold Skipes—one of those eccentric billionaires—hid a treasure cache on the island. At least, that's the rumor that's got everyone stirred up. Earlier today, I passed two kids on Sunset Strand arguing over a treasure map so creased it looked like it had been through a washing machine." She talks with her hands, her fingers slicing through the air in dramatic circles as she speaks.

"Treasure mania has this whole town in a frenzy. It's so bad that it's got the Coast Guard in a tizzy, so they've pulled in NOAA authorities. Now, everyone diving near the Drop has to have a permit." Ding jumps on the couch and snuggles in next to her. His eyes close as she strokes his coat.

"Whoa… This is exhausting."

So much for living a quiet island life.

"You've got that right. And it's all gone viral on social media. Celebrities are getting in on the hype. Wes Harrington and his crew are expected to arrive sometime this week. They're staying right here at the inn."

"Who?" I haven't looked at the list, but more guests are arriving soon.

"You've never heard of Wes Harrington?" Her eyes widen in disbelief. "Last year, he rappelled into a cenote in the Yucatan with just rope and his GoPro. Edge-of-your-seat clickbait. His channel tripled overnight. He claimed he found valuable artifacts." She giggles as Ding licks her hands. "The locals claim he faked the whole thing. He's a charmer, at least on camera. Look." She pulls up his channel on her phone. "Over two million followers and a ton of fan channel spin-offs. He's a real celebrity daredevil." Her face spreads into a grin. "Not to mention he's hot."

I shake my head and laugh. "This is nuts. It sounds like I won't be bored."

"Ha… that's an understatement." She gives me a big hug. "Welcome to Maverick Key. You're going to love it here."

♥

After Hannah leaves and Ms. Connor and I share a quick dinner, I linger on the inn's front porch, my gaze fixed on the horizon.

I picture Nathan's face and the first dive we took together so many years ago.

"The sea has a way of pulling us in, Mads."

Deep water enveloped us, a boundless expanse of wonder and mystery. The beauty of the deep lies in its endless and mighty embrace of all within it.

"Look at you… you're a natural." His face was full of pride.

We both loved the sport, and he made it an important part of his life. My mentor. My hero. He dedicated his life to exploring the ocean's secrets, a path I might have also taken, but I didn't. When I went to college, I had a different plan for myself. To break out of the mold and not live the same life as Mom and Dad, or Nathan. I wanted so much to be my own person. Now, I'm not sure who I am. My vision of his face vanishes as I turn my head away from the shore.

In the next few weeks, I'll focus on preparing to open my animal clinic. Make connections with the locals, do house calls, etc.

This is what I want, isn't it?

But tomorrow—tomorrow, I'm going to take a day off for myself—one last break before I'm too busy with this new life.

Maybe I'll go swimming.

CHAPTER 2

SCOTT

I break the surface with a kick. Sunlight hits my face as I pull my dive mask down and spit out the regulator. Bracing, familiar air rushes into my lungs, and the taste of the ocean clings to my lips as I climb the ladder. Man, I love this shit. It never gets old.

"Welcome back," Jamie calls from the boat, grinning as he reaches out a hand. "Find anything good down there today, boss?"

I grab his hand and haul myself onto the deck, my dry suit clinging to my shoulders. "No hidden treasure, if that's what you're asking. Just a whole lot of rocks and silt."

He snorts. "So, we're not rich yet?"

"Not unless you can cash in on dead ends and frustration."

Margaret had dived with me today to collect the animal bones we'd spotted on our last dive. I'd started a recon on the first entry point and found it went nowhere.

"Damn." He stomps a foot. "I guess I'll have to cancel the check for the yacht I just bought." He tosses the clipboard aside dramatically.

I pull off my fins and lean against the railing. The sun warms my face—a welcome relief from the cool, oppressive darkness below. Every descent into the Drop is a negotiation, a balance between curiosity and caution. One wrong move and the deep will swallow you whole. It has no mercy.

A bark interrupts my thoughts. I glance to the other side of the boat and spot Denver, my Belgian Malinois, his ears pricked and tail wagging furiously. Jamie follows my gaze.

"What's up with him?"

"He's got no patience for the sea life today." He barks again, his tone more demanding this time. I give him a quick nod, reassuring him I'm okay, before turning back to Jamie. Liam joins us, stepping up to the helm to take the wheel.

The engine roars to life, drowning out the ocean waves as Liam steers *Adeline* from the Carter's Drop descent point back toward Maverick Key. Jamie settles down beside me, flipping through the day's notes on his clipboard. Margaret, my first mate, quietly catalogs her bone samples at the back of the boat.

"Think we can wrap this up early?" Jamie asks, rubbing his nose. "I wouldn't mind getting a good night's rest for once."

I shake the drying salt from my hair. "You're assuming Garrett Harlow gives a fuck about your sleep schedule."

"Yeah, well, the man doesn't care about much beyond slapping his name on a museum plaque and science journal." Jamie's scribbling away on his clipboard, pretending like he's working. "He talks a good game about preserving history and advancing human knowledge. I'm just not buying it." Liam and Margaret both chime in with their agreement.

"Garrett's never seen a blue hole up close or explored a cave in his life. But he talks like he's got an oxygen tank strapped to his back." Jamie's never gotten over Garrett's comment that I should fire him. I'd never do that. He does a damn good job when he works and he's family. Once I take someone on as part of the crew, it's ride or die.

"Welcome to academia." I give him a pat on the shoulder.

The sharp ring of my satellite phone cuts through the air.

"Speak of the devil," Jamie mutters.

I sigh, fishing the phone out of the dry box. Sure enough, Garrett Harlow's name glares on the screen. I hesitate before answering. "Rickter."

"Scott. How's the progress out there?"

I move to the stern, away from the engine noise. "Still scoping the first tunnel entrances. We've found nothing worth going deeper yet, but we're narrowing the options down."

"That's not good enough. I need some results," he huffs, like a spoiled brat. "I'm trying hard to be patient here, but the funding isn't endless. I have to give the university an update tomorrow. Give me something."

I bite down a curse. If it weren't for the money and the opportunities for more work like this down the line, I'd let Garrett know just how much I care about his problems. The guy's a jerk, but the fact is we all need the money, and projects like this are rare. The crew is counting on me for this job. Garrett dumps his shit on everyone else. He's under pressure since the first investors pulled funding and it's been a slow sell to get the university to approve more. Now that he has it, he's over-promising and under-delivering. So daily, I'm dragged into his temper tantrums. I try to keep it from the crew.

"You hired me to do this right, not fast. I'll get you the results, but we're not—"

"Okay, fair enough." He talks over me before pausing. "Oh, there's one more thing. I almost forgot. Wes Harrington's crew arrives tomorrow. He'll also be diving in Carter's Drop."

"Harrington. Why?"

"He's chasing down his own thing. Something about boosting views on his channel. It's got nothing to do with our project, so let him do what he wants and stay out of his way."

It's convenient he has all the details of Wes's plans. I doubt his interest is benign. Garrett doesn't play that way. "Easier said than done." I ball my fists. "We'll be working in the same waters. It's going to get crowded."

"You can make it work." He snickers and adds slowly. "You might even learn a thing or two from him. I understand he's the best cave explorer in the business today." I roll my eyes. Garrett's weaselly voice really grates at me.

"You done?" I pause, letting the silence sink in. "Thought so."

"Watch it. Anyway, there's no room for any egos on this. It's too important. Be the grown-up. I look forward to tomorrow's update."

The line goes dead.

I stare at the phone, resisting an urge to hurl it overboard. Losing a phone won't hurt Garrett, so why bother? Jamie glances up from the clipboard, his good humor disappearing as he catches my expression. "Bad news?"

"Wes Harrington." I shove the phone back into the dry box. "Garrett expects us to play nice."

"That guy on that urban exploration channel? Wes UrbEx, I think it is. Why's he coming here? Doesn't he stick to old abandoned manmade structures?" His eyes widen. "Actually, his show is pretty wild. I once saw him—"

"All right. Enough." I wave him off. "Yes. He's the guy. He considers himself an explorer of all trades. I won't deny he knows his stuff. But his showboating puts lives in jeopardy. In my book, that makes him an asshole. I don't want him anywhere near our team."

Wes and I were both tagged to a sea salvage rescue a few years back. As experienced technical cave divers, we're on a short list of people called for when rescues require those skills. Fortunately, no one had died. He'd shown real courage and intelligence, but his antics and exploitation of the victims' trauma for profit left a sour aftertaste.

Margaret doesn't look up from her samples. "If Harrington or his followers get within five feet of our work, I'll feed them to the sharks."

"Hey, seriously, do you think he might let me in on one of his videos?" Jamie asks hopefully, combing his fingers through his curly blond hair. "Girls go nuts over those."

"Sorry, J, there's not enough room on his show for two pretty boys," Liam says. We all burst out in laughter at Jamie's expense. He shrugs and joins in.

The crew's voices fade into the background as they work to anchor us back to the docks. As I look toward the sea, my thoughts drift. What a beautiful day. I close my eyes and say a prayer. It's the same one I say every time my crew makes it home safely.

Then I see her face.

I still hold on to pieces of her—my partner, best friend, and beautiful wife. No matter how many dives I make or what I find out there, the truth follows me, haunting every descent.

Whatever circus Harrington brings with him, the ocean won't care. But I do, and I need a plan to handle him before he wrecks everything in his path.

♥

Sweat trickles down my temples as I walk up the sandy path to the Driftwood Inn & Cottages. I don't bother to wipe it away. My mind is too busy going through what has to be done this week. Denver pads alongside me, his dark coat shimmering in the sun. His pace is steady, head swiveling as he surveys our surroundings.

Jamie tosses a water bottle from one hand to the other.

"Think Garrett's going to micromanage us even while he's out of town?"

"Without a doubt." I don't break stride. "He'll call two more times before the day is over."

Margaret trails a few steps behind, her arms filled with maps, while Liam brings up the rear.

"Let's hope breakfast makes up for it," Liam says. "I'm starving."

"Didn't you just eat a donut a few minutes ago?" Jamie looks up at Liam, incredulous.

"I need at least five thousand calories a day to survive, J. One donut won't cut it, man." Liam's six-foot-five muscular physique showcases his Samoan heritage, making him a towering figure among us.

Ms. Connor's breakfasts are legendary—fluffy pancakes, crispy bacon, and whatever tropical fruit dish she's concocted. They make up for the aggravation of working for Garrett. Almost.

A breeze drifts in, carrying the faint floral scent of the inn's garden. Overhead, gulls squawk as they circle the sky. This is shaping up to be a good morning.

Denver's ears perk up, his tail wagging as he spots a shaggy dog lounging under a tree. As we get closer, the other dog lifts his head, one floppy ear twitching in mild skepticism. Black and gray fur with white-tipped paws. We're an inconvenience he's debating whether or not to deal with.

"Looks like Ms. Connor's got a new security system." Jamie motions toward the dog.

"Denver's going to size him up." His tail wags faster as he trots forward, sniffing the air toward the lounging dog. The two stare at each other briefly before the other dog flops his head back down with a huff, deciding Denver isn't worth getting up for.

"Lazy mutt," Jamie says. Denver's ears flick in agreement as he returns to my side.

We reach the front door, and I knock, the solid sound echoing in the quiet morning. Denver sits at attention beside me. I knock again, thinking Ms. Connor may not hear us if she's in the kitchen. The door opens faster than I expect and I take a step back from the woman who greets us.

Clearly, not Ms. Connor.

Her light brown eyes—the color of desert sand—meet mine with a warmth that throws me off balance. Damp, honey-brown curls frame her face and brush against her cheeks, the color perfectly matching her eyes. A fine dusting of freckles crosses her nose. She's gorgeous, no doubt, but what catches my attention, and the rest of the crew's, is what she's wearing.

A tiny, tight blue bikini. The straps of her top tied loosely behind her neck, exposing her toned shoulders. A yellow beach towel is wrapped around her waist, barely covering the tops of her long legs. Her face flushes a deep rose as she fumbles with the towel, clearly aware of the five sets of eyes on her.

Jamie lets out a low whistle.

Margaret glares at him. "Really?"

Denver barks once, agreeing with her assessment.

Liam raises a brow.

"Not what I expected for breakfast," Jamie says nonchalantly, making her cheeks darken even more.

The towel slips.

She gasps, her eyes wide with horror, scrambling to grab it before changing course to snatch a T-shirt from a nearby chair. She tries to pull it over her head.

"Dang it," she mutters, talking to herself as she struggles with the shirt.

She's not quick enough to prevent a peek of the bikini bottom and a clear view of her toned ass. After she gets it on, the oversized shirt barely skims her thighs, doing little to hide the skin beneath.

"Sorry, I was swimming… I didn't… uh…" She clutches the hem of the shirt, trying in vain to pull it down. "I thought it might be an emergency."

I stoop to pick up the towel and hand it to her, our fingers brushing briefly.

Something about her—the way she stands, shoulders back, trying to reclaim her composure—pulls me in. I clear my throat, recovering faster than the rest of the team. Ms. Connor must not have given her a heads-up we were coming.

"I'm the one who should apologize for the intrusion." I keep my voice steady and try to ignore Jamie's smirk I feel radiating from behind me.

"I'm Scott Rickter." I shake her hand, noticing the firmness of her grip. "My dive team is chartered for a university research project led by Dr. Garrett Harlow to explore and chart Carter's Drop. We hold our dive briefing here every Monday morning with Ms. Connor's permission." I motion to the others, saying, "This is Margaret, Liam, and Jamie." The crew waves and smiles at her. Denver adds a friendly bark.

"Nice to meet you. I'm Maddie." Her voice is strong despite her embarrassment.

"Maddie Carter."

Jamie straightens slightly. "Carter? As in related to Nathan Carter?"

Her expression falters. "He was my brother."

Sympathy hits me. Carter's disappearance is still a fresh wound for many people on the island. How hard is it for her?

"I'm sorry for your loss. Your brother was a good man—a hell of a diver. It's an honor to continue his work."

"Thank you." She glances up hopefully. "Did you know Nathan?"

"Our paths didn't cross too often, but his reputation preceded him. We all feel we knew him a little." I press a hand to my chest. "He was famous, here on the Key."

"Everything about this place reminds me of him." Her sweet face looks down at Denver. "You're a good boy, aren't you?"

She rubs behind his ears, and he nuzzles against her hands.

I catch myself staring at her.

What am I doing?

I force myself to refocus. This isn't the time.

Before the awkwardness lingers, Ms. Connor's familiar voice rings out from behind us. "What are you all doing, standing around like a pack of loiterers? Move aside… I've got groceries."

She's bustling up the path, arms loaded with bags. We hurry to help, grabbing the bags. I hold the door open as she ushers everyone inside.

"It's good to see you again. I hope you slept well, honey," Ms. Connor says. "Join us this morning. You can listen in and see what these troublemakers are up to."

Inside, Ms. Connor gets started on breakfast, and Maddie excuses herself to go change. I hope she's coming back to eat with us. She's a good-looking woman. I'm going to have a hard time getting her and her little blue swimsuit out of my head later on.

As we wait in the living room, Jamie goes on and on about Nathan's hot sister, and the rest of us try to tune him out as we prepare for the dive briefing.

"Wow, did you get a good look at that body?" He asks, excitement in his voice. "Mmm. and those gorgeous eyes. Seems sweet, too. I wonder if she's single. Ms. Connor probably knows—"

I thwack his shoulder. "Ow."

"Shut the fuck up." I give him my boss stare.

Soon, the savory smell of bacon permeates the air, mingling with the bright, citrusy scent of freshly squeezed orange juice. I make a beeline for the coffee pot, pouring myself a steaming cup and taking a long, satisfying sip.

Maddie returns, and the team peppers her with questions as we wait for the food to finish. Her answers are gracious, and she listens attentively with genuine interest. She's a delight to be around but guarded. Denver thumps his tail against the floor, approving of her presence.

She's a real sweetheart. And she's drawing us all in. Me, the most.

"Time to eat, friends," calls Ms. Connor, setting plates of pancakes, bacon, and biscuits on the table. Chatter fills the dining room as food is passed around.

At first, Maddie sits at the table quietly. Her posture is rigid, her shoulders tight, and her movements are tentative as she puts food on her plate. For a while, she just eats and observes. She's way too shy for this group. I'll fix that.

"Now that you've been here a couple of days, what do you like most about the Key?"

She looks at the ceiling for a moment. Inhaling deeply, she moves her gaze back and locks eyes on me. "The air." She closes her eyes like she's let something go. "I can finally breathe again."

My heart just takes off. This woman, she's got layers. Layers, I want to unwind.

"You're already fitting in," Jamie praises Maddie after she tells a funny joke. "Careful, though. Margaret's the only one who can out-snark Liam."

"I've got no snark, man. I'm the teddy bear," Liam says with a straight face.

Maddie leans back in her chair, relaxed.

Reaching for the syrup like she's been sitting at this table for years, she eats in earnest. Over the course of one breakfast, she's no longer an outsider. She's a new friend.

For a little while, the tension from Garrett's call this morning and all thoughts of Harrington's impending arrival fade away, and I feel… alive.

"Are they always like this?" Her bright sandy eyes meet mine again. The directness of her gaze makes me catch my breath.

"Every day." I shrug. "You get used to it."

"Take us or leave us," Jamie says, jumping in.

Maddie glances around the room, the warmth in her expression spreading over me. "I think I'm going to keep all of you."

Who is this woman?

Despite myself, I hope she means it.

CHAPTER 3

MADDIE

We all pitch in to clear the breakfast dishes. The lively chatter from earlier fades into a quieter, more focused tempo as the dive team shifts into work mode.

Scott stands at the foot of the table. There are maps and notes spread across its polished wood. Neatly combed dark brown hair, broad shoulders, and poised demeanor reveal a military background even before he speaks. His sun-kissed skin and muscular build suggest he's no stranger to hard work. Focused hazel eyes miss nothing as he surveys the group. I stare at the black dog tags resting against his chest and the deep, jagged scar running along his neck. I shiver and close the collar point of my shirt, pulling the fabric closer to my skin.

He commands the attention of those in the room with a voice of authority as he outlines the tactical plan for their next excursion.

Jamie lounges in his chair, twirling his pen. Margaret sits in a corner by herself, taking notes, while Liam is the closest to Scott, pointing to lines on a laminated map of Carter's Drop's caverns. Liam's a gentle giant with dark brown hair, eyes, and skin. I get the sense he and Scott have known each other the longest.

"Garrett agreed to another reconnaissance dive before we push deeper into the cave tunnels." Scott taps the map with his knuckles. "We need to confirm which tunnels are worth focusing on before committing to an exploration route. He wants us in there as soon as possible, and I've assured him the last thing we want to do is waste time on the dead ends."

Jamie tips his chair back onto two legs. "The guy's been out of town for days and still wants his signature of approval on everything."

Margaret crosses her arms. "His university grant is funding this." Her soft voice is matter-of-fact. "It's not shocking he wants to know where his money's going." Even though she's a petite, unassuming brunette, her words carry a punch.

"Is it true Garrett is bringing another university bigwig with him when he gets back to the inn?" Jamie asks, and scoffs. "Another Egghead. How stuffy is this place going to get?"

"Elaine Fischer is well respected." Scott levels Jamie with a flat, no-nonsense stare. "The grant's investors are insisting she join the project." The corners of his mouth twitch. "Not sure Garrett is too pleased about that."

Obviously, he doesn't like this Garrett guy either.

I think of the guest list. The doctors will both be staying here at the inn.

"Anyway, back to it." Scott gestures to the map.

Liam leans forward and taps on a shaded section near the bottom corner. "These sections we analyzed last week don't look too promising.

If we want to stick to Garrett's timeline, we're better off focusing here. The conduits are wider, and it'll be easier to navigate."

Scott pulls out a chair and sits, the wood creaking under his weight. "I was thinking about that, too. But if we take this path …" He traces a finger along another route. "It might save us time in the long run. There are a few more siphons and restrictions this way, which bring more risks and take more time, but the passages open up to larger rooms that may bear more fruit."

I lean closer, drawn in by the intricate lines of the overlay map. A network of tunnels branch out like veins under the skin, a maze impossible to navigate.

Which tunnels did Nathan go into? What drove him to explore the depths of those caves alone, knowing how dangerous they were?

Denver pads into the room, his black coat shining. He settles in beside Scott's chair. His presence is as commanding as his handlers. Scott reaches down to scratch behind his ears, and the brief softening of his expression tempers the hard edges of his appearance. I find myself staring at the muscles in his shoulder as they move against his shirt. Oh, my.

Denver's ears perk up when Ding trots into the room. He sniffs the air as he approaches. The two dogs circle each other, tails wagging, before agreeing to an unspoken truce. Ding flops down beside Denver, resting his head on his paws.

Jamie's bright blue eyes twinkle when he spots the two dogs. "Ahh, look at that—fast friends. Ding, I think you've met a buddy who's going to whip your ass into shape."

Ding gives him a blank stare and huffs.

Scott glances down at the two dogs, his expression warming even more. "He's smart. Knows Denver's the real deal."

"Is he part of the team?"

Scott regards me, his hand still on Denver's head. "He's more reliable than most people I've worked with." He glances at Liam and Margaret. "Present company excluded. He's been with me since I left the Navy. A goodbye gift from my unit."

"Is he military-trained?"

"He was young back then, only about a year old, but already one of the best. He's saved lives. My SEAL team pitched in to match us at my Hail and Farewell. They thought he'd be good company for the civilian life. They were right."

Jamie chimes in, a teasing lilt in his voice. "Denver's the real alpha of this operation. Scott just follows his lead."

Scott rolls his eyes but doesn't argue. He picks up where he left off. "If we start here and move along this shaft, we'll avoid the stronger currents and get a better read on these deeper collapse zones," he breaks off, turning to me. "Do you have a question?" His voice is softer, his expression open.

I hesitate. I don't want to interrupt the flow of their work. It's serious— life and death. But I'm intrigued by the technical details of their plan and just how much is involved in it. I'm getting a tangible sense of the dangers of cave diving.

The faint scratch of Margaret's pen breaks the silence. "Recon tomorrow morning?"

"Early. The current's been stronger later in the day. I want to be in the water by sunrise."

He turns his gaze back to me. "On a recon dive, we're assessing the tunnel entry points. We'll lay lines, set markers, and do some preliminary exploration of the tunnels to ensure flow and stability."

Heat rises up my neck. He's taking the time to explain for my benefit. I soak in every word.

"Do you enter the caves diving open circuit, or do you use rebreathers?"

He stands and moves to the chair beside me, smiling as he glances over the notes I've been adding into my phone. His nearness makes it hard to breathe. And those dimples. It shouldn't be legal for Scott to smile. The heat from my neck blooms and spreads to my chest and face. "Have you done much diving?"

Eagerness zips through me. "I used to, in Sarasota. I was really into it for a time, dive club and all. No closed circuit, though." I'm excited to share a connection with the team—especially him.

"When's the last time you've been under?"

"Five years ago."

His expression changes, the light in his eyes dimming. I don't mention how, after Nathan's death, I struggled with aquaphobia for years. I've only recently been comfortable even approaching water, let alone diving beneath the ocean.

He gives me a moment, then continues. "We usually use our rebreathers, full-face masks and dry suits for all dives. This is more for routine than necessity. It's more comfortable and makes communication relays topside easier. From time to time, we go open circuit if we don't have all our gear or are diving with buddies. But we always use rebreathers for the penetration dives. They're deeper and longer."

"I don't know much about cave diving, just what Nathan shared with me. I didn't want him to do it, especially not alone."

"Alone?" Scott raises his brows.

"Yes, he told me a few weeks before he disappeared that he'd be doing some diving into the blue hole alone." I don't mention he'd promised me he wouldn't go. "I'm not sure why, but he wanted me to know."

Scott's jaw tightens, but he doesn't comment. Instead, he finishes explaining the recon dive procedure and logistics.

Jamie groans, tilting his chair even farther back. I worry that he's going to fall over. "Before sunrise, really? Are you sure? You know, that's still the middle of the night."

Scott's lips twitch. "This isn't a spa retreat."

"Hey, I've got an idea…" a familiar voice chimes in from the dining room doorway. "Bring some strong coffee to wake him up." Hannah strolls into the room and sits next to me. "Or maybe a pillow so he can nap on the boat ride."

Jamie points at her. "See? Now, that's support. What brings you to the inn so early?" He doesn't wait for an answer. "Or… should I ask, *who* brings you here so early?"

Hannah's face turns bright red, her confidence faltering for a split second. "I thought you all might need a hand," she shoots back, but she's not fooling anyone.

Scott raises an eyebrow but stays out of it. I stare at my orange juice. I hope Wes Harrington lives up to the hype for Hannah once he gets here.

"Do you always plan your dives in this much detail?" I ask Scott.

"Yes. Every dive's a risk." He pauses. He seems unsure whether to continue. "Especially in overhead environments like Carter's Drop." His jaw tightens, and his gaze drops a beat. Is he thinking of Nathan's solo dive or something else?

"Sonar shows Carter's Drop is a complex system—an advanced technical cave dive once you get past the initial tunnel entrances." He's attempting to avoid getting into too much detail, summing up the rest. "The more we plan, the better our chances of returning successful and, most importantly, safely." He takes a sip of his coffee.

"You seem interested in the project." He tilts his head forward.

"I am."

He rubs his chin thoughtfully. Like he's trying to figure me out.

Jamie jumps in. "You should come with us to the marina and see us in action. Watch us load the boat and prep for a dive. It's pretty cool."

I turn to Scott, my heart beating a little faster.

"Would that be okay with you? If I tag along?"

His eyes linger on me for a moment. "Sure. We'll be there early tomorrow morning if you want to watch… just don't expect it to be glamorous."

"It's 100 percent grunt work," Jamie says.

He turns to Hannah, eyes glinting. "You should come too. I'll bet you Wes will be there."

"Do you want to come?" I ask Hannah.

"Let's do it." She blows Jamie a kiss.

♥

I close my sweater, the crisp early morning air refreshing against my skin. The moon's still in the sky, fading fast. There's not much time left before daylight. Maverick Key is waking up.

Hannah stands waiting for me at the entrance to the marina, coffee in hand for Jamie.

"Ready for the show?" She nudges me toward the docks.

Ding jogs beside us, his ears perked up, excited to be here.

"It's been a while since I've seen this part of Nathan's world. I'm finally connecting the dots of his past."

Her eyes flick ahead to the rows of ships tied to the pilings. "Well, you're here for the connection, and I'm here for the view." She motions to all the men working on the docks. "Of the ocean, of course." She chortles. "Let me go find Jamie. I'll be right back."

The wooden planks creak under my feet as I step onto the pier. The smells of brine, fish, and diesel mix with the cool breeze, a distinct and oddly comforting blend. Men and women move with choreographed efficiency, hoisting tanks, testing equipment, and shouting clipped instructions to each other. The occasional clang of metal and the splash of ropes hitting water punctuate the hum of activity.

My gaze settles on the boat docked at the end of the pier. *Adeline*—its name painted in bold, weathered letters along the bow. It sways with the tide as Scott's crew moves across the deck. Scott stands at the stern. His broad frame silhouetted against the pale light of dawn. He's focused on coiling rope. Liam hoists tanks onto the deck like they weigh nothing while Margaret is working at the helm, checking the tiller. Hannah's getting off the boat after waving goodbye to Jamie, who's crouched near the motor housing, mumbling under his breath as he tinkers with a fuel line. He pauses and takes a sip of his coffee, looking Hannah's way.

She turns to me. "He's like the annoying little brother I never had." Her face is flushed.

I laugh and point at the crew. "They're a well-oiled machine."

Hannah leans against a post, folding her arms. "Well, they have been at it for months."

I look closer at the boat. "Adeline. That's a beautiful name. Where did it come from?"

Hannah hesitates, her expression dampening. "Scott named it after his wife."

I blink. "His wife?"

"His *late* wife," she clarifies gently. The sparkle in her brown eyes dims. "She passed away a few years ago… in a diving accident. Scott was with her."

"Oh." The gravity of her words sinks in.

I want to ask her more, but a strong voice cuts through the air, pulling my attention to a man speaking to a cluster of people gathered at the end of the pier.

"That's Mark Glassier," Hannah whispers, leaning closer. "He's a Coast Guard lieutenant. The lead here in Maverick Key. His coast guardsmen are the only thing keeping our waters from spiraling into chaos."

Mark radiates composed authority, his calm voice softening the rigid edges of his unyielding expression.

"This area is restricted. If you don't have the proper permits, you'll need to leave the pier."

A man shoves a piece of paper at him. "I've got a permit right here."

Mark glances at it. "That's a fishing permit, not clearance to dive Carter's Drop. Sorry, this isn't negotiable."

Another man raises his voice in frustration. "We didn't come all this way to get blocked by red tape. We're just here to swim, man."

Mark doesn't flinch. "The rules are in place for a reason. Carter's Drop isn't a recreational dive site. If you want access, get the proper permits and come back."

Grumbling ripples through the group, but eventually, they stomp off.

"Mark and Nathan were college buddies. You'll want to connect with him."

I start to walk over when Hannah's hand on my arm stops me. Her voice drops to a whisper, and her eyes brighten with excitement. "There he is."

"Who?" I ask, but it's obvious who she's spotted by the way she's bouncing on her heels.

Hannah's eyes lock onto another gathering of people at the checkpoint. At the center stands a man who commands attention. Tousled, rust-blond hair, and sharp, chiseled features give him the air of someone who thrives in the spotlight. His eyes sweep over the pier, lingering on Mark before scanning the rest of the scene. He moves with the confidence of someone accustomed to being noticed—and accommodated.

"That…" Hannah breathes, awe in her voice. "Is Wes Harrington. Internet sensation, modern-day explorer." She giggles. "And some say a pain in the ass."

Wes hands Mark a set of neatly folded documents, his movements thoughtful and precise. His smile is winsome, but it has a polished edge. It's practiced.

Mark scans them. "Welcome to Maverick Key, Wes. It's been a while." Wes shakes his hand. "You're cleared for Carter's Drop."

"Much appreciated," Wes replies, his tone easy as he claps one of his crew members on the shoulder. "All right, let's go."

"Stay out of trouble." Mark gives him a stern look and frowns when Wes salutes him with a grin.

As his team heads toward their boat, Wes straightens as his eyes lock on Scott.

"Rickter," he calls, his voice carrying over the buzz of the pier.

Scott turns, his expression unreadable. "Harrington."

Wes saunters closer, hands tucked in the pockets of his windbreaker, every movement deliberate and calculated. Provocative like he's daring Scott to react.

"Still running your operation like clockwork, I see."

Scott's shoulders go rigid and a muscle ticks in his cheek. "Some of us focus on work, not cameras."

Wes chuckles, low and amused. "My cameras pay for the work. You should try living in the big leagues one day. You might like it."

Scott doesn't respond, but the tension in his muscles speaks volumes.

"I'll see you at the Drop." Wes lingers for a moment, then strolls back to his boat and climbs on. The sleek vessel roars to life, slicing through the water and disappearing toward the horizon.

"Well." Hannah exhales, blowing out a low whistle. "That wasn't subtle. I could taste the testosterone from here."

"Do they know each other?"

"Yeah, they cross paths from time to time in the caving circuit. There's a wager going around the island which one will kill the other first." She shivers, biting down on her lip. "I'm at a loss where to put my money."

My gaze drifts back to Scott. He's unruffled, but the way his fingers curl into his palms betrays the tension he's holding back. He's so handsome.

I step closer, hoping he'll notice me.

Scott pauses what he's doing, his eyes meeting mine. Surprise flashes across his face. He dips his head. And then gives me a big, genuine smile. I catch my breath as his attention snaps back to his team, focusing on the task at hand.

Hannah nudges my shoulder. "Look at you, softening up tough old Scott. I think you've made an impression on him. That's not an easy thing to do."

I'm not sure about that, but the man has left one on me.

As the boats pull away from the pier one by one, my gaze lingers on the horizon until *Adeline* disappears.

I'm sitting cross-legged on the rug in my cottage, my back pressed against the couch, with Ding sprawled beside me. I have a bowl of Skittles within arm's reach. Through the open window, a faint, briny scent from the ocean blends with the earthy aroma of the aged wooden furniture. The small cottage, tucked behind the inn's main building, was once Nathan's home. His research and notes are now enshrined within its walls.

Nathan's notebooks are stacked in front of me. Their cracked spines and dog-eared pages show the wear of years spent in his restless hands. I reach for the top one, brushing my fingers over his name on the cover. I flip through it, the pages bursting with detailed sketches of objects, geographical features, and dense blocks of notes. I comb through one notebook after another, losing track of time as hours go by.

What were you searching for?

When I open the next journal, newer than the others, a folded sheet of paper flutters to the floor.

A poem, in Nathan's handwriting.

Between waves, a memory sings
Whispers of a touch
The sea calls, but it will not claim
I hear her

Rereading it, I sigh.

Nathan was such a romantic.

He was fond of classic authors and poets and their timeless words, quoting Keats and Shelley at the funniest moments. But this is personal. Folding the poem to return it to the notebook, a faint sketch catches my attention. A seashell, the spiral patterns subtly forming the shape of a heart. Nathan liked to sketch, but it seems like an odd thing for him to draw.

I put the notebook down and head toward the desk in the room's corner.

The desk creaks as I pull open the drawers. They're cluttered with pens, papers, and an old flashlight—ordinary things. The inside of the bottom drawer is different from the other two. It's not the same size. Running my fingers along the wood, I tap lightly until I find a thin, nearly invisible seam.

My breath hitches. With trembling fingers, I grab a letter opener from the desk and slide it carefully into the seam, prying upward. With a soft pop, the false bottom gives way, revealing a hidden compartment.

The scents of aged paper and leather rise as I pull out a small bundle of objects wrapped in cloth.

Inside, there is a collection of folded papers, a slim leather-bound journal, and a strange object—a stone?

The stone feels heavy and solid in my hand. Smooth and dark, intricate carvings cover its surface. But what sends a shiver down my spine is the warmth—it's unnaturally warm. What is it? I trace the grooves of etched symbols with my fingertips and look for a crease to see if it's running on a battery or something. Nothing, it's completely solid. So strange.

As I place the stone on the desk, another piece of paper catches my eye. I unfold it and read the hurried words scrawled across it.

Call me tonight. It's important.

The handwriting is feminine and unfamiliar.

I spread the rest of the papers across the desk. One is a hand-drawn map marked up in Nathan's distinctive style. It isn't the map Scott's team showed me. This one is more detailed and handwritten, with some sections marked in red ink.

My brow furrows.

You were exploring deeper than we thought, weren't you?

Among the papers is a sheet full of symbols, a chaotic scrawl, uniform and consistent. I tilt my head, squinting.

A startled breath escapes me. Nathan, you genius.

Ding stirs, lifting his head.

The code. A language we'd created as kids—a private shorthand for secrets. I recognize the first combination immediately. He'd used it so many times. It says *Maddie*.

He wrote this to me.

It'll take time to decipher the rest of the message, but one scribbled note, uncoded, an absentminded doodle, stands out like a warning.

I don't trust him.

CHAPTER 4

MADDIE

An earthy aroma of rosemary, garlic, and onions sizzling in olive oil wafts from the pan. Adjusting the flame until the crackling vegetables simmer, I wipe my hands on a striped dish towel and peer out the window at the gravel driveway. No one's out there. We're expecting the rest of our guests tonight and I offered to prepare the main dish, one of Nathan's favorites. I'm a pretty good cook, but it's been months since I've made a hot meal for myself. I hope I'm not rusty.

"Dinner smells delicious," Ms. Connor says from the kitchen island. Expertly, she slices through a crusty loaf of bread, the knife thudding against the cutting board with each downward motion.

"Thanks. I just hope it's edible."

"Don't be modest. You've been a blessing these past few days. I'm going to keep you."

She directs me through another task—folding napkins. Helping with the inn chores has been comforting, and I've quickly picked up on the routines of the place. Between jobs, I've continued to go through Nathan's things, but I put aside the coded words. I'll need to dig through my old journals to find keys to decipher his coded messages. I cringe when I think of the multiple boxes of old junk I have in storage. It's going to take a small project to get through all of them.

Ouch. A sharp sting pulls me from my thoughts. "Dang it." I put the bottom of my palm to my mouth, trying to soothe my hand.

"Careful, honey."

I walk over to the sink and run cold water over the red welt. Once the stream takes the edge off the pain, I return to the pan and stir the food. The crunch of tires on gravel pulls my attention away from the stove. Ding, snoozing near the front door, perks up and heads to the sounds. Low, animated voices carry through the open windows, followed by the heavy thuds of car doors closing and footfalls.

"They're here," Ms. Connor announces, wiping her hands on her apron as she bustles toward the front entrance. "Keep an eye on that pan, dear. You don't want it to burn."

Curiosity gets the better of me. I wander over and stand by the kitchen entryway. A group of men step onto the porch. They could all use a good shower, filthy after what appears to have been a long day's work. One man stands out with his athletic build and rust-blond hair ruffled just enough to appear effortlessly styled. His rolled-up sleeves reveal muscular forearms and faint scars marking his skin—hints of a risk-taker's life. There's tension in his shoulders, a subtle weariness.

Wes Harrington.

His name was tossed around all week, and I'd seen him from a short distance at the marina. But up close, his presence is magnetic, like an exotic animal at the center of a zoo exhibit. He's used to turning heads.

Ms. Connor ushers the group inside. Wes's voice rises above the others, smooth and confident. "Ms. Connor, it's a pleasure finally meeting you in person." Instead of shaking her hand, he kisses it.

"About time you showed up," she replies, pulling her hand away and wagging a finger at him. "Dinner will be done soon. You've still got some time to clean up." She eyes his wrinkled shirt.

"Sorry, I'm late. We promise to be presentable and on time for dinner." He pulls off the video camera which was hanging from a strap around his shoulder. "We've been stuck out on the boat for a couple of days but got some great footage of the island's surrounding waters." He shows Ms. Connor the screen. "Today, we filmed in Carter's Drop." He turns the camera off and puts the strap back over his shoulder. "We ran into Scott and his crew while we were there."

She purses her lips. "You need to stop messing with Scott. Everyone's talking. He's been through enough and doesn't need the drama."

"Me? I was nice to him. Promise." She narrows her eyes.

I get ready to slip back into the kitchen when his gaze shifts from Ms. Connor and locks onto mine. My breath catches. His intense green-gray eyes are arresting, bright with curiosity. They narrow and his brow lifts just a bit. Then his lips curve up.

"You must be Maddie Carter." He steps forward and extends his hand. His grip is firm but not overbearing, his touch soft, surprising me.

"And you're Wes." Heat rises to my cheeks. "A friend told me all about you."

"All good things, I hope."

"Mostly."

Approval flashes across his face. "I like her already." He looks over his shoulder at Ms. Connor. "Nathan always said his sister was a spitfire."

The mention of my brother catches me off guard. "You knew him?"

His expression shifts, the charm giving way to sincerity. "Yeah, we worked together while he was exploring The Great Blue Hole in Belize. Had some beers—played pool. Got into all kinds of trouble. Brilliant man. He was one of the good ones." His voice softens. "I'm sorry about what happened." His eyes gleam with a hint of moisture.

He pauses, then continues. "He talked about you sometimes—how you put yourself through school." His expression turns serious. "He shared all sorts of embarrassing photos." I cringe.

"I heard about what happened to your mom and how you stepped up to care for her, putting your own life on hold. You're the person who does anything for the people you love." Leaning in a little closer, he lowers his voice. "That's a trait I admire, Maddie. Deeply."

He stares at me in silence.

My throat tightens. "That sounds like him. He loved me too much to be objective."

We chat a few more minutes before his focus drifts. Then his expression darkens. "Are you in touch with his girlfriend?"

"Girlfriend?" I frown. "No, I didn't know he was seeing anyone. Who is she?"

He shrugs. "Nathan mentioned her to me a few times. It seemed he was in deep the last time we talked in Belize. He never talked about his personal life, ever. But he told me he had someone in his life. Someone permanent. Sorry, I don't know much else."

Before I press further, Hannah appears in the doorway, her flame-colored hair catching the light. She's wearing a sexy black silk dress. I glance down at my simple blue cotton one and wince.

She gasps and clutches at her neck. "Wes Harrington." Wes looks her way, his gaze starting with her face and working down.

"Guilty as charged. And who are you, sugar?" he asks smoothly.

"Hannah Rodriguez." She bites down on her bottom lip. This makes him catch his breath. He opens his mouth, then closes it. He shakes her hand.

"I'm a lucky guy, meeting two beautiful women in one night. I think I picked the right inn." He turns to Hannah. "Are the rumors true that this is the best bed-and-breakfast in Maverick Key?"

"Rated the best B&B on this coast. Ten years in a row." Hannah launches into her sales pitch. "Ms. Connor's dinners are legendary, and you won't find better amenities on the island. She's a beast."

"Is privacy a problem?"

"Well… you'd better be on your best behavior. She'll set you straight if there are any crazy shenanigans in this place."

"I wouldn't dream of stepping out of line," Wes says lightly and turns to me. "And what about you? Are you going to keep me in line, too?"

I laugh nervously, heat creeping to my neck. "I think Ms. Connor's got that covered."

"Hmm… maybe."

Ms. Connor claps her hands from the kitchen. "All right, that's enough of you for now. Go clean up before dinner. Your room is ready. It's the second one on the right."

"Yes, ma'am."

As Wes heads upstairs, he calls, "Raincheck on that next story. I'll see both of you lovely ladies at dinner."

As soon as he's out of sight, Hannah whirls to face me, eyes wide. "Did that just happen? I can't believe we just met Wes Harrington up close and personal. He's even more gorgeous in person and smells good, too."

I choke, then laugh. "He smells like he's been out to sea a few days… Anyway, if that banter was any sign, I think he was just as interested in you as you were in him."

"Please," she shoots back. "He was looking at you hard. The guy's a certifiable flirt."

"Good luck with that," I tease.

I head back to the kitchen to finish dinner.

The connection between Wes and Nathan has my head spinning. And then there's Nathan's secrets.

I'd intended to dive headfirst into the animal clinic's renovation plans, but staying close to what's happening with the Carter's Drop project may need to be my priority until I figure all this out.

♥

Candlelight bathes the dining room. A low murmur of voices blends with the soft piano melody drifting from a radio hidden in the corner. The air is rich with the aroma of roasted chicken and garlic potatoes and the faint perfume of fresh flowers arranged as a centerpiece. Tonight's dinner is a welcome home for all our inn guests. I kick myself for not inviting Scott and his crew to dine with us.

Ms. Connor sits at the head of the table, charming everyone as she pours wine and makes sure all the guests are comfortable. Her down-to-earth nature provides a balance to the eclectic mix of personalities at the table. Dr. Elaine Fischer sits poised to her left, sipping her wine between comments. She's a tall, elegant woman in her late forties. Her dark hair sprinkled with silver streaks and styled into a bob. Dr. Garrett Harlow sits across from Elaine, his relaxed posture belying the shrewdness in his eyes. If it weren't for those eyes, he'd be the embodiment of a gentile college professor, a spitting image of Henry Higgins from *My Fair Lady*. His fingers tap against the stem of his glass. Hannah beams, her beautiful hair catching the chandelier's light as she leans in toward Wes Harrington, who sits beside her. Her doing, of course. Wes, seated directly across from me, splits his attention between us. Although his charm radiates like a second skin, exhaustion lingers in the shadows beneath his eyes. He catches me looking and offers a slow, sleepy smile.

It's going to be an interesting year.

The rest of Wes's team sits at the far end of the table and engages in their own conversations. Their chatter juxtaposed with the more serious discussion among the scientists. One young man gestures with his fork, entertaining the woman beside him. Another quieter member of the group adds a dry, well-timed comment, eliciting jokes from the others.

Ms. Connor clears her throat, setting her wineglass down with a clunk. "All right…" Her expression is playful. "Now that everyone's fed," she announces, "let's talk about all the excitement that's gotten this island buzzing. Carter's Drop. Lost treasure. With all the scientists and treasure hunters—and let's not forget the celebrities…" She winks at Wes. "You'd think our tiny island is the world's next wonder. Who wants to start?"

Dr. Fischer dabs the corner of her mouth with a napkin, her serene expression focused. "Well, that may very well be true for Carter's Drop. The cavern system is extraordinary—an intricate network of passageways and chambers stretching farther than anyone's been able to map physically. We can glimpse its beauty on sonar, but Nathan's finding may be one of this century's most remarkable archaeological discoveries."

Garrett leans forward, his fingers steepled in front of him. The expensive, woodsy fragrance of his aftershave drifts toward me—pleasant but cloying. "What he found before his final dive laid the foundation for this current expedition." He looks at each of the faces around the table, double-checking that everyone is paying attention. "Finding the hole itself was nothing short of a miracle—hidden by an outcrop of coral and shell, sitting just at the right depth on the shelf to remain invisible from aerial scans."

He takes a sip of water and clears his throat. "The fossilized remains he discovered in the cavern alone are groundbreaking. Even a speculative link to a cultured civilization could redefine our understanding of ancient human history."

"What kind of remains?" Hannah asks, tearing into a piece of bread. A crumb sticks to the corner of her lip until she brushes it away.

"Human bone fragments, so far," Dr. Fischer replies, eyeing Garrett. "Enough to confirm civilization, though the evidence is tenuous. It doesn't yet indicate sophistication—they could be primitive human remains."

Wes leans back in his chair. I can't tell whether he's listening intently or bored with the conversation. Candlelight flickers across his face. For a split second, his pensive stare reminds me of my brother's. I feel a tug on my heart.

A brief lull in the conversation gives me an opening. I take a breath and speak.

"Nathan believed they were more than just bones." My voice comes out as a whisper. I clear my throat and continue. "He believed that the people he was searching for were ancient and intelligent. He was looking for the truth, and I believe he found it."

I think of the stone, warm and marked with distinct, complex patterns. It must be important. I'll keep the stone and map to myself until I know who I can trust.

The room falls silent, my words hanging in the air. Even Hannah stops mid-bite, glancing toward Garrett as if waiting for his response. I fold the ends of my napkin, hesitating before speaking again.

"I've been going through his things. There are dozens of notebooks and journals in his cottage. He was getting close to finding what he was looking for."

Garrett's eyes gleam. "Unpublished work?" He leans in. "What kind of information is in his notes?"

I hesitate. "Observations and sketches. He was meticulous about documenting each of his dives."

"Is there anything specific about the cave system?" Dr. Fischer asks, folding her hands in her lap. "Admittedly, his hypothesis about the settlement of an advanced civilization in the Gulf has more merit than what many of us in the archaeological community considered." She exhales. "Fantastical stories of lost cities and mystical people have distorted true science for generations—sometimes with grave consequences when wielded by those with bad intentions. You can imagine why the idea of a superior civilization, absent evidence, can be dangerous."

I nod and continue. "There's some information about Carter's Drop in his journals. But it's technical and coded. I'll need time to review everything to determine what is important. But I can do it."

Garrett gapes.

Before he asks more questions, Wes jumps in, shifting the conversation to another topic. "Nathan always had a knack for creating suspense." He pours himself another glass of wine. "And seeing potential in other people." He meets my gaze, then looks at the others. "I worked with him during one of his underwater expeditions in the Great Blue Hole in Belize. I was a rookie cave diver—young, cocky, a pain in the ass. Still, he took a chance on me when no one else would." He shoots Garrett a hard look. "Even then, his sights were on Maverick Key's waters, following the evidence. Everyone blew off his theories, but he didn't stop until he found Carter's Drop."

Garrett's expression remains neutral, but there's a threat in his eyes. Beneath his benign exterior, he's dangerous. His cordiality is an artifice. My skin crawls.

"It sounds like Nathan left you an important legacy, Maddie," Garrett says smoothly. "If you're willing, working with Scott's dive team might help you make sense of it and your access to Nathan's research could fast-track this project."

My heartbeat picks up. Excitement rushes through my veins. Being a part of this exploration wasn't even on my radar. Am I qualified for this? And what about the animal clinic?

"Oh… I'm not sure that's a good idea. I'm not a scientist or a technical diver."

"Yet."

Dr. Fischer jumps in, agreeing with Garrett. "Fresh perspectives are invaluable. You'll bring that to the team."

I glance at Hannah, seeking reassurance. She gives me a thumbs-up and mouths, "You've got this."

"No pressure," Garrett coaxes. "But by the look in your eyes, I'd say you've already decided."

He's smug. I don't like Garrett Harlow.

Despite my misgivings, I agree to act as a consultant on the dives. We move to a more casual discussion as the dinner guests begin to excuse themselves.

Hannah leans closer to Wes, her voice teasing. "Tell me, Wes, what's the craziest thing you've ever done?"

Wes looks at her innocently.

"Let me clarify, the craziest thing you've done—on the job? Don't hold back. I've seen all your videos."

Wes launches into a story about escaping an unstable abandoned warehouse in Spain. His voice rises and falls with the cadence of a natural storyteller, and his hands—beautiful artist's hands, with their long, elegant fingers—move animatedly as he describes the danger and his survival. Hannah hangs on his every word as he mimes his dodge of a falling ceiling.

"You're insane." Her cheeks and neck flush to a red that matches her hair. "And brilliant. How do you stay so calm in those moments?"

"Years of experience." He casts a sexy smile my way.

"You need to tell that story again at the Blue Fin tonight," Hannah says, her eyes sparkling. "The whole island's going to eat it up."

My stomach flips. "You're going out tonight?" I glance at my watch. It's already ten-thirty. "It's pretty late."

"Oh, the night's still young. We're all going out. Right, Wes?"

Wes leans forward into the candlelight, focusing his vivid eyes on me. "I'll go if Maddie goes. What do you say? Are you ready to come out of your shell a little? I'll show both of you ladies a real good time."

Ms. Connor calls out from the kitchen. "Y'all girls, go and have some fun. This place will be waiting for you when you get back."

I hesitate, my pulse quickening. "I'm not much of a bar person…"

"That's fine. Come with us, and I'll make sure no one bothers you— unless you count me." He flashes another megawatt grin. "Can't make any promises there."

"Okay, I'll go."

My heart races with excitement. There's no denying the pull of Wes Harrington's charisma, even though it's another's face on my mind as I walk to my cottage to freshen up.

CHAPTER 5

SCOTT

I descend toward Carter's Drop. As I sink deeper, the surface world disappears, leaving only the occasional whoosh of the regulator and release of carbon dioxide. In every direction, the endless expanse of the ocean stretches before me.

I glance at my depth gauge—it's dropping. Ahead, the dark maw of the cavern looms, jagged and uninviting, like the mouth of an ancient and hungry beast. No matter how many times I enter the Drop, my pulse always kicks up.

"Visibility's good." Jamie's voice crackles through our comms.

"Margaret, how's the weather looking topside? Over." I scan the area, my focus sharpening. The cold water hones my senses.

"All good," Margaret says. "Keep the comms clear and check in once you've reached the tunnels for an update. Over."

"Copy. Out." I take a deep breath and switch on my dive light.

We advance into the cavern. The natural light from above fades into near blackness.

"All right. Jamie, you're with me this time. We'll continue to drop cookies on the offshoots and run traverse into the tunnels we flagged last time. Liam, verify the main line tie-offs—lay temp traverse if the passage looks stable. Mark the distances with the knotted line."

"Got it." Liam checks his gas. Jamie gives me an OK sign.

We enter the first tunnel. My beam catches a detail we missed on our prior dives. A faint line of algae-covered nylon trails along the rock of the tunnels, an old dive line left behind by someone who's been here before. I point it out to Jamie. "Mark this."

"Done," Jamie says, scribbling on his slate.

We move slowly, adjusting our BCD and trim as we navigate to avoid clouding the water. The quartz veins in the walls glimmer under our lights. This is the fun part, seeing areas of the cave for the first time and taking in the natural beauty. Some smooth areas of the walls in this tunnel are out of place from the Swiss cheese texture of the limestone. I reach out and brush my glove against a flat patch of stone. Interestingly, it's warmer than the surrounding water. Before I investigate further, Jamie's voice blasts through the microphone.

"Heads up—movement at your three o'clock. I can't tell what it is."

I turn my light toward one of the subsidiary shafts, catching a flicker of motion. Small particles scatter as another beam cuts through the murk.

"Looks like we're not alone." My jaw tightens as three silhouettes emerge into the passage.

Wes Harrington's team.

Their clumsy movements stir up silt plumes that soon reduce our visibility. Fine particles cling to my mask, swirling in the water. Through the haze, Wes emerges, his dirty blond hair unmistakable even in the murk.

"Watch your buoyancy, boys." He turns his head my way. "Rickter. I didn't expect to run into you guys down here yet. Not on our first day."

I'm willing to bet running into us is exactly what he expected.

"Funny," I reply as I keep my tone clipped and gesture toward the three divers by his side, two struggling to control their bulky underwater video equipment. "They're going to get stuck." I bite down a curse at the sheer recklessness. "In case you missed the memo, this passage is a little tight."

"A little squeeze doesn't bother me…" Although the regulator hides his smirk, I see it in his eyes. "We're getting in a short swim and some footage before heading over to the Driftwood to check in and get some dinner." He pauses, then adds. "I get to meet Nathan's little sister, Maddie, tonight. He told me so much about her, and the word is she's cute. All the guys in town are talking. Have you met her yet?"

I knew Wes and his crew were staying at the inn, but Maddie's name on his lips makes my ears throb. There's no way I'm going to sit here and have a friendly chat with this guy. I couldn't care less about his dinner plans.

"I guess this is your show now, Harrington." I gesture toward the walls of the tunnel.

"Get ready to see how this gets done." He's got the gall to wink.

One of his divers fumbles with the camera, kicking up another wave of silt. Unconcerned, Wes navigates easily into one of the narrower offshoots with his usual theatrics. The camera flares, casting dramatic halos in the murky water. The guy has excellent skills himself, but it's criminal he has these guys down here. Typical.

"This is what people tune in for," he declares, his voice dripping with showmanship. "Tight squeezes, the risk of death, and the thrill of the unknown. Make sure you're getting all this, boys."

I roll my eyes. "Let's move." I motion to Jamie. "We've got real work to do."

We slip past Wes's crew without a word as we return to the main cavern. When we enter, the silt cloud disappears. I signal to Liam as Jamie and I approach the second tunnel. My light sweeps across the walls, another faint line of nylon, a breadcrumb from someone's previous journey.

"Get this one, too." I point. "Mark as B. Spool and tie-off more line—keep it tight. Let's get the first twenty feet mapped."

We continue working, the silence of the underwater world broken only by an occasional crackle of the comms and chatter from Wes's team, which blessedly stops.

Margaret's voice chimes in. "Check your gauges. How does it look? Over."

"Productive. We've got two promising leads to explore further the next time we go down. We're good on gas, over 70 percent. Over."

"Copy," Margaret says. "By the way, Wes's team just surfaced. The Drop's all yours. Out."

"Thank God," Jamie says. Liam chuckles from the main cavern. We continue to work, capturing markers. After half an hour, we're ready to wrap it up.

"All right. Let's head back."

We pack up and start the ascent. The water brightens fast as we rise, and a faint pull of the current guides us upward. Breaking the surface, I pull off my mask and take a deep breath of salt-laden air. The hum of *Adeline's* engine greets me.

Margaret leans over the side of the boat, extending a hand.

"We made a lot of progress today, despite Harrington's shit." I strip off my fins and set them aside. "We'll go deeper next time."

After we dock, I lean against the boat railing and dial Garrett. The line connects, his abrasive voice cutting through. "What do you have for me?"

"Two promising tunnels. We'll begin exploring them next time."

"Good. As you map them, make sure the work is thorough and clean. I don't want any amateur shoddiness."

Margaret grimaces, and Liam arches a brow.

"Okay, understood." I hang up and shake my head. What a bastard.

I turn toward the team. They don't deserve Garrett's disrespect. "How about we hit the Blue Fin tonight?"

Jamie tosses his towel onto a bench. "Now you're talking. You buying the first round?"

"Yeah. Drinks are on me."

I can't think of a better way to let the day's tension ebb away. Tomorrow we'll deal with more shit and do it well, but tonight, a few drinks for this crew are well-earned.

♥

The Blue Fin Tavern thrums with energy as we claim our usual corner spot at the back of the outdoor beach bar. The combined scents of saltwater, coconuts, and seafood drift through the warm evening air. A live band plays island tunes, their melody blending with the waves. It's the kind of night Maverick Key does best, laid-back and brimming with life.

I sit back, nursing my beer as Liam and Jamie launch into their latest debate about dive spots, arguing over the hidden gems versus well-trodden tourist traps. Margaret's flipping through a laminated dive chart, getting ready for the next dive, no doubt. I need to convince her to leave her work at home. I'm worried she has no life away from the water. The rise and fall of voices, clinking glasses, and the crunch of sand underfoot surround us as servers weave in and out between tables.

My gaze drifts toward the shoreline, into the darkening horizon. The cool breeze ruffles my hair as I take another sip. The stress of the day easing away—until I spot them.

Hannah's bright hair shines like a beacon as she approaches the tavern. Beside her, Maddie's blue dress flutters in the breeze, her simple grace catching my attention. Her loose honey-brown hair frames her face, and her smile is even softer than I remember, real and unguarded. My heart rate picks up and I sit up straight. I'm glad I put in a little more effort into cleaning up for tonight than I typically bother with.

Trailing behind them is Wes Harrington, his casual stride unmistakable. Of course, he's here. His charm is as phony as his personality. He gestures animatedly, bringing more attention to himself. I see girls all over the bar whip out their phones and aim. But what's getting under my skin is that he's here with Maddie. The asshole works fast. My grip tightens around my beer bottle.

"Fucking Wes Harrington."

Jamie tracks my gaze and lifts a brow. "Here comes trouble."

"Always making a grand entrance." The girls who were filming him have now gathered into a massive swarm, staying at a somewhat discreet distance.

"Stealing the spotlight—and the ladies," Liam says, a grin tugging at his lips as he casts me a knowing glance.

I don't reply, and my focus locks on the hand Wes rests on Maddie's back as they make their way toward the bar where they get their drinks. Hannah spots us first and waves enthusiastically as she drags the others along.

"Hey, guys," she calls, her excitement infectious.

I stand out of habit, my southern roots kicking in. "Hannah. Maddie." My gaze lingers on Maddie a beat too long before shifting to Wes. "Harrington."

"Rickter," Wes replies, his expression challenging. "Small island, huh?"

"Very." I motion to the table. Maddie hesitates, her fingers brushing the back of a chair.

"Let me get that for you." Wes pulls out Maddie's chair with a flourish. Hannah nudges Maddie.

Maddie sits and glances at me before moving her attention back to her friends. The faint scent of her perfume drifts toward me—warm, gourmand, understated. So sweet. I wonder how she'd taste. Heat rushes up my spine. I shift my focus to my drink, forcing my thoughts elsewhere.

As the night wears on, the conversation flows. Hannah and the others fire off questions to Wes about his adventures. He eats it up and shares story after story. Hannah lights up as he recounts his near-death experiences and daring escapes. A few times, women come to our table to ask Wes for his photograph. He obliges them and gives them a light touch or kiss. I sit back, drinking my beer. Maddie is quiet, too, her fingers tracing the edge of her glass. Every so often, her gaze flicks in my direction. I might just be imagining it.

"All right, it's an open call for the piano." An energetic man announces to the crowd as he wheels a well-worn piano to the stage. "Any brave souls out there who want to play tonight?"

Hannah's face lights up as she turns to Maddie. "You have to," she urges Maddie. "Come on."

"No way," she murmurs. Her cheeks burn bright pink, but her fingers twitch in her lap.

"Don't be shy," Wes says, his voice full of enthusiasm. "You'll be incredible."

Hannah grabs Maddie's hand, pulling her to her feet. "I know you can play. Let's see you blow them away."

I sit up straighter as Maddie allows herself to be led to the stage. Compared to the loud, intoxicated crowd, she's so small and quiet. Fighting an urge to get up and start corralling them away from her, I stay put, eager to see what she does. Hannah returns and lifts her arms, hands in fists, cheering Maddie on.

Maddie scoots around on the stool for a few minutes, getting comfortable, as she nervously glances over the bar. Returning her gaze to the piano, she takes a deep breath. Her hands hover above the keys, and she begins to play. The tempo is tentative at first but grows stronger. The song's melody envelops the silent crowd like a spell. Maddie's slender shoulders rise and fall as she strikes the keys.

I can't look away. Her emotion pours through every note, raw and unfiltered.

The room erupts into applause when the song ends. I've stopped breathing. My heart is racing.

Maddie rises and makes her way back to the table.

She's only a few steps away when a man stumbles into her path, his drink sloshing precariously close to her dress. "Well, aren't you special?" he slurs, reaching out toward her. "Can I get your autograph, pretty girl?"

Maddie freezes, eyes wide.

I don't think. I'm on my feet, closing the distance between us.

"Get away from her."

The man blinks, swaying as he registers my presence.

Wes stands, too. "You heard him, buddy. It's time to move along."

Without a fight, the drunk mutters, and stumbles away. Maddie is trembling. I brush my hand across the back of her neck and rest it on her shoulder.

"Are you okay?"

Her skin is still flushed. "Yes, thank you." Her gaze moves between me and Wes. "Both of you."

There's a loud crash. Chaos erupts near the bar. A swarm of drunk tourists and locals shout, their argument escalating into a full-blown scuffle. Chairs topple, glass shatters, and everyone nearby scrambles to get out of the way.

"Here we go," Jamie says, shaking his head. He stands with Liam, getting ready for anyone coming our way.

Maddie and Hannah don't need to be in the middle of this.

I turn toward Wes. "Go home. Get them out of here." I tip my head toward them.

Wes guides them toward the open beach. I stay behind, stepping into the fight with Jamie and Liam.

"Calm down. Take it somewhere else if you need to."

By the time the police arrive, the crowd has dissipated. As I give my statement, my mind drifts to Maddie—the melody she played, the softness of her features, and the way her eyes lingered on mine. For a fleeting moment, she'd looked at me as a man she could rely on, and I'd liked how it felt—a lot.

My body burns with thoughts I shouldn't entertain. I remind myself she's not for me. No one is. The truth settles in my chest, heavy and unshakable, lingering long after the bar falls silent. I get into my truck and drive home.

CHAPTER 6

MADDIE

The Coconut Grill Café bustles with the midday crowd. Voices around us blend with the clinking of plates and the soft beat of island music drifting from the speakers. A fun, pirate-themed centerpiece showcasing boxed crates and treasure chests stands in the middle of the restaurant. Capturing the spirit of the island. I sit across from Hannah on the shaded patio, where the bright orange umbrella above casts dappled light across the table. We're settling in for lunch after a long morning at my first vet house call—a sweet little tabby cat named Rascal and his owners, Bob and Edith Clark. Poor Rascal has an upset tummy but should be as good as new in a few days.

Last night was interesting. The lively dinner, chaos at the Blue Fin Tavern, and all the quiet moments in between. The cheers of the crowd, Wes's easy grin, and Scott's heated gaze.

Our server sets our waters on the table, condensation trailing down the glasses. The tangy scent of lemon drifts up from the slices floating inside. I take a sip, letting the coolness chase away the lingering heat of the day. Hannah hasn't been herself all morning. She was the life of the party last night, but today, she's uncharacteristically quiet.

"This place…" Hannah says, flicking the wrapper off her straw with ease. "Isn't it like a permanent vacation?" She drops the straw into her glass and blows a bubble into the water. "That's what I tell myself on the weekends, and then Monday morning comes around."

Hannah's small shop at the center of town sells handmade island trinkets with a mystical flair. Candles, charms, local art. She does well enough, picking up side gigs where she can to fill in the gaps. I offered to pay her for her help with Rascal today, but she politely refused.

I open the menu. Fresh-caught tuna with tangy wasabi aioli. My mouth waters. I wave the server over and place my order. Hannah orders a house salad.

"Extra croutons, please."

I raise an eyebrow. "Living dangerously?"

"Don't judge me." Her lips twitch.

The server disappears, and I lean back in my chair, letting the ocean breeze wash over me. My fingers drum against the table as I debate whether to bring up Nathan's notes. The weight of what I've uncovered grows heavier by the day, but if there's anyone I can trust on the island, it's Hannah.

"I've been going through more of Nathan's notes."

Hannah's gaze sharpens. "What kind of notes?"

I hesitate, "So, remember I mentioned he was working on a theory about an ancient civilization that he believed existed thousands of years ago?"

She leans in, her focus on me, tuning everything else out.

"He believed they were descendants of Atlantis—people who fled when their homeland sank into the sea. His hypothesis was they settled on an island system in the Gulf. Later, he discovered traces of their existence in Carter's Drop."

Hannah blinks, leaning forward. "Atlantis? That's… wild. Do you think he was right?"

"Yes, I know Nathan. If he believed it, I do too. He wasn't the type to chase fairytales. If he wrote it down, he had the evidence. His notes suggest he was very close to finding what he was after. But…" His coded words flash in my mind. "He wrote some of his notes using symbols—he was keeping a secret. I'll need to find some of my old journals to decipher them. He was using a code we created as kids."

Hannah stares at me like I'm from outer space.

"Code? Like the Klingon language or something?" She giggles.

"Hey, scientists raised us—it's how we kept each other entertained as kids." My heart pulls with the memories of our childhood. Playing with no other cares in the world.

"He also wrote the words: **I don't trust him**."

Her brows knit with concern. "Do you think his disappearance may not have been an accident?"

"Until I figure that out, I can't trust anyone with what I've found." I meet her eyes, my voice firm. "Promise me, Hannah. Don't tell anyone."

She reaches across the table, her fingers brushing mine. "I promise, Maddie. Whatever you need, I'm here."

The server returns with our food, interrupting the conversation. My ahi tuna sandwich is picture-perfect. The seared fish glistens under a drizzle of soy glaze, paired with crisp greens nestled between toasted ciabatta bread. I take a bite, savoring the tangy heat of the wasabi against the tender fish.

Hannah's salad is a colorful mix of greens, cherry tomatoes, cucumbers, and golden croutons glistening with olive oil. She picks at it, her thoughts drifting elsewhere once more.

"All right. That's it." She's pushing a crouton around her plate. "What's on your mind? You've been thinking about something all morning. I thought something was cooking between you and Wes last night, but today, you're acting like someone broke your favorite toy. Spill."

She sighs, stabbing a tomato with her fork. "Okay, fine. After we got back to your cottage last night, and you and I said goodbye, I realized I'd forgotten my purse in the inn's kitchen. When I went back inside, I noticed Wes and Garrett speaking in the hallway. It didn't look friendly. They seemed… intense."

My stomach twists. Garrett and Wes? "What were they talking about?"

"I couldn't hear much," she admits. "But it gave me a weird feeling. I thought those two barely knew each other." She frowns. "Wes saw me. He didn't let on. He just kept talking to Garrett."

Her eyes squint. "He's so hot and cold. One minute, he's all charm and the next, it's like he's hiding something and… he's always looking at you, Maddie. I'm sure you've noticed it. I thought he might just have a crush on you. You're just so sweet and gorgeous… not to mention smart. But now I'm convinced that's not it. I'm not sure what it is about him, but he's giving me bad vibes."

Wes's spat with Garrett is odd, but my instincts tell me I can trust Wes.

"I'm sure I remind him of Nathan. We look alike. Since they were friends, it may be déjà vu when he looks at me. Heck, I feel that way when I look in the mirror."

Hannah tilts her head, her eyes squinting.

"Also, Wes is exhausted. There is something or someone weighing down on him. I know that kind of fatigue when I see it."

Uncertainty flicks across her eyes. "Maybe."

I move to another topic. "Hannah, did Nathan ever tell you anything about his personal life? Like whether he was seeing anyone or had a steady girlfriend?"

"Nathan?" She sets her fork down. "No." She pinches her chin. "I didn't see him every day, so I guess he could have been seeing someone. He was private. Women noticed him, of course, he was—successful, handsome, mysterious—but I never saw him on a date."

I glance down at my hands, Nathan's poem flashing in my mind. "Wes mentioned Nathan told him about a girl in his life who was important to him, and I found a love poem Nathan wrote. Keeping a secret like that doesn't match the brother I knew. I feel like he would have told me if he had someone."

"That's interesting. If there was a woman in his life, maybe he was keeping it quiet to protect her." She pauses. "Do you think this relationship could be connected to what happened to him?"

"I'm not sure, but I think there is more to his disappearance than a diving accident. There had to be a reason Nathan was diving alone and couldn't trust the people he was working with."

I swallow the tears in my throat. "Why didn't they find his body, Hannah? I'm convinced someone harmed him or worse. If that's true, I can't move on until I find the answers."

"I understand. Nathan always carried so much responsibility on his shoulders. I see the same resolve in you. Whatever I can do to help you, I'm here. You tell me. I'll spy, maim, kill. I'm on it."

I laugh. "Okay, another topic… I noticed Jamie talking to you last night. The two of you seemed pretty cozy."

Color creeps over her cheeks. "Jamie's sweet. He told me he likes having me around."

Amusement tugs at my mouth. "He has a crush on you."

Hannah lets out a breath and shakes her head. "Jamie? No, we're just friends."

"Are you sure about that?" I tease.

She ducks her head, hiding a smile.

The rest of lunch passes with light conversation, and all the earlier tension is gone. Hannah and I make plans to go through my storage boxes on a quest for my old journals. We'll make it fun with a movie, wine, and food. After we pay the bill and gather our things, my mind is already turning to my next move.

"I think I'll share a little more information with the dive team tomorrow."

"Really? I thought you didn't trust anyone."

"I don't. But Garrett said I could be part of the team. If I want to stay involved, I need to contribute something… I'm just not sure how much to share."

Hannah rests a hand on my arm, her gaze steady. "You'll figure it out."

We grab our purses and rise from the table.

"Come on." She puts an arm around me and leans into my side, laying her head on my shoulder. "Let's get some ice cream."

CHAPTER 7

SCOTT

I lean back in my chair with my coffee, watching the team as they fall into their usual cadence. At the far end of the table, Garrett is discussing research findings with Dr. Elaine Fischer, the sharp-eyed academic that has just been aligned with the project. I like her. She's got a cool head and seems to be here for the science not the fame.

"Scott, you look very nice today. Blue is your color." Ms. Connor's lips turn up as she puts a honeybun on my plate. I thank her and take a bite.

Maddie's gaze moves between the maps and the people around the table, like she's deciding whether to speak up. Her fingers fidget with her napkin, folding it into shapes. It makes me want to grab the napkin so I can take away her anxiety and feel her skin. I've noticed she has a habit of fidgeting when she's thinking about saying or doing something. It's cute. Hannah leans in and whispers into Maddie's ear, coaxing a smile from her.

Sitting across from Maddie, my eyes linger on her face, her soft lips moving as she speaks in a low hush to Hannah. I follow the long lines of her neck to the edge of her collarbone, partially hidden beneath her white linen button-down. She's wearing a gold necklace with a jade elephant pendant, cradled against her heart. I imagine her pulse softly beating there. It makes me want to get closer to her, to erase the few feet of distance between us. She doesn't quite fit into the chaos of our world yet, but she's determined to join us.

Wes strides into the room.

"Morning." He walks over to the coffeepot and pours himself a cup without waiting for an invitation.

I keep my expression neutral, tightening the grip on the mug. Wes isn't part of the team. He doesn't belong at this table. But he's got a knack for inserting himself into things—including our breakfast.

Standing beside him, Ms. Connor gestures to the table. "Make yourself at home."

"Thanks. Just for a minute. We're about to head out to the reef to get some pretty pictures of the coral and the tourists." He kisses her cheek and grabs a bagel. Then he pulls out an empty chair and slides it in next to Maddie. I can't hear what he's saying to the women, but they burst into giggles.

Frowning, I finish my food and give Garrett a wave, signaling that it's time to start.

Garrett clears his throat, silencing the chatter. "All right, everyone, let's focus. Scott, walk us through the plan."

Wes excuses himself, clearly not interested in the minutia we're about to jump into. He gives Maddie a quick squeeze on the shoulder, and leaves.

I set my mug down and point at the map. "We've identified two stable main entry tunnels with signs of prior exploration. It's not conclusive who the diver was, but there's a strong chance it was Nathan."

Maddie's eyes snap to mine. I swallow, my words stumbling out. I force myself to slow down and lean forward.

"We'll do another recon on Thursday. We expect the currents to be the calmest this week. On this dive, we'll focus on charting and continue to look for leads to identify the chambers most worth pursuing."

"That's logical. So what about tomorrow?" Elaine asks.

"Shallow dive. Near the surface."

I was glad to find out Maddie would join our team in a consultation role—a good move on Garrett's part for once. The woman's as smart as she's beautiful, and the insight she'll bring from Nathan's private research will be immensely valuable to the project. But damn. I just want an opportunity to see her underneath the water. I'm going to ask her to get in.

"Another day in the open ocean. I'll take it," Jamie says.

"Don't get too comfortable. Thursday's dive will make up for it."

Maddie's fingers fidget as they play with her cup. She clearly has something on her mind she wants to express. When she speaks, her voice is steady.

"I've gone through more of Nathan's research." She opens a small notepad filled with a neat, bulleted list. "You all know he believed Carter's Drop might hold evidence of an ancient civilization. I've learned he believed they were the actual descendants of Atlantis—people who escaped when their homeland sank into the sea. He found evidence that supports this theory in Carter's Drop."

The room stills. Garrett's gaze locks onto her with an intensity that borders on predatory. I don't like it.

"Atlantis? He never talked about Atlantis. That's ridiculous. What kind of evidence?" he asks, his tone condescending.

"Hey." I give Garrett a stern look and he closes his mouth.

Maddie hesitates, her grip on the glass tightening. "Carvings on a small stone-like object he found underwater. He believed it was evidence that linked the human activity he was searching for to the myth of Atlantis. The stone appears to be made of a material that he wasn't familiar with. But nothing is confirmed."

Garrett squirms in his chair, taking off his glasses and rubbing his eyes.

"Did he document this in his journals?" Elaine asks.

"Some. I've connected the stone to a journal entry noting where he found it in the blue hole's tunnels. He traced the markings to text found in research about the lost city." Maddie takes a quick breath and continues. "But the rest of his notes are in code. It's like he was trying to protect some of the information. I haven't translated it yet."

Garrett leans forward, his voice cutting. "Coded how? What exactly did he say? Can I look at the stone?"

"Ease up, Garrett." I cut him off. "Let her finish." He leans back in his chair, jaw tight. He wants to argue, but he's holding back in front of Elaine. Good. His gaze doesn't move from Maddie.

She looks up at me, relief in her eyes.

"I'm impressed you've gleaned so much already," Elaine says.

"I just want to understand what he was looking for. And why he kept so much of it to himself. I want to know why he dived alone." Her lips quiver.

I study her for a moment. She's composed, but the pressure of not having the answers about what happened to her brother is pressing in on her.

"Maddie, if you're interested." I stand and walk over to her. "You can join us on tomorrow's dive. It's shallow and safe—a good opportunity to get back in the water and familiarize yourself with the area. You can see the hole yourself… from a distance."

Her eyes widen. But it's with excitement, not fear. I like that.

"I haven't dived in years. Not since Nathan disappeared." She hesitates. "I'm not sure I'll—"

"It's like riding a bike." I take the seat Wes abandoned and sit beside her. "You haven't forgotten how to do it. We'll go at your pace. Make sure you're safe and comfortable. You'll do great."

Hannah nudges her. "You should go. It'll be good for you."

Doubt flickers across her face. She takes in an audible breath.

"Okay. I'll come. Thank you."

Then she leans over and gives me a big hug. My heart stops as I wrap my arms around her. She's so soft. Her curves press against my chest and I can hear the flutter of her heart. My breath hitches, and I try to control my body's reaction to her touch. Reluctantly, I let go when she pulls away.

After the meeting, I linger by the window and watch as Maddie helps Ms. Connor clear the table. The sunlight catches the soft waves of her hair and highlights the freckles on her nose. She's stirring a promise of desire I thought was long gone. My mind is on the hug, the sweet pressure of her body against mine, her smell. I want…

I approach her as she sets down a stack of plates. "Hey. Got a minute?"

Her light brown eyes meet mine. "Of course."

I swallow before speaking. "I wanted to apologize for last night. It wasn't the best introduction to our island's nightlife. I promise the locals are decent people, and nights at the bar are usually fun."

She shrugs it off. "That's okay. At least it wasn't boring. I had a lot of fun."

"That song you played on the piano last night was beautiful. What was it?"

Her expression softens, and she glances down. "It's a song my mom played for Nathan and me when we were young. She taught me how to play."

"You've got a gift." My pulse quickens, exciting possibilities overtaking any practical thought. I feel ten years younger.

She blushes and breathes in deeply. "Thank you."

The words are out before I stop myself. "If you're free Saturday, maybe I can take you fishing. A break from all this chaos. My personal welcome to the island."

She drops the rag she was using to wash the dishes into the sink. "I'd like that." She licks her bottom lip. The urge to kiss her hits me hard. I force myself to look away for a moment, trying to shake it off.

"Great. I'll pick you up at eight on Saturday." I give her a gentle caress on her shoulder. "And we'll see each other bright and early tomorrow morning for the dive."

"I can't wait." Her husky whisper tells me she may be affected, too.

We say goodbye, and I get out of there before I grab her and kiss her in front of everyone.

In my truck, I start the engine and try to clear my head. This isn't loneliness or missing Adeline.

This is new. And it's dangerous.

But I don't care.

CHAPTER 8

MADDIE

Adeline glides through the waves as we head toward Carter's Drop. I grip the railing. No one knows about my crippling aquaphobia. After Nathan's death, in my nightmares, I was always drowning—alone in the dark, in the cold merciless waters of the blue hole. I'd wake up breathless. Covered in sweat. Simple things like brushing my teeth or showering would trigger panic attacks. It's taken years, but I've fought my way back. Today, I'm going to take my biggest step yet.

Into the ocean.

The crew is busy preparing for the dive. Scott's steady gaze fixes on the horizon. It's too soon to have these strong feelings, but I want to get closer to him. I'm enjoying the thrill of our encounters and the attraction. Maybe it's just physical for him, but I believe it could be more.

I put on my wetsuit, adjusting my arms and pulling up the zipper with trembling fingers. Today, everyone is diving in wetsuits.

"You ready for this?" Hannah asks. She's wearing a pink sundress, she doesn't swim. "By the way, you look great in the suit."

"Thanks. I think I'm ready. It's been a while."

"Don't worry." Jamie walks by us. "Like Scott said, diving's like riding a bike. Except it's underwater, with tanks and no wheels."

"Smartass," Hannah quips.

"That's… not as reassuring as you think, Jamie."

Liam adjusts his mask. "Relax, Maddie. If you forget anything, we'll just point at you and laugh. Then we'll rescue you. You're safe with us."

Margaret rolls her eyes. "Just ignore them. You've got this."

Scott walks over. He hands me my mask and places the tanks by my feet. Resting his hands on my shoulders, he rubs them before letting his hands glide down my back, lingering a moment before pulling away. I hold my breath.

He takes my hand and gazes into my eyes. A question flashes across his face.

"Were you thinking of your first dive or the last one?"

We both sit down on the boat bench.

"My first, how'd you know?"

He watches me for a moment. "Your face… I know that look." He glances out at the ocean. The waters are calm, broken only by the wake of small waves and the froth trailing behind the *Adeline*.

"You always remember your first dive and your last. I was fourteen when my dad took me out for my first time. Hard to believe from looking at me, but he was a Wall Street banker." He laughs, shaking his head. "He loved the sport. How old were you?"

"I was ten," I tell him proudly.

Scott's brows lift and he opens his mouth in surprise. "Really?" The word slips out on a breath, and a faint flush climbs his neck. His eyes are gleaming.

"Nathan was already a pro by the time he was fifteen. Already diving solo. Mom and Dad let him take me out for my first swim." His lips curl, and I shoot him a *don't lecture me* stare. "I know it wasn't legal, but they trusted him. It was a special day—just for us. They were on the boat."

His grin widens.

"My parents were so young back then. They were both marine biologists, and they raised us to be fearless."

"You're full of surprises."

His face is relaxed. His pupils push aside the hazel in his eyes. My breath catches. I lean in.

"Returning to this place, to Maverick Key…" My chest is lighter as the words leave me, saying them out loud—it's intimate. I want to share this with him. "I'm returning to myself. The person I was before… life got hard."

He's quiet. A steady, thoughtful gaze. Then he stands and reaches out for my hand. I take it.

"This is a shallow dive. It's going to get you back in the water. There's no pressure today—just an easy swim. Let's enjoy the reef." The tone of his voice is steadfast. I exhale.

"Thanks… I need to get in there and remember why I used to love this."

He cups my face with his strong hands, sharing all his confidence with me.

"Trust me, Maddie."

His simple, sincere words fall over me like a warm blanket. I believe him. He'll keep me safe.

"I do."

I take hold of his hands and close my eyes. Breathing in. He brushes his lips across the top of my head. This makes me jump, and we pull away from each other, taking a parting glance. Then he returns to the helm to steer. My heart is beating in my ears, and my hands are shaking.

Adeline slows as we reach the descent point. The sea is a brilliant turquoise, with sunlight filtering through its surface, creating watercolor patterns beneath.

The blue hole is down there.

Waiting for me.

My heart is still racing as Liam tosses the anchor and the boat rocks.

"All right," Scott announces over the engine thrum. "It's the buddy system, as always. Stick together, watch your gauges, and enjoy the dive. This one's just for fun. Maddie, you're with me."

I put on my tanks, then turn back to the water. The dark ripples appear benign, welcoming even. But the surrounding air is thick, and it's hard to breathe. I pinch myself, trying to push the fear from my mind.

This is where Nathan took his last dive. It's where he died. Will the blue hole look the same as it did in my nightmares? Will it take me too?

Scott returns and checks my gear. I shiver at his touch as he brushes back the loose hair that's fallen over my eyes. He tilts his head.

"You good, sweetheart?"

"I think so."

"You're gonna be fine. We'll take it slow." He squeezes my hand. "Nathan wants you to live, Maddie… let's go." I put on my mask.

We enter the water, and the sea wraps around me, cool and weightless. The noise of the boat disappears. I stay close to Scott as the rest of the team follows.

The underwater world opens up, vibrant and alive. Schools of brightly colored fish dart around us, their scales shimmering like tiny rainbows. I move cautiously at first, my breathing loud in my regulator. Then I relax and look around.

Scott points to a cluster of yellow fish that scatter as we approach. A sea turtle glides past, slow and majestic, its flippers moving in unhurried strokes.

This is incredible. Can you see this, Nathan? Wonder fills my chest, replacing some of the fear. For the first time in five years, I'm happy to be underneath the water.

Scott writes on his dive slate. **Beautiful, isn't it?**

I nod, grinning behind my regulator. He grins back, and everything around us feels natural. I watch all the weight on my heart, carried for years, float away into the abyss like rising bubbles.

We swim farther, the underwater landscape shifting beneath us. The light dims as we approach Carter's Drop, and the water grows cooler. The entrance to the blue hole looms ahead—a vast, dark void in the ocean's floor, its coral and barnacle-covered edges teeming with life. Crabs scuttle across the sand. Fish dart through the crevices. A bounty of color surrounds a pit of endless black.

I hover near the edge, a wave of emotions crashing over me. My heart freezes. This is where Nathan disappeared, where the unknown swallowed his final moments.

Scott places a hand on my arm, his touch calming me. He writes on his slate. **We're not going in. We're just taking a look.**

I swallow hard, staring into the depths, half expecting Nathan to emerge from the void, his face breaking into one of his lopsided grins. But there's only darkness, vast and unyielding.

Scott motions for me to take my time, his gaze tender. I stare into the hole for a few more minutes, then relax. The weight of Nathan's loss eases just a little bit more.

This is what he loved. This is where he wanted to be.

Scott holds my hand, and we glide around the hole, taking in all the beauty surrounding us. For the first time in years, I feel pure joy.

We linger there awhile before Scott signals to the group it's time to ascend. As we move away, I glance one more time at the blue hole.

Back on the boat, my limbs are heavy with exhaustion, but my spirit is lighter than it's been in years.

"Not bad," Hannah says, handing me a towel.

I wipe the water from my face. "Thanks. It felt good… better than I expected."

Scott appears beside me, his expression thoughtful. "You did good out there. You're a natural." I catch my breath at his words. You're a natural, Maddie. That's what Nathan told me—when we dived the first time—when I fell in love with the ocean.

"Thanks." For a moment, the noise of the boat fades. He moves closer like he's about to say more.

Then the sound of wakes crash beside us. A sleek black and silver boat approaches, cutting through the water. Wes stands at the helm, his face visible from the distance. He waves.

"There's your new best friend," Hannah teases.

I lift a hand to wave back. Wes salutes before turning to his crew. Beside me, Scott's jaw tightens. Not saying a word, he starts securing the gear.

As *Adeline* heads back to Maverick Key, the team's focus shifts to preparations for the evening.

"Bonfire tonight, anyone?" Jamie calls out.

Hannah claps her hands. "I live for those."

Scott glances at me, his tone lighter than usual. "Are you up for an island tradition?"

After today, I'm ready to leave my comfort zone.

"Why not?"

Scott pulls me into his arms and gives me a squeeze, his nose brushing against my neck. I want to stay there, wrapped up in the strong warmth of him, and never let go.

"Today was amazing," he murmurs, his fingers raking through my hair. "Let's do this again."

"I'd like that."

He smiles and walks off to the helm.

As the boat nears the island, I lean against the railing, the wind teasing my hair. It's soft, but not the same as Scott's fingers. He stands at the helm, steering us home. Our gazes meet a few times, charged but still hesitant. What are we afraid of?

When we pull into the docks, his eyes are closed, and when he opens them again, he doesn't notice me. His gaze is fixed on the horizon.

♥

Hannah and I weave through the crowded aisles of the Maverick Key General Store, gathering provisions for the bonfire. The store is packed with tourists, their sunburned shoulders peeking out from their flowered tanks. The smell of coconut and banana sunscreen mingles with the recycled, air-conditioned air. Outside, the golden light of the late afternoon sun spills across the island.

I steer the cart down the baking aisle, scanning the shelves for marshmallows and graham crackers. The cart's rubber wheels squeak, blending into the surrounding chatter.

"Were you able to get in touch with Mark?" Hannah asks as we stroll down the candy aisle.

"Not yet. I tried to reach him at the Coast Guard office. But it seems he's going to be hard to pin down. One of his officers said he'd get back to me soon when he has time." I frown. "If they were as close as we thought, I would've expected to hear something back by now."

"They were college buddies. I promise you they were close," she says with a huff, shrugging. "Well, maybe you can meet his wife. She's a sweet woman. She'll get you the meeting." She grabs some matches. "Anyway… This bonfire is going to be fun," Hannah says, grabbing a large box of chocolate bars and tossing them into the cart. "This will be a perfect opportunity for you to hook up with Scott."

I choke. "Umm, I don't think that's going to happen."

Hannah adjusts the goods in the cart. "Oh, come on. You know I'm not blind. I felt the sexual healing on the boat today." She pinches my chin playfully. "Look, Maddie, you're choosing well with Scott. He's a gentleman, and he's hot. I'm sure he'll be great in the sack, too." Her eyes get large. "But don't dare tell him I said that. It'd get weird."

I roll my eyes. "Scott's attractive. But I'm not in the headspace for a relationship, and I'm not looking for a one-night stand." I pause before adding. "Though I'd be lying if I said I hadn't imagined it." I don't tell her about all the dreams I've had over the last week. It's been so long since I've had sex, or even thought of it. I may have forgotten how it's done. But I doubt I'd forget Scott, though.

She cackles. "Suit yourself, but it's inevitable. I can read tea leaves, you know." She pauses for effect. "And they say that you and Scott are definitely going to do it. Sooner or later. Let's hope for sooner."

I'm as red as a tomato as we pass a group of tourists gathered around a display of metal detectors. Their excited voices carry across the store, and their eagerness tells me they've just arrived on the island.

"Tonight's the night," a man in a tropical shirt announces to his friends. He gestures grandly toward the stack of detectors. "The treasure of Maverick Key. It's out there somewhere, and this is a small island."

His friend scoffs, and they move to the snack aisle.

"Don't zone out," Hannah says, waving a pack of buns in front of my face. "Let's get back to Scott."

I bite my lip, trying to ignore the warmth creeping up my neck. The memory of Scott's deep voice and large presence lingers. I can't shake the memory of the tingles that ran up my body when he held me after the dive. It's unnerving how quickly he's gotten under my skin.

"Fine." I lower my voice. "The dive was fun. He… surprised me."

"How so?"

I run my fingers along the cart's handle. "He's not the stern, no-nonsense leader I thought he was. There's more to him. He's careful, reliable, but…" I can't find the right words.

"But hot," Hannah supplies with a grin.

I laugh despite myself. "That's not what I meant."

"Sure, sure. If you say so, Maddie," she teases, nudging me. "But hey, no judgment here. You two will be terrific together. He'll keep you from doing anything without a plan, and you'll make him smile more. It's win-win."

I chuckle as she basks me with more of her matchmaking wisdom.

"Oh—nature calls. Can you handle the rest without me?" She's already rushing off.

I push the cart forward, scanning the shelves for skewers.

A soft voice interrupts.

"Excuse me."

I glance up. A young woman stands at the end of the aisle. Her blond hair is pulled into a sleek ponytail. She's dressed nicely but looks out of place in the store. Her expression is polite yet tinged with discomfort. She seems afraid to be here.

"Are you Maddie Carter?" she asks.

I freeze. "Yes, that's me. Can I help you?"

She stares at me in an intimate, unnerving way.

"I thought it might be you. I've… heard of you. Your brother was Nathan Carter."

The mention of Nathan jolts me. "He was. Did you know him?"

She studies me, then jumps when she hears something nearby and her eyes flick toward the store's front doors before returning her gaze to me.

"I'm sorry to bother you. I just wanted to meet you and say… I'm sorry. Nathan was… important to me."

She looks back at the doors.

"I should go." She turns and starts to walk away. "I hope you're enjoying yourself on the island."

"Wait." I step forward, but she's already retreating outside, her steps quick and purposeful.

I hesitate, deciding whether to go after her or stay and wait for Hannah. I rush outside, but she's already gone.

Hannah is waiting for me when I get back inside. "What happened?"

"It was strange," I mumble, my thoughts racing.

"This woman came up to me. She knew who I was and told me Nathan was important to her. Before I could ask her anything, she left in a panic."

"What did she look like?"

"She was thin and had pale blond hair."

"Well," Hannah says, dropping skewers into the cart. "There are a lot of blondes on this island, but it's small. You're bound to run into her again."

We finish gathering supplies and head to the register. Outside, the sun sets as the first stars emerge. Hannah loops her arm through mine as we walk toward her car, chatting about the bonfire plans and setting me up with Scott.

I should be listening, but my minds on the strange woman's words.

Nathan was important to me.

Who is she? Why did she run?

CHAPTER 9

SCOTT

The bonfire burns ahead, casting shadows on the faces of those already gathered. The smoky tang of burning wood mixes with the sweetness of marshmallows roasting over the flames. I carry a cooler and a few folded chairs toward the group. Jamie, Liam, and Margaret are already at the fire, their chatter cutting through the crackle of the flames.

There's Maddie.

She's at the edge of the group, her pink dress swaying in the breeze. Her hair falls in loose waves, framing her beautiful face. She's talking to Hannah.

For a second, I forget to keep walking, my feet rooted in the sand.

"Hey, Scott," Jamie says, his voice snapping me out of my daze. He waves me over. "You going to join us… or just stand there like a statue?"

"I'm coming." My voice is rough. Jamie looks at me but says nothing. I set the cooler down and get started on unfolding chairs.

Jamie pops the cooler open with a flourish, pulling out a beer. "Now it's a party," he declares, tossing one to Liam before cracking open his own.

"Please tell me someone brought crackers," Jamie says as he flops down beside Margaret. "It's not a real bonfire without s'mores."

"I've got you covered." Maddie waves a box of graham crackers.

I settle farther back, letting the group's energy wash over me. My eyes drift to Maddie as she prepares s'mores with the marshmallows Jamie roasted. She's lively tonight, more outgoing than usual. I lose myself in her—every movement, the highlights in her hair, her beautiful skin. I know what that skin feels like. Soft and kissable. She doesn't need the fire to glow. When she settles down on a beach blanket, I grab another beer from the cooler and walk over, joining her on the blanket. Her warmth, the scent of her, engulfs me.

"Thought you might be thirsty." I crack open the can and hand it to her.

"Thank you." Her fingers brush against mine as she takes it, and I'm hyperaware of each movement she makes. I watch her lips as she drinks her beer and I feel a thrill each time we accidentally touch. On the dive, Maddie was so at ease and happy under the water. And brilliant. She's good at it. There was one moment when we approached the hole that I thought she may have lost her confidence, but it didn't last long. The woman is full of surprises. Diving at ten years old. I shake my head.

The night settles into an easy rhythm of jokes, stories, and togetherness. Sparks spiral into the night sky as the fire pops and crackles. Jamie launches into another fishing trip story.

"And then," Jamie says, unable to contain his enthusiasm, "A guy on the dock yells, 'Shark! Shark!'... I swear, I've never swum so hard in my life. I barely got out of there alive."

"It wasn't even a shark, J," Liam chimes in, shaking his head. "It was a floating log."

"Ha. Those are just details." Jamie waves him off. "Facts are overrated."

The group bursts into another round of laughter. As it fades, I catch Maddie looking my way, her eyes filled with curiosity. Her gaze makes me want to touch her.

"What about you?" she asks, her voice drawing the group's attention.

I blink, surprised. "Sorry, what about me?"

"Most embarrassing story," Hannah prompts.

I sigh, scratching the back of my neck. "I don't get embarrassed."

"Oh, come on," Maddie teases. "Scott, there has to be something."

My name on her lips electrifies me. A vision pops into my head—Maddie beneath me in bed, whispering my name. I forget where I am for a moment as the image lingers and my muscles tense. Jamie's voice snaps me out of it.

"What about the pool?"

I groan. "You're not bringing that up again."

"Oh, I am," he shoots back. "It's classic."

I frown. "Fine. I was trying to impress someone. Thought I could dive off one of those Olympic platforms and look cool. Turns out, I wasn't wearing the right swim trunks… and had to get out of the pool sans attire."

This time, I'm the one at the center of the laughter, and even I have to chuckle. Maddie's laugh stands out to me—loud and full, making the embarrassment worth it. I glimpse her long legs through the slit in her dress when she crosses them. The bright pink color of the dress is a pretty contrast against the light tan of her skin. My heartbeat picks up.

"Did you?" She bites her lip, waiting for my answer.

"Did I what?" My throat turns to dust.

"Impress her."

Her voice is soft, and she's no longer smiling. Her eyes pierce through me.

I clear my throat. "I never saw her again." I pause. "Turns out I don't do casual well."

I can't pull my gaze from her lips.

"What do you do well?"

I stop breathing.

"Whoa, it's getting a little hot over here," Margaret says, giggling. It's the first time I've ever heard her giggle. The entire crew is looking at us like they know something we don't.

Maddie and I take another sip of our beers, taking down the temperature.

The night carries on.

Liam's tale of his first kiss leaves everyone in stitches, and the topic of first kisses sticks.

"All right, Maddie, it's your turn," Hannah says. "Tell us about your first kiss."

Maddie's cheeks flush, and she looks at her hands. "There's not much to tell."

"Come on…" Hannah presses. "Everyone's sharing."

Maddie shrugs, uncomfortable. "I've never been in a serious relationship. I dated a little, but nothing ever felt… right for more than a few dates and some fun. Sorry to say, no kisses worth mentioning."

"Why not?" Jamie asks, curious.

Maddie's gaze shifts to the fire, her expression softening. "I guess I was always in love with the idea of love and never saw it in just one person. Then I had to focus on other things, like school, caring for Mom, work… Nathan's death." Her voice falters. "The men I dated only wanted casual." She glances at me. "And I guess that's all I wanted too."

She doesn't say she's afraid—afraid of letting another person in, then losing them. Like Nathan. Like her mom. I reach over and squeeze her hand. I recognize the pain. But I'd endure my own grief a thousand times over rather than trade away a single moment I had with Adeline. Suspecting someone as selfless as Maddie might fear love—makes me ache.

Hannah brightens, trying to lift the weight of the moment. "Well, it's their loss. Those guys should have fought for you. You're a catch, Maddie."

Maddie brushes it off, but sadness lingers in her eyes. "Thanks."

When the attention shifts back over to me, I hesitate, then shrug, taking a long sip of my beer. "Not much to tell. You all know who my first kiss was. I married my high school sweetheart, and it's now been four years since I buried her. Adeline was an amazing woman. I was lucky for the years we had."

My voice catches. I don't admit my biggest regret—never giving Adeline what she wanted most in this world—a family. I thought we had time. But I was wrong. And selfish.

Maddie's gaze lingers on me, silent and thoughtful.

The fire burns low as the group begins to scatter, their voices fading into the night. Maddie and I stay behind, gazing at the ocean as we lay on the blanket. The night is quiet now.

"Thanks for inviting me tonight."

I turn my head to her, my voice low. "I'm glad you're here."

We lie there for a while, the ocean stretching before us. We listen to the waves, the birds, and our hearts. When she sits up and gazes at the water toward the Drop, her expression is unreadable. What is she thinking about?

She stands to go and takes my hand, pulling me up. She gives me a shy smile that makes my chest tighten. Then, standing on her toes, she presses a sweet kiss to my lips. I don't want to say goodbye. She does it for me.

She walks up the path, her figure disappearing into the night.

I can't wait for Saturday.

CHAPTER 10

MADDIE

My bare feet brush against the smooth deck of the *Adeline*. The lightweight sweater I threw over my sundress flutters in the wind. Scott stands at the helm, steady and confident, his hand resting on the throttle. His sunglasses mask his expression, but the ease in his posture says it all. This is his world—he fits into it effortlessly. The sea and the boat are extensions of him.

"This spot should work," he calls out, stopping the engine. The low rumble fades.

I squint against the sunlight, turning to him. "Do you keep all the good fishing spots to yourself? Or do you share them with others?"

The corner of his mouth tilts up. "Well, I don't like to share, but with you, I'll make an exception. Been here in the Key a long time. Stick with me, and there's a lot I can teach you."

He pulls out the tackle box and sits down next to me on the bench. Tying a lure—his strong hands move with practiced ease, deft and efficient. He motions for me to try, and when I mimic him, my fingers fumble over the line.

"Here, let me help you." He slides closer. His hands brush against mine, rough and steady, as he guides me through the knot. "Like this."

His warm breath tickles the back of my ear. A nervous giggle escapes me and I can't hide my shiver. Pleasant heat flows from my neck to my core.

I glance up, catching his gaze before refocusing on my task. "Thanks. Not sure why I'm a mess. It's not like I haven't fished before." My voice comes out thick.

"You're doing fine."

Once we cast our lines, we sit in silence for a while, enjoying each other's company and the beauty of the day. Tension I didn't know I was holding dissolves with the gentle rocking of the boat and the warmth of the afternoon sun. I take off my sweater, relishing the rays on my shoulders. Scott catches and releases a snook, and I almost catch a grouper. A couple of hours go by before the bites slow down, and we unpack our lunch.

"This is nice." We've finished eating and are just enjoying the sky and the water now.

Scott leans back against the bench, sliding his sunglasses up to rest on his head. "It is. There's so much out here to see. It's nice to just sit and breathe."

We watch the lush cropping of the mangroves on the distant shore and the terns diving into the water to catch their lunch. We lay out on the boat deck for a little while, then Scott stands and pulls me up.

"Let's get in." He nods toward the ladder.

I hesitate, but the water sparkles like an invitation, and the afternoon sun has me longing for a cool plunge. "Okay. But I didn't bring a swimsuit, so… undies?"

"I don't mind…"

Smiling, I turn away, peeling off my sundress, the sun warming my bare back. Thankfully, I'm wearing modest white underwear, which provides a whole lot more coverage than my blue bikini did, anyway. Well, at least they will while they're dry. Oh well.

When I turn around, Scott's already stripped down to his black boxers, descending the ladder. I follow him in. Soon we're neck deep in the water.

"Want to fool—" he grins, "I mean, swim around?"

I laugh and splash at him playfully.

We swim, tease, and drift like we're the only two people in the world. It feels like a secret—just us, the water, and the sun. We're both excellent swimmers. The deeper we go, the more competitive we get, sprinting underwater, racing to imaginary finish lines.

After what must be over an hour—me in the lead this time—Scott grabs my ankle and tugs me backward.

"No fair, you're a cheater," I call, laughing at the innocent look he shoots me in return.

The water's getting colder, sinking into our bones, and we know it's time to get out. At the ladder, Scott pulls me toward him, steadying me as I climb. I feel his hands linger low on my waist.

Back on the deck, I'm a wet rat—dripping and chilled. When I turn, I catch him staring. His expression is unreadable at first, but his gaze becomes fixed, intense. I realize my nipples are visible and hard through the soaked see-through fabric. I grab a towel from the bench, wrapping it around me.

"That was fun."

"Oh yeah," he replies, slinging a towel around his neck. His gaze is still on my towel covered body.

We quench our thirst and settle back on the bench. Side by side, we let the sun dry us off the rest of the way.

"So," I begin, looking up at him. "How did you end up here, in Maverick Key? Why this place?"

His expression softens as he looks out over the water. "After the SEALs, I needed a fresh start and a place to settle down." He rubs his hands over his face. "Adeline and I wanted to live somewhere untouched. The island felt right. Close to the water, away from the noise of a busy town. Her family moved here with us."

I tilt my head, intrigued. "What made you choose to join the SEALs?"

His hands flex against the edge of the boat bench. "I chose the military for financial security and opportunities. I had a new wife, and the service was a sure way to protect our futures. The SEALs, because I wanted a challenge. Something to push me, to make me better. And it did. But we wanted more, something of our own. Adeline and I were both lovers of the sea. Maverick Key was perfect for that dream."

"How did you get into cave diving?"

"I'd always loved diving, and did it professionally with the SEALs, but cave diving came later. Adeline got me into it." His expression turns somber. "She was a dive instructor and when she got to Maverick Key, she started to cave. Long before Carter's Drop was a blip on anyone's radar, we'd take weekend trips to the Caribbean to dive blue holes. We were living life." He pauses and blinks. "Adeline was fearless. Maybe reckless. But she had this way of making you believe she could do anything."

"You named your boat after her."

He nods, a bittersweet smile tugging at his lips. "She loved the ocean. Being out here was her favorite thing in the world."

I hesitate. "Can I ask what happened?"

His jaw tightens, and his free hand grips the edge of the bench. "We were diving a cavern system in the Bahamas. She wanted to push deeper than we'd planned. It was risky, but she was stubborn and thought she could handle anything." His voice quiets. "The current shifted, and she got caught in a tight passage. I went after her. Managed to get her free and get us to the surface, but…" His voice breaks on the last word. "There wasn't time to stop on the way up. She took on too much nitrogen. Decompression sickness. She made it to the hospital alive, but it was too late…" Scott stops and swallows.

"We never got to say goodbye while she was conscious." He closes his eyes tightly. "I…"

My heart clenches at the raw grief in his voice. I reach for his shaking hand. "Scott, I'm sorry."

His gaze is distant. "I keep thinking about what I could've done differently. If I'd called the dive sooner, insisted we stick to the plan, or not gone in the first place…" His voice is heavy.

"You went for her. You did everything you could."

"It wasn't enough." Anger flashes across his face. "She was everything to me, and I didn't save her."

I squeeze his hand. "From just the little you've shared about her, Adeline wouldn't have wanted you to carry any guilt. She'd want you to keep living, to keep diving. You honor her every time you go out there."

His eyes meet mine—raw, vulnerable. "Sometimes it feels like the ocean took her from me. Other times… it feels like the only place I can still feel close to her."

I reach up and gently cup his face—my thumb brushes along the rough line of his jaw. "You're a good man, Scott. Adeline knew that. And I can see it too."

The air between us is charged, thick with yearning. He lets out a soft gasp. His gaze flicks to my lips before returning to my eyes. His breath is warm against my hand, which he has pulled to his face like a blanket.

"Maddie," he whispers, his voice barely audible.

My heart pounds as he leans in. The world narrows to just the two of us, his closeness, the scent of salt and his cologne, the way his breath feathers across my skin.

Then he pulls back, his expression torn. "This means something to me." His face is flushed and his voice hoarse. "You mean something to me. I just… I need to be sure."

His words hit me harder than they should. "I understand."

He exhales slowly, his gaze lingering on my face before returning to the ocean.

CHAPTER 11

SCOTT

Cool sand presses against my bare feet as I stand in my yard, staring at the starlit sky. The moon hangs low, casting silver light over the water, turning the waves into a shimmering icing coating the sea. My house is tucked behind the dunes and sits dark except for the small lamp in the living room.

I rake a hand through my hair. The air around me is quiet, but my mind buzzes like static, stuck on her. Maddie. How I've thought of her these past two weeks. Swimming bravely beneath the water, sultry and alluring at the bonfire, and today on the boat—her hands holding mine with quiet strength and compassion. She clings to me.

What are you doing, Rickter?

I make my way to the house. The porch steps creak as I push open the door. It's a simple, functional home. Old rugs soften the hardwood floors, and bookshelves crammed with novels, diving manuals, and other pieces of my life—line the walls. A pair of fishing poles lean in one corner. Framed photos hang above them—my family, my time in the Navy, Adeline.

I grab a beer from the fridge and sink onto the couch. The leather groans under me, and I stare at the blank TV screen.

Maddie.

Her beauty turns me on, sure—but it's more than that. She enthralls me. I'd forgotten what my own heartbeat felt like until I met her.

She's stronger than she realizes, carrying a weight she shouldn't have to. She's open and honest. And she looks at me like she sees through me. It's unsettling. And thrilling.

I lean back and close my eyes. The can is loose in my hand.

Admit it, Scott. You want more.

I want *her*. I want to know what makes her laugh and what keeps her up at night. I want to see the dreams she doesn't share with anyone else. I want to understand how she sees the world—how she sees *me*.

She's searching for answers in Carter's Drop like she's lost. And when her eyes meet mine, it's like she's searching for me, too.

I take another sip, then set the can down on the table and rub my hands over my face.

This island doesn't need more complications. Neither does my life. Fortune hunters have turned Maverick Key into a circus, with Carter's Drop at the center of it all.

Garrett Harlow pushes the team too hard, and Wes Harrington skulks around with his secrets. The way they watch Maddie sets my teeth on edge. I won't let them hurt her.

Pacing my living room, my gaze lands on a photo of Adeline. Her carefree grin frozen in time. Guilt is always there, a shadow I carry every day. It's why I keep my guard up and don't let anyone too close. I can't bear to fail like that again.

And yet, Maddie makes me want to try.

I stop at the window, staring out at the waves. My reflection stares back at me in the glass, weary and conflicted. How do I balance my desire for her with what's at stake? When I think about how she gives herself so willingly, even when she's scared, I know I'm already in too deep.

I sink under the navy-blue comforter on the bed, staring at the ceiling. The room is silent.

When sleep comes, it's the restless kind.

I dream of being back on the boat with Maddie, the sunlight sparkling on the water. Her smile is bright and alive. Without thinking, I reach for her, our lips meeting this time in a kiss, real and consuming. I pull her closer.

Our kiss starts tentatively, then quickly deepens. I'm out of my mind with desire. My lips trail down her neck, moving lower, reaching the secret spot beneath the open buttons of her linen shirt. I let my fingers trace her collarbone and clasp the golden chain around her neck. I want to devour the saltiness, vanilla, and jasmine on her skin. I want to bury myself in her.

"Scott, I need you. Please."

Her sweet sighs set me on fire. Now she's in the blue swimsuit, the one she wore the day we met. I pull at the straps, revealing more of her. Her hard nipples invite me to taste them, and I eagerly take them in my mouth. Moving my fingers down, down, down—underneath the blue fabric, I stroke her softness in slow circles. She gasps.

"Let me touch you."

She's moving against me now, taking control, releasing me from my pants.

And then…

We're underwater, floating in a world of color and light. Her hair is haloed around her face as we hold each other.

Then, the dream shifts.

The water darkens, and menacing shadows emerge. Carter's Drop looms in the distance, its mouth wide and hungry. Reaching for her, the current grows stronger, and pulls her away. Pulling her into the blue hole. I swim harder, my lungs burning, but I can't reach her. She stretches toward me, her fingertips brushing mine before her mouth opens in a silent scream.

Then she's gone.

I wake with a jolt, my chest heaving, sweat clinging to my skin.

Sitting on the edge of the bed, I drop my head into my hands, trying to steady my breathing. I'm getting too close. Letting her fall, only to risk failing her like I failed Adeline.

It's unbearable.

I want her.

But can't let myself have her.

CHAPTER 12

MADDIE

Hannah and I wave goodbye as I step off her porch and start walking down the narrow sandy road to my cottage. We just finished going through all the moving boxes I brought over for our girls' night while we drank wine and watched scary movies. My purse holds several old school notebooks, each containing keys to the code Nathan and I created as kids.

Even though it's late, I'm eager to decipher Nathan's coded notes tonight. A few hours of focused effort should do the trick. I also found some old library books of his, including science texts. One dogeared chapter covered the myth of Atlantis. There was an illustration that seemed more like science fiction than science, featuring people in white robes gathered around an object with etchings that look just like those on the stone I found among Nathan's things. The more I find of his past, the stranger this all becomes.

My thoughts return to Scott. On our fishing trip, his tough guarded shell had softened, revealing a glimpse of vulnerability and fun. My heart races as I think about our swim and how we nearly kissed. Not a quick, sweet peck like I'd given him at the bonfire, but a real kiss. He wanted to—I know he did—but it wasn't the right time.

I shake my head to clear my daydreams, the warmth of the memories shielding me from the cool night air. I've been on Maverick Key for two weeks, yet Scott Rickter already occupies more space in my mind than I care to admit.

The walk home is quiet, with long, dark shadows stretching under the swaying palms. Gravel crunches beneath my sneakers as I get closer to the inn. Ding isn't with me tonight, making the silence heavier.

Suddenly, a shift in the air prickles the back of my neck, and I sense another presence. I glance over my shoulder, my steps quickening. The night's shadows press closer, and every rustle of leaves is sharper and louder than it should be. A nervous laugh escapes me. I'm just being paranoid. I clutch my purse closer, my fingers brushing against the cool leather as if it might somehow protect me.

A twig snaps behind me.

I freeze. Every muscle in my body locks up. My breath catches, and my heart pounds in my throat. I have to know what it is. Slowly, I turn, scanning the shadows. Nothing moves except the palm fronds, their rustling magnified in the stillness.

"Hello?" I whimper. My voice is barely more than a whisper, fragile and uncertain.

Silence.

Except for distant waves and chirping cicadas. Swallowing hard, my mouth dry, I force my feet to keep moving. The road stretches ahead, now endless, my cottage and the inn still not in sight. My breathing grows louder in my ears as I focus on my steps.

There's a harsh scuff of heavy shoes against gravel. Fear jolts through me, and this time, I don't pause. I don't want to know who or what is behind me.

I walk faster. Just a little further.

The glow of my porch lamp is finally visible through the trees ahead. Relief floods through me—but it's fleeting. The weight of unseen eyes presses against my back, suffocating and insistent. There's a sudden rustle in the bushes to my left. I jump, my breath hitching.

Spinning around, I peer through the thick brush. "Who's there?" My voice is louder this time, edged with fear.

More silence.

Then—movement. A tall, fleeting shadow flashes to the side of my vision, slipping deeper into the trees. Now, I don't stop. Panic surges through me, and adrenaline propels my legs forward. My sneakers slip against the gravel as I sprint the last stretch to my cottage. My lungs burn with every gulp of air, and my heartbeat roars in my ears as I stumble up the porch steps.

My hands tremble as I fumble for my keys, the cold metal slipping through my fingers before I get the right one into the lock. The door swings open, and I throw myself inside, slamming it shut. My trembling hands twist the deadbolt into place.

I'm safe.

My gaze sweeps the room, and the air in my lungs turns to ice.

The cottage has been ransacked.

Papers are scattered across the floor, drawers yanked out and left hanging. The couch cushions are tossed aside, and the bookshelves topple over each other, their contents scattered. My mind struggles to make sense of it.

Then—A figure stands in the shadows near the open window. It's a man, but I can't make out any details of his face or body. I catch a faint glint of metal in his hand and hold my breath.

Moving slowly, he creeps closer to the window toward me.

I scream.

CHAPTER 13

SCOTT

A loud sound jolts me awake from a restless sleep. It takes a moment to clear the fog from my head and figure out the source of the noise. My cell phone. I reach for it on the nightstand and force my eyes open. Hannah's name glows on the screen.

A tight knot of dread grips my stomach. I bolt upright.

"Hannah?" The clock flashes 2:30 a.m.

"You need to get over here right now. Someone broke into Maddie's cottage and attacked her."

The room spins as adrenaline surges through me. "What? Is she all right?" I'm already out of bed, grabbing last night's clothes from the floor.

"She's shaken up pretty bad, but she's safe. She wants you."

"I'm on my way."

The phone falls onto the bed as I slip on my jeans and boots and grab my keys and jacket.

My truck's engine roars to life, and I'm on the road before I even register if I've closed the door. The dark, empty streets of Maverick Key blur beneath the glare of my headlights. Who would do this? And why? The thought of Maddie, alone and scared, makes me tighten my grip on the wheel until my knuckles ache.

I pull up to her cottage and jump out. Maddie sits on the steps, a blanket draped over her shoulders. She's so small. Her pale face stares at the ground. Wes sits beside her, his arm resting across her shoulders, while Hannah paces nearby, talking into her phone, her movements restless. Ding is curled up beside Maddie, his head resting on her lap.

She lifts her head, meeting my eyes.

Wes gets up and steps aside, giving us room. I crouch in front of her, scanning her for signs of injury. "Are you hurt, sweetheart?"

She grips the edge of the blanket. "No, I'm okay. Just… scared."

Wes and Hannah fill me in on what happened to Maddie. Thankfully, no one touched her.

Relief washes over me—overshadowed by the tightening tension in my stomach. "The important thing is that you're safe," I murmur, brushing my hand over her knee before withdrawing it. "We'll figure this out."

Inside the cottage, it's a war zone.

"Whoever did this didn't care who heard them. I'm surprised the noise didn't wake up the whole inn," Wes mutters, his jaw tight as he surveys the destruction.

I turn to Maddie, my stomach in knots at the thought of her walking into this chaos—of someone tailing her home.

"Do you know what they were looking for?"

Her fingers tighten around the blanket. When she speaks, her voice wavers.

"Nathan's research. All his notes are gone."

I step closer, my brow furrowing. "Are you sure they took everything?"

"Yes."

I swear under my breath, my fists clenching at my sides. "This wasn't random. Whoever did this knew what they were after."

The four of us sift through the wreckage, but it's clear the intruder wasn't interested in any valuables. Maddie stays close to Hannah, her movements stiff.

"Is there anything else missing?" I crouch near the overturned desk. "Anything other than the rock and his notes?"

"No. I've been reviewing his notes and was about to decrypt the coded ones," she sniffles. "Now they're all gone."

Wes exhales. "If someone's willing to tear this place apart to get to Nathan's notes… there must be something valuable down there."

"Or they might be trying to hide something," I retort, meeting his gaze. "Covering something up."

The tension between Wes and me is palpable, but Maddie's soft voice cuts through it.

"It doesn't matter why they did it." Her hands tremble. "They won't stop me. I'm going to figure out what Nathan was searching for and finish his work."

I stand, meeting her determined gaze. There's fire there, stronger than her fear, and it fills my chest with pride and worry.

"You won't do it alone. We'll figure this out. Together."

We've done all we can for the night, but one thing is clear. The intruder followed her home for a reason. He wasn't just here to steal. He wanted to get to Maddie. My gut tells me he planned to harm her. Fuck.

"Hannah." I turn to her. "Can Maddie stay with you? I don't want her to be alone tonight."

"You bet she is," Hannah replies right away, stepping closer to Maddie like a protective shield.

Wes straightens. "I'll keep an eye out here at the inn. If anything comes up, I'll call." He's worried. It's a new look for him. I give him a curt nod, but my attention remains on Maddie. She's still scared, but she trusts us. She trusts me to keep her safe. That's why she asked for me.

"We'll find out who did this, sweetheart," I promise, tucking a loose strand of hair behind her ear. I straighten the elephant pendant that's been slung around her neck, putting it back in place. "And we'll make sure this doesn't happen again."

I press a gentle kiss on her forehead.

"Thank you." She pulls back her shoulders, dismissing her fears, and lets me help her stand.

We all help clean up the cottage and ensure it's secure for the night. I make calls to a few guys I know to have them install window locks and security film tomorrow. As I prepare to leave, I take one last look at Maddie while she and Hannah pack her overnight bag. "Get some rest tonight."

Outside, the events of the night weigh on me. Whoever broke into Maddie's cottage is sending a message. This reeks of someone trying to cover their tracks. Nathan must have been in over his head. Did they find what they were looking for, and what else do they want from Maddie?

My jaw tightens as I scan the shadows, clenching my fists.

They might think they can scare her off.

But they don't know her.

And they don't know me.

CHAPTER 14

MADDIE

"Ready?" Wes's voice snaps me out of my thoughts.

I've been waiting for him on the porch, reading and reflecting on last night's break-in and what it means for my quest to uncover what happened to Nathan. All his coded notes are gone. Why didn't I decode them sooner? Also, I haven't been honest with my friends. The thief didn't take everything. Nathan's poem and maps are still in my purse. I'm not sure if they'll lead me to answers, but I'm keeping their existence to myself for now.

Wes stands by the swing. Sleeves rolled up.

"I'm ready." I close the book I'd been reading. "Hannah can't join us. She needs to handle an issue at the shop."

Hannah and I had agreed to join Wes for a wine tasting on the mainland—some fun to distract us from our island worries. Spending time with Wes today seemed like a safe choice, a chance to learn more about his friendship with Nathan and a welcome distraction. However, not telling Scott nags at me. Now, with Hannah backing out at the last minute, it's just Wes and me on this trip. Is that okay? How will Scott feel about it? What exactly are me and Scott, anyway?

Wes reaches out, his fingers curling in invitation. I hesitate for a moment before slipping my hand into his. He helps me off the swing, steadying me as I rise, then pulls me toward him. His grip is warm and firm.

"Good wine. Good company. You'll feel better soon. Trust me."

We head toward his rental Jaguar. I had no idea you could rent a Jaguar, but apparently, Wes can.

As we pull out of the driveway, he turns on his playlist. The tunes of *Explosions in the Sky* envelop us. The music is uplifting, cathartic.

Focusing on the road, he glances my way as we talk.

"What type of wine do you enjoy? Red or white? Sweet or dry?"

"I've never given it much thought. Maybe red? I'm not a fan of anything sweet."

He laughs.

"What?"

"I figured you'd like sweet." He pats my leg.

"I've never been to a wine tasting. Hopefully, I won't embarrass you."

"You couldn't embarrass me if you tried," he huffs. "May I suggest we order a flight with a regional variety? And maybe we'll drink just one sweet wine to finish?"

"I'll follow your lead." The excitement of the trip is lifting my spirits. "This is fun. I never do fancy things."

"You deserve fancy."

We discuss various topics while driving, such as my veterinarian residency and our families, even though Wes is vague about his childhood. It's like his life began in adulthood. I plan to press him for more one day.

However, I sense there's a dark memory from his distant past he's trying to overcome and wants to forget. I'll give him time to share. Being in Wes's company is easy, and I'm appreciating how genuine he is, away from the cameras and crowds. No one can replace Nathan, but I feel light and free with Wes, like I did when I was with Nathan.

When we reach the vineyard, neat rows of grapevines stretch for acres. Near the vines, an elegant stone and wood building stands, with parking spaces in front. Two are filled, so Wes parks the car in the third spot and opens my door.

"Muscadine grapes are the varieties grown in this climate."

"Aren't those the ugly grapes?"

He laughs. "Yes, but they're delicious in wine and juice. They also have a lot of health benefits."

As we step inside, I absorb the romantic energy of the Italian-style winery. The host greets Wes and leads us to a private tasting room. We sit at a small table, a large charcuterie board in the center, accompanied by two tall glasses of iced water. The rich aroma of cheese and cured meat makes my stomach rumble.

"Hungry?"

I give him an abashed look and sit down.

"Just relax and enjoy this."

I take a sip of water and let my shoulders drop, allowing the atmosphere to soak in.

The sommelier enters with a cart full of wine bottles and glasses. "Mr. Harrington, Ms. Carter." He bows. "Good afternoon, and welcome to *Beau Fruit du Coeur.*"

"Fruit of the Heart," Wes translates.

"I've curated a selection of wines that showcase the regional beauty of our vineyard. If there is anything in particular you'd like to explore, please let me know."

He starts with muscadine white and red wines, followed by a rosé and a semi-sweet blanc. Wes has let me tell all my wacky stories about growing up and diving. I fill him in on my diving adventure the other day and how much fun it was. Amused, he listens, enjoying the wine and food.

"Hmm." He takes another olive and pops it into his mouth. When I raise my brows, he continues. "It's interesting what's on your mind. The past, the ocean, the project."

"So?" I'm not sure what he's hinting at.

"Well, I'm curious about what you want now. The animal clinic, your goals…"

"Finding out what happened to Nathan is the most important thing right now. I'll get to those other things later."

"Yes, well, a big part of life is learning to let go at the right time—so you can hold on to what you're meant to. Right?"

"Okay, Aristotle."

He winks and jumps back into the topic of wine, doing all the work for our host. I'm captivated by the history and essence of each variety and have immersed myself in the experience by the time we reach the dessert wine.

"We end with our Key Lime Dessert Wine, per your request, sir," the sommelier says, with a slight bow to Wes.

As the expert I now consider myself, I eat a small cracker to cleanse my palate, swirling the wine and observing the thick, pale-yellow legs as they run down the glass. I inhale deeply, catching citrusy floral notes with a hint of honeysuckle. I take a sip.

"What do you taste?"

"It's tart and creamy."

"And?"

"Okay… it's delicious."

Wes smiles and gulps his down.

♥

After returning to the inn, we relax in the living room, discussing the highlights of our day. We're on the couch, and Wes leans in closer to me.

"You remind me of Nathan," he says, a shadow of memory clouds his face. "Intelligence, curiosity—that quiet fire. You're much stronger than you think."

"I don't think I'm much like Nathan at all. He knew what he wanted, and he was so fearless. I'm just… trying to figure things out. I feel pretty useless right now."

Wes shakes his head, not having it. "Nathan believed in you. And I see why. You have so many great things ahead of you. You just need to take a breath and figure out what you want."

He's right. I have no idea what I want. The animal clinic? I should be excited about opening it and building a life here, but am I?

"I'd like to interview you." His request comes out of the blue. "It's a piece about Nathan and your time on the island. Tomorrow morning?" I'm a bit taken aback by the abruptness of his request, but I agree.

I hope I don't regret it.

A noise comes from the kitchen—Garrett. He steps out, holding a glass of tea.

"Good evening." He's staring at us, curiosity in his eyes. "It's quite late. Am I interrupting?"

Wes looks up. "Yes."

Garrett snorts. "Excuse me, then. If you have a minute, Harrington, I'd like to discuss some business with you before you turn in for the night. I'll be in the kitchen." He frowns at Wes, then smiles at me. "Goodnight, Maddie." Garrett walks back to the kitchen.

Wes rubs a hand down his face and breathes in through his nose.

"So, what's next? Have you decided how you want to deal with all this?"

"I'm not sure what to do. Nathan's research, Carter's Drop, and the break-in are connected, but I can't figure out how." I pull my hair back from my face. "It's like trying to finish a puzzle with half the pieces missing."

"Well. If I can help you…"

"Why are you so nice to me?" The question slips out before I stop it.

"Easy. I respected Nathan." His green eyes catch the light and hold it. "And I care about you."

He means it, leaving me at a loss for words. This is friendship, but I'm confused by what he's seeking. It seems to be more. But what?

"So… is there something going on between you and Scott?" He flashes a wicked grin.

I blush. "What makes you think that?"

"Um. The way he looks at you as if you're the only person in the room." His grin stretches wider. "It's hard to miss."

"It's not like that," I protest, though my racing heart tells a different story. "Scott's been kind. We're just… getting to know each other."

"Fair enough. But for what it's worth, Scott's a good guy. He has some rough edges, sure, but he's real."

"Why do you guys hate each other so much?"

I need to know. They've been trading sharp jabs at each other since I got here. And if looks could kill, they'd both be dead.

"Oh, we go way back. I wouldn't say it's hate. We just…" he pauses for a moment. "Rub each other the wrong way, I suppose. Like the opposite sides of two magnets."

"I wish you'd get along. You both are my people now."

"Since you asked so nicely, I'll give it a shot. Can't vouch for Scott, though."

We both laugh at that.

"Thank you for everything."

He shrugs. "That's what friends are for. Remember… whatever you need, I'm just a few steps away."

Warmth blooms in my chest. "I'll keep that in mind."

He playfully salutes before turning to leave, his relaxed stride taking him up the stairs, ignoring Garrett, who's still waiting for him in the kitchen.

CHAPTER 15

SCOTT

I walk into the Sand Dollar Dive Bar. The sharp tang of liquor and fried food surrounds me. The room is loud, with overlapping voices, bursts of laughter, and the soft strains of an old country tune pouring from the jukebox in the corner. Couples are line dancing in the center, surrounded by cheering onlookers.

I scan the crowd, spotting Liam waving me over from a corner table, smiling ear to ear. I wave. His earlier text about getting engaged sent shockwaves through the team, sparking this celebration, which is clearly in full swing. We knew he was dating and really into his girl, but none of us expected it to move this fast. Good for him. Glasses are raised, voices louder than usual, and judging by Liam's smile, he's enjoying every second of it.

Before I head to our table, I find the two faces I'm looking for sitting at the bar—Daniels and Graham, the detectives handling Maddie's break-in. Adjusting course, I walk over to talk to them.

"Evening." I lean against the counter of the bar. "Got a second?"

Daniels raises his beer while Graham nods with a somber expression.

"Rickter," Daniels greets me gruffly. "What can we do you for?"

"Do you have any updates on the break-in at the Driftwood?" I keep my tone light, but my stomach is in knots, bracing for the answer.

Daniels shakes his head. "Not much. We found his footprints near the cottage. Size ten, male. Looks like he went in through the door and out the window. The strange part? We think he followed her back after leaving hours earlier."

"What the fuck? Hours—" I exhale. "Then it's personal? A stalker?"

"Maddie said she saw someone outside after the break-in. He was carrying a weapon, possibly a knife. He was wearing gloves, so there were no prints, and he bailed after she screamed. Probably assumed the guests in the inn could hear her." He pauses, uncertain whether to continue. "We also found some masking tape in bushes near the cottage. That suggests he planned to take her but didn't move fast enough."

"Damn it," I mutter, running a hand through my hair. My mind races, piecing together the implications. "Whoever this is, they're not just after Nathan's notes. They're after Maddie."

Daniels's face is grim. "That's how it looks. But we've got nothing definitive yet. Whoever it was knew what they were doing. Like we said, no prints, no fibers—professional, if I had to guess."

Frustration simmers beneath my skin. "Let me know if you find out more."

"You and Maddie will be the first to know," Daniels assures me. "Now go enjoy your night before your friends drink the place dry."

I head toward the corner table. But my thoughts are still on the stalker and wondering what the hell he wants with Maddie.

Liam is at the center of the group, his arm slung around his fiancée, Jill, who's perched on his lap. She's petite, with sparkling dark eyes and curly black hair. She fits in like she's always been part of the crew. Jamie and Hannah are teasing each other, and Margaret's here, too, for her friend. Even Wes is acting like a normal human being tonight.

"There he is!" Liam shouts, lifting his glass as I approach. "Rickter, meet the future, Mrs. Mitchell."

I reach out to shake Jill's hand. "Congratulations, Jill. You're a saint to put up with this guy."

"Thanks. I think I just caught him at the right time."

"Caught me?" Liam feigns indignation. "More like reeled me in." He mimes catching a huge fish.

Everyone's happy, and the mood is infectious—the dark weight of the last few days lifts. At some point, everyone in the bar chants to the lovebirds, "Kiss! Kiss! Kiss!"

Never one to back down, Liam dramatically dips Jill and kisses her to thunderous applause. She kisses him back passionately, holding her own.

Hannah leans over to me. "Who knew Liam had it in him to be a romantic? He was so shy with the ladies."

"Not me. Jill brings him out of his shell. I'm happy for them."

Nearby, Jamie sidles up to Hannah. "Any chance I can buy you a drink?" he asks, feigning casualness. The guy has it bad. I don't like to get into the personal business of my friends, but I've told him on more than one occasion he should go for it. They're clearly into each other, and Hannah's awesome.

Hannah raises an eyebrow. "You think one drink is enough for all the years I've put up with you?"

Jamie pauses, pretending to mull it over. "Two drinks, then."

I look at Maddie. She's relaxed and happy.

Wes strolls over and tells Hannah and Maddie he's heading out.

"Early night, Harrington…" Jamie quips. "Are you planning on a threesome with the locals?" He tilts his head toward two beauties at the bar, both eyeing Wes eagerly.

Unruffled, Wes shoots back, "Nah, I'm a one-woman man… at least, a one-woman-at-a-time man." He gives Jamie a pat on the back before returning to the bar momentarily, then disappears into the night with his admirers.

I glance at Maddie. She doesn't seem bothered.

Later, Liam and Jamie drag me onto the karaoke stage. Before I protest, the opening chords of *Simple Man* by Lynyrd Skynyrd fill the bar. Rolling my eyes, I grab the microphone. By the second verse, the room has quieted, the song's recognizable chords pulling everyone in to sing along. When I finish, the room erupts into cheers.

Back at the table, Maddie claps, her eyes bright with surprise. "You didn't tell me you could sing," she teases.

"There's a lot you still don't know about me," I reply, leaning in.

Her cheeks flush. A slow song plays, and I extend my hand.

"Dance with me?"

Maddie slips her hand in mine. "Yes."

The music wraps around us as I lead her to the dance floor. Her hand rests lightly on my shoulder, and the soft sway of her dress is brushing softly against my jeans. For a moment, the world narrows to just the two of us.

"You've got moves," she murmurs, her breath hitting against my shirt in soft puffs.

"Well… if you like those…"

We laugh and snuggle in closer.

"Hey! I found something!" We hear the shout from outside the bar.

Curious, we walk outside with other patrons to see what's going on. Heads are turned toward the beach. A man stands waving his hands in the air, his voice hoarse with excitement.

We spill out onto the sand, joining the small crowd gathering around him. He holds up a diamond ring, its facets catching the moonlight.

"Is it the treasure?" someone asks breathlessly.

"No. Just a ring. Probably someone's wedding band. I wonder if it's a real diamond."

Jill's eyes flick to her hand—ring intact—she sighs.

Excitement ripples through the crowd, breaking the tension and triggering the suggestion from a group of tourists to do another late-night treasure search around the island. It's becoming the norm these days for locals and tourists both to prowl the island late at night, looking for Skipes' hidden treasure. Liam claps the man on the back. "Guess you'll have to keep searching for the real loot. At least it's not a total loss." He gestures to the ring.

"Naw, I'll post it in the classifieds. I'm sure someone is looking for it, and I'm not going to get in the way of love, man. My old lady would kill me." He walks off, shoulders slumped in disappointment.

Back inside, the celebration resumes. It's two a.m., but the bar doesn't close until three. I walk back to Maddie, but Jamie approaches me, his face serious.

"We've got a problem."

Straightening, my instincts sharpen. "What kind of problem?"

"Not here." He scans the bar. "Let's talk back at the inn. We may need some privacy for this…"

Reluctantly, I tell Maddie goodnight and arrange for her to walk home with a trusted buddy. She's still having fun with Hannah, and I don't want her night cut short. She needs some fun.

The cool early morning air greets us as we step outside, and unease tightens in my chest.

Whatever this is, it's not good.

♥

On the inn's patio, the tension in the air is thick. Liam, Jamie, and Margaret are nearby, their postures rigid. Jamie's phone lights up his face as he scrolls through video quicks, his frown deepening with each one. I've got an inkling of what's going on and am trying hard to keep my anger tamped down. And I'm failing miserably.

"All right," he mutters, pausing. "Here's the one. He posted this last night. Over half a million views already." Jamie recoils as I peer over his shoulder at the screen.

Crossing my arms tightly, I try to contain my frustration. "Let's see it."

Jamie taps play and the video rolls. Wes Harrington's smug face fills the screen, his white teeth gleaming.

"Hey there, explorers…" His voice rings out, oozing fake enthusiasm. "It's your boy, Wes, bringing you an exclusive look into one of the world's most mysterious and dangerous places—Carter's Drop."

The video cuts to dramatic shots of Wes standing above the ocean's surface, gesturing theatrically toward the water.

"Word has it there's treasure down here—maybe even the missing hoard of billionaire Harrold Skipes himself… But will we find the gold in the caves below or hidden somewhere on this island? We're here to find out."

Underwater footage follows—dark, moody shots of the caves heavily edited for maximum drama. Wes's voiceover hints at ancient artifacts, untold riches, and buried secrets, each exaggerated word fanning the flames of chaos and inviting disaster.

When the video ends, Jamie looks up at me, his mouth set in a grim line. "It's bad. The comments are filled with people saying they're cashing in on their 401ks to come here to dive."

"The Coast Guard is furious. Glassier called me thirty minutes ago. He's threatening to shut down all diving at Carter's Drop," Margaret adds.

Liam scratches his chin, frowning. "Can they do that? Shut us down?"

"If they think it's a safety risk, yes, they can." I grit my teeth. "And thanks to Wes, they've got all the justification they need. One call to NOAA, and we're done."

Without another word, I turn and head for the stairs. My boots thud against the wood as I march toward Wes's room, anger building with every step. I pound on his door, my fists rattling the frame. I don't care if it wakes the whole inn.

The door creaks open, and there stands Wes, shirtless, bleary-eyed, like he just got out of a fight. His hair is a mess, and the faint scent of spicy perfume clings to the air. Inside, ripped condom packages are strewn across the floor, and a blond woman lounges on the bed, scrolling through her phone, completely unbothered.

"Rickter," Wes groans, rubbing his face. "What the hell, man? It's the middle of the night."

I shove the door open, stepping inside without waiting for an invitation. The girl looks up at me and smiles, then turns her attention back to her phone.

"Your video is a problem."

He blinks at me, still half-asleep. "What video?"

"The one that's gone viral," I snap, my patience thin as paper. "The one turning Carter's Drop into a fucking joke and putting the Coast Guard on our backs."

Recognition dawns on his face, followed by a flicker of irritation. He raises his hands in surrender. "All right, all right. Let me get dressed, and we'll talk."

"There's no time."

I'm pissed. "Put on a shirt. You're coming with me to the Coast Guard station. Now."

♥

Inside the Coast Guard station's back office, a small group of tired and cranky officers is gathered—none too thrilled to be called into work so early. Lieutenant Mark Glassier stands by a computer monitor with his arms crossed. On the screen, Wes's video loops, frozen on his stupid face as he gestures toward Carter's Drop like he's selling tickets to a theme park.

I lean against the wall, my glare locked on Wes. He slouches in a chair, rubbing his temples, more tired than defiant. His swagger has evaporated, leaving behind a man who's scrambling to cover his ass. If I didn't have restraint in this moment, I'd happily wring his neck.

Glassier's voice slices through the room like a whip. "Harrington, do you know what chaos you've stirred up?"

Wes opens his mouth, but Glassier's hand shoots up, silencing him. "Don't. Don't say a damn word until I'm finished." He jabs a finger at the screen. "That video has half the country believing there's treasure just sitting in those caves, waiting to be scooped out. We've had nonstop calls. Professional divers and amateur thrill-seekers are planning to show up here and dive without authorization. Your little stunt has every idiot with a GoPro gunning for Maverick Key."

"Publicity never hurt anyone," Wes quips.

Mark's eyes flare and for a moment it looks like he's going to ring Wes's neck for me.

"This isn't just about bad publicity. It's a safety nightmare. Someone's going to get killed."

I push off the wall. "Lieutenant, what needs to happen to keep the dives open?"

Glassier's stern gaze shifts to me. "First, that video comes down. Immediately. Second, Harrington posts a public retraction, making it crystal clear that Carter's Drop isn't a playground for treasure hunters—with a statement from Mr. Skipes confirming he hasn't put anything in the waters."

Wes shifts in his chair, raising a hand in protest. "Look, I—"

"Shut up," I snap, my words like ice. I clench my fists. "You'll do it. Now."

Wes raises his palms.

Glassier steps beside us, shouldering in. "And let me be clear—if there's anything else, another video, post, or whatever the hell else might stir up more attention, I'll shut down Carter's Drop indefinitely."

His words press down on the room. "Understood." I turn to Wes. "Harrington?"

Wes sighs and pulls out his phone. His muttering doesn't conceal his irritation as he works on taking the video down. "Fine. Retraction. Whatever you want."

Across the room, a young officer waves his arm and calls out, trying to get Harrington's attention. "Hey, Wes, man, didn't know you had a thing for the Carter girl… Sweet ass. I really hope you're tapping that…"

The words hit like a gut punch.

I turn, my fists clenched. "What the fuck is that supposed to mean?"

The boy's eyes widen and he gestures quickly toward another monitor, where a paused thumbnail shows Wes and Maddie standing by the pool at the Inn. Her face is lit with that effortless smile that draws me in. The sight of them together sparks something volatile in my chest—a combination of protectiveness and anger that's hard to contain.

Wes glances at the screen, his expression unchanged. But he swallows. "That? It's nothing. Just a casual chat."

I step closer, my voice a low growl. "Casual? You're dragging her into your shit now?"

"Relax, Rickter. It wasn't like that. We were talking about Nathan. That's all."

Instinct tells me there's more, and the knot in my stomach twists. Is there something going on between Maddie and Harrington? "If this spotlight brings trouble her way, you'll answer to me. Do you understand?"

Glassier clears his throat, his commanding tone cutting through the tension. "Enough. Harrington, get the video down. Rickter, keep your team in line. We've got enough fires to put out without adding more." He looks at me.

"A woman like her has got no interest in the likes of him."

Wes bristles but says nothing, focused on deleting the video and drafting his retraction.

His antics are the immediate problem, but dragging Maddie into the mix has lit a fire in me. She doesn't deserve this. Not the attention or the danger.

CHAPTER 16

SCOTT

I sink into my leather couch, balancing my laptop on my knees. The dim glow cuts through the room's darkness, casting jagged shadows that mirror my mood. I've been in a sour funk all day. Wes Harrington's video carousel plays on a loop, with each episode more maddening than the last. Hand curated for his audience. I told myself I was looking through his videos to find out if there was anything else to worry about, but there's only one video on my mind.

The next thumbnail stops me cold.

Maddie's head is tilted, her expression bright and unguarded. She's with Wes at the pool, and the sight freezes me. My pulse quickens as I click play.

Wes opens the footage with his usual bravado, standing near the pool, his voice smooth and confident. The camera pans across the grounds before landing on Maddie, her sweet smile lighting up the frame.

"Here's the lovely Maddie Carter," Wes announces, his charm dialed up to eleven. "The legendary Nathan Carter's sister. She's agreed to share insight into her brother's incredible discovery—Carter's Drop."

Maddie flushes, tucking her soft, honey-brown hair behind her ear. "He loved the water and loved history. He was very passionate about his research and his dreams."

Wes leans forward, his eyes sharpening like a predator circling its prey. "Passion often leads to greatness… and Nathan was one of the greats."

I watch him work—turning their conversation into another performance. Maddie talks about Nathan's love for his family and dedication to his work. Wes ricochets more questions off each of her responses and weaves their Q&A into a narrative he's eager to sell.

My fists clench.

As the video continues, my frustration deepens, rising to the top until I'm ready to explode. I slam the laptop shut.

What she does with Wes isn't my business. If she wants him, I'll have to respect it.

I try to ignore the desire, the primal urge to make her mine in every way.

I fail.

"Damn it," I mutter into the silence. Wes is dangerous and careless, and he's pulling Maddie into his orbit like a black hole.

Grabbing my keys, I head to the Driftwood Inn. It's not far, but each passing second fuels the fire burning in my chest.

The soft light from Maddie's cottage window spills onto the porch, a warm invitation against the dark. I stride up the steps and knock.

The door opens.

She's barefoot, wearing an oversized T-shirt that slips down one shoulder. Her hair is tousled, and sleep lingers in her eyes. She's gorgeous.

Desire, mixed with anger at Harrington, has me so confused I just stare at her for a moment.

She tilts her head, a curious smile on her lips. "What's going on?"

I hesitate. "Can we talk?"

Her brows knit together. She steps aside, motioning for me to enter. The familiar warmth of her living room greets me. It's like home. The scent of lemon and the sight of Ding sprawled lazily on the rug tugs at my heart.

Maddie leans against the arm of her small couch, arms crossed. "What is it?"

I get straight to the point. "I saw one of Wes's videos."

"The one about Carter's Drop?"

"No." My voice is tight. "The one with you."

She glances down, exhaling. "Oh. That." She pauses. "It was just an interview. Wes asked me to talk about Nathan."

"Yeah, I get that." I swallow to keep my voice calm. "I just want to make sure you're okay with it. Wes has a way of turning little things into problems."

Her eyes narrow as she studies me. "Are you worried about me or about what Wes is doing?"

"Both," I admit. "I know Wes isn't a bad guy, but he's careless. He draws the kind of attention you don't want. I don't want you caught in the middle of his mess."

Her posture softens. "I can handle myself." She takes my hand, guiding me to the couch to sit. "But… thank you. For looking out for me. I'm grateful."

Some of the tension in my chest eases, but not all of it.

"I don't want anything bad to happen to you." I pause, swallowing. "Or for someone careless to break your heart."

The truth is, I don't want her to want Wes. I want her to want me.

She lets out a startled laugh, though it doesn't quite reach her eyes. "I don't think Wes is going to break my heart." Her gaze lifts to mine, her eyes filled with longing. "But that doesn't mean my heart isn't at risk of being broken."

Her words throw cold water on me.

I inhale, pushing down my reaction, and change the subject.

"The police found footprints. A man, heavy boots, size 10. He was waiting for you. Beyond that, they've got nothing useful."

Her shoulders sag, worry flashing in her eyes. "So we still don't know who it was or what they wanted."

"No. Until we do, you have to be careful. Stick close to Ms. Connor and Hannah. Don't stay here alone—especially at night. You should move into a room near Ms. Connor."

"I'll be careful. I promise."

I rest my hand on her waist and gently squeeze. She's soft, warm. "If you need anything—day or night—you call me. Got it?" I'm staring at her lips, wishing this was the time and place I could taste them.

Her eyes meet mine, filled with trust. It soothes the restlessness inside me.

"I will. Thank you." She rests her hand over mine, sending a jolt of electricity to my heart.

I give her hand a squeeze before saying goodbye and turning toward the door. As my hand touches the handle, her voice stops me.

"Scott?"

My heart picks up when she says my name. I turn back to her. "Yeah?"

She beams at me. God, I don't want to leave.

"Goodnight—don't let the bedbugs bite." Her sweet smile melts my heart.

I laugh. "Okay, goodnight sweetheart."

CHAPTER 17

MADDIE

I spread Nathan's hand-drawn maps across Hannah's kitchen table, their edges curled with wear. She sits across from me, her arms crossed. Her expression is a mix of concern and frustration.

"I can't believe you still haven't told anyone else about these."

Guilt stirs in my chest. "You're the only one I trust with this right now. I'm not ready to share it with anyone else yet."

Hannah leans forward. "With all the things that have happened to you recently, that's understandable. But these maps could be the key to finding out what happened to Nathan or, at the very least, what he found in the caves. You know Scott would want to see them."

I run my finger along the winding tunnels and Nathan's meticulous notes—unstable, at risk of flooding, unknown depth—all the dangers of the deep he dived into head-on.

"I want to tell him." I trace circles with my fingers across the map. "I do, but I'm afraid he'll never let me do what I'm considering."

Hannah's eyebrows shoot up, her stare sharpening like a blade. "What exactly are you considering?"

The words stick in my throat, heavy with meaning. I push them out.

"I'm going to learn technical diving, specifically cave diving—I'm going to follow where Nathan's maps lead and get there first."

The room is still. Even Ding, sitting by the door, doesn't lift his head. Instead, he stares at me and barks once. Telling me no.

Hannah bursts into laughter. When I'm silent, her eyes become saucers. "You're joking, right?"

I meet her stare with determination. "No, I'm very serious. If I don't go down there myself, I'll never understand what Nathan found or what happened to him. And I need to be the one to follow his path. I don't trust anyone else to put Nathan's work first."

Hannah crosses her arms tightly. "You know cave diving is hazardous. People die doing this—extremely experienced, qualified people. Before the other day, you hadn't dived in years, let alone in caves. Sweetie, you know this isn't something you can just decide to do. It takes years to learn."

"I know." I take a breath. "But Nathan hid these maps, and the coded messages for me. He trusted me to figure this out."

"And you can figure it out without risking your life," she shoots back, her voice rising slightly. "Scott and his team are trained for this kind of thing. Let them handle it."

I clench my hands into fists, the tension spilling over. "They're not looking for the same things I am. Scott's focus is on the logistics and the technical dive. But this…" I gesture to the maps spread across the table, my voice catching. "If I don't go down there, I'll never see it with my own eyes and know."

Hannah rubs her temples, exhaling slowly. "I love you, but this is crazy. You don't even know where to start. You aren't thinking straight. Nathan wouldn't want you to risk your life like this. Curiosity is going to get you killed."

"It's not curiosity—" I snap, my voice cracking under the weight of my emotions. "This is my brother's life's work. I owe it to him to finish what he started. Don't act like you know what Nathan would have wanted. He would have stood by me on this. He believed in me."

Her expression softens. "All right, you're right. But what about Scott? Do you think he's just going to let this slide? You need his help."

I swallow hard. "That's why I haven't told him. He lost his wife, Hannah, in a cave. I don't think he'll understand. He'll shut me down before I even get the chance to try."

Hannah reaches across the table, taking my hand, her voice gentler now. "He's protective, yes. But that's why you need to tell him. He knows the risks better than anyone, and he can help you. He won't let you go in blind."

"No. If I tell him, he'll say no."

Hannah slumps back in her chair. "You're putting a lot of pressure on yourself and you're not giving Scott a chance. He may surprise you… promise me you'll think this through. This isn't something you can just jump into."

"I'll think about it." My mind is already made up, and it's racing ahead, the fire in my chest too strong to ignore.

We continue to pore over Nathan's maps, dissecting every line and note. I point out some sections he marked—possible artifacts and anomaly detected—explaining the most intriguing notations. Hannah listens, her skepticism giving way to a cautious interest as she watches me piece it together.

"You're serious about this, aren't you?"

"Nathan gave everything for this. I owe it to him to see it through."

Her hand squeezes mine firmly. "Okay, just promise me you'll get the help you need."

"I promise."

CHAPTER 18

MADDIE

The sun blazes over the tarmac, casting heat waves against the horizon. American flags line the makeshift pathways, their bold reds, whites, and blues vivid against the cloudless sky. Patriotic country music drifts through the air, mingling with the crowd's excited chatter.

I stand among the spectators, waiting for the Naval Air Show to begin. Families cluster together, and children wave little flags, their faces painted with the stars and stripes. Everywhere I look, people are smiling with their eyes turned skyward, waiting for the aerial spectacle to begin.

"Wow," Hannah says beside me, adjusting her sunglasses and fanning herself with a program as sweat drips down her temples.

"Exciting, isn't it?" I shield my eyes with my hand and gaze ahead at the distant runway. Planes are lined up and ready to go.

"Exciting indeed," she mutters.

I follow her gaze—and my breath catches.

Scott strides toward us in his crisp white Navy uniform, his medals gleaming in the sunlight. His broad shoulders fill out the sharp lines of his coat, and he carries his hat tucked neatly under one arm. His confident stride draws every nearby pair of eyes, especially the female kind. Beside him trots Denver, tail wagging in sync with Scott's steady steps. Denver's own medals of honor are displayed on his vest.

Hannah lets out a low whistle. "I mean. Come on."

My stomach flutters. Wow.

"Ladies," Scott greets us, his voice deep. His gaze lands on me. I'm standing there with my mouth half open. "Enjoying the show?"

"We are now," Hannah quips. "You clean up pretty well, Rickter."

Scott chuckles, the sound a low rumble in his chest. "Thanks. I'm going to take that as a compliment."

"You should," she replies, elbowing me. "Don't you agree, Maddie?"

I nod. My cheeks are already pink from the heat, but I feel them get hotter. "You look…" I pause, searching for the right word. "Distinguished."

"Distinguished," Scott repeats. He looks up like he's giving my word some thought, his lips twitching. "I like that." His voice is husky as his gaze flickers from my eyes to my tank top and short denim shorts, then back to my eyes. "You look nice too, sweetheart." He inhales.

Denver nuzzles Scott's leg. His expression turns to pride. "Denver's been the big star today."

"I believe it," I reply, crouching to pet Denver. He leans into my touch, his black fur warm and soft beneath my fingers. "You're my good boy, aren't you?"

Denver wags his tail enthusiastically. I wipe away some of the sweat pooling on my forehead with my shirt and stand, taking Scott's hand as he helps me up. He averts his gaze from my bare stomach and clears his throat.

"Hey."

He leans in—stiff, his face all serious. Is he nervous?

"I'll just spit it out." He exhales. "Will you let me take you out tonight?"

"Yes," I answer too quickly.

"Thank God…" He lowers his voice to a whisper. "You just made my day."

Gently, he pushes his fingers through my hair, tilting my head back slightly before pressing a sweet kiss to my mouth, just the faintest trace of his tongue crossing my lips. Enough to tease me. My heart pounds.

Before I recover, Jamie and Liam approach, each precariously balancing a tray of food. Jamie holds out a hot dog smothered in mustard and onions. "Anyone hungry? We grabbed extras."

Scott reluctantly leaves us to it, flashing me a private smile. The rest of us grab our food and sit, anxiously waiting for the show to start. Scott's so handsome. What am I going to wear for our date? I want this to go somewhere. Is this what love feels like?

Stop it, Maddie.

You're twenty-eight years old, and Scott's in his thirties. This is what grown-ups do. They date and find out if they're compatible. They don't dream about love before they've even French kissed.

An eerie sensation washes over me. I'm being watched.

Scanning the crowd, I scold myself. There's no threat here.

Then, I spot the woman from the general store.

She's stunning, dressed in a simple white dress today. A little girl, maybe four or five years old, clutches her hand. She has big blond curls, just like her mom. The mother appears nervous, shifting on her feet and skittishly jumping away from anyone who gets too near her in the crowd. Something's off. Her make-up's too heavy, and there's a dark shadow on her cheek.

This is wrong. I need to speak to her.

Handing my leftovers to Jamie, I step cautiously toward her. As I approach, her eyes meet mine for a moment.

She bolts.

"Wait," I call, picking up my pace. She picks up the little girl and runs, disappearing into the crowd.

Not able to find her among the hundreds of people, I return to my friends and pull Hannah aside.

"What's wrong?"

"I saw the woman from the general store. I tried to approach her, and she ran."

"What in the world? Why would she run from you?"

"I'm not sure, but I think she's in some kind of danger." I explain the bruise and makeup.

"She also has a little girl."

Hannah frowns. "We need to tell Scott and the police. Her behavior just doesn't make any sense, especially with the little girl involved. I don't like it."

I agree, we need to find some way to find her.

The announcer's voice booms over the speakers, and the crowd cheers as the first jet streaks across the sky with a roar.

"God, that's incredible," Jamie mutters, craning his neck as the jets loop and dive. "How do they do that?"

The cheers grow louder.

For the finale, they soar high into the sky, leaving behind a red, white, and blue starburst. Applause erupts, thunderous and heartfelt.

We all enjoy the rest of the show, but my thoughts keep returning to the woman and her little girl. It doesn't make sense for her to avoid me. After the break-in and stalker, danger seems to be all around. Why did she run? What's she hiding? And most importantly—who's hurting her?

♥

Scott and I walk hand in hand along the sandy path leading from the beachside restaurant to the Driftwood Inn. A warm breeze carries the faint scent of salt and blooming jasmine through the air.

I break the silence. "That was the best red snapper I've ever had."

"Told you. Best seafood on the island. You just have to know which night their supplier comes in."

"Insider knowledge."

He glances down at me, his hazel eyes catching the moonlight. "You're picking up on island life fast." He nudges me with his hip. "You know I'm going to share all my secrets with you." He smiles sweetly. "Besides, you've already got my team wrapped around your little finger—I'm no exception."

I roll my eyes, though I can't stop the grin from spreading across my face, and I feel a twitch of female pride. "Hardly. They're just being nice because I'm the new girl."

Scott stops walking to face me fully. After a long pause, he lifts my pendant and smiles. "This is pretty. You wear it all the time. Is it special to you?"

"It's my spirit animal." His brows raise with a question.

"An elephant."

He chuckles. "I can see that. What made you choose a spirit animal?"

"I didn't. He chose me."

"Well, I don't know much about spirits, but it suits you."

I hold my breath.

"I like everything about you." He lets go of the pendant and gently brushes his fingers over my collarbone.

My heartbeat quickens, and I wonder if he can hear it. How he looks at me like I'm the only thing in the world makes it hard to think. I learn more about Scott every day and it has me yearning for more. Over dinner, I shared my plans to open an animal clinic, and Scott shared his dreams to open a dive shop once he has time to focus on it.

Scott breaks the silence, pointing toward a small outcropping of manmade stones overlooking the beach. He tugs on my hand. "Come on. The view's better from there."

I walk with him, my hand in his, the soft sand beneath my feet giving way to the smooth stones as we climb the short incline. When we reach the top, the ocean stretches endlessly before us.

"This is beautiful," I murmur, awestruck, as much from the simmering between us as the scenery.

Scott lowers onto one rock, patting the space beside him. "This is my favorite spot on the island," he admits. "Whenever things get too crazy, I come here—to clear my head."

I sit down beside him, tucking my legs in beneath me. "I didn't peg you as the guy who needs to clear his head."

"We all need that sometimes. Even me."

I study him, noticing how the moonlight softens the sharp edges of his face. He's gentler here, serene. "What do you think about when you're here?"

He keeps his gaze on the horizon, the silence stretching so long I think he might forget to answer.

"A lot of things. I think about my time in the Navy. The people I served with. The ones I lost. Other times, I think about the dives, the risks, the rewards. And sometimes…" His jaw tightens.

"What?" I prompt.

Scott turns toward me, his hazel dark with intensity. A shiver runs down my spine. "Sometimes I think about what it would be like to stop running and just hold on to what I have in front of me."

His honesty moves me.

"What are you running from?"

He looks down at the space between us, his voice raw. "Regrets mostly. The things I can't change. Mistakes I've made."

I reach out to him, resting my hand on his forearm. "You're not running now."

His gaze moves to my fingers, then back to my eyes.

"No." His voice is barely audible. "I'm not."

My fingers trace the jagged scar along his neck. "How did you get this?"

Scott stiffens for a moment, then exhales, his hesitation brief. "We were deployed to Yemen on a hostage rescue mission. Everything went smoothly and right to plan—until it didn't. We got all our men out, but not without a fight. It was the first and only time I've killed a man." His voice is calm but heavy. Like a chain around his neck. "I'm glad I have this to remember." He gestures to the scar. "Anyway, because of this, my six-year tour in the SEALs ended five months early."

I swallow, my fingers tightening around his and pulling his hand to my heart. "I'm so sorry you experienced that."

The space between us is smaller now, and the ocean carries away our silence. The intimacy of the moment compels me to share something personal.

"When I was little…" My voice trembles with bottled-up emotion. "I always dreamed of living somewhere beautiful where my family would keep growing, where we would always be safe and live together forever."

My eyes water up and I feel a tear escape. "I didn't know death. I was so afraid to lose them."

Scott slides his arm around me, pulling me closer. He brushes a soft kiss against my cheek to wipe away my tear.

"When Dad died, it was just the three of us. Nathan was sixteen and had to grow up fast to take care of us. There was never enough time." I exhale slowly, my voice shaking. "And Mom worked so hard. But no matter what, no matter how tired she was, Mom made time for us. She would play us a song on the piano every night. She'd tell us it's not the number of hours you have, but how you use them. Make them count."

Scott turns toward me, his gaze stormy. "The song you played at the tavern?"

"Yes. When Nathan disappeared and Mom couldn't play anymore, I kept playing. And when Mom passed…" My voice catches. "It's my connection to them all. A way to keep them with me."

Scott doesn't speak right away, but his warm hands caress my shoulders and back. "Hearing you play that song was the most beautiful thing I've ever heard," he murmurs, his voice rough with emotion.

Heat rises to my cheeks. "Thank you," I whisper. "I want that again one day… a family of my own… to love." I inhale. "But I'm afraid."

Scott shifts, his thumb brushing lightly over my knee. The hem of my dress flutters in the breeze. He's staring at my legs. My eyes drift to his neck, where his skin flushes against the white of the scar.

"I…" He hesitates, his voice thick. "You've made me want to stop running. You're worth staying put for."

His words send my heart into freefall.

Our faces are so close now, I feel his breath. The ocean fades. There's electricity snapping between us.

Scott leans in, deliberate and careful, giving me a chance to pull away.

I don't.

When his lips meet mine, the world disappears.

His palms cradle my face as he weaves his fingers through my hair, rough against the softness of my skin. His kiss is slow and tender, filled with gentle intensity. He moves with a deep longing to explore, gliding his tongue against mine like a slow dance. No haste, just pleasure and an understanding between us that we want to follow this path. We want to discover where it leads together.

We're breathing hard, our hands moving over our bodies now, wanting more than a kiss. When we pull apart, Scott rests his forehead against mine.

"I've wanted to do that for so long." His words pour out breathlessly.

"Me too." I reach back out to him and pull his face to mine.

As the hours pass, we remain on the rocks all night, surrounded by moonlight and the crashing waves—talking, laughing, and kissing. And dreaming of tomorrow.

CHAPTER 19

SCOTT

I park my truck at the edge of the cemetery. Dark clouds of an approaching storm cover the sun. A gust of wind stirs the scent of pine and damp earth, and as I step out onto the ground, the quiet void wraps around me. My chest is heavy from the weight of my decision to come here today and from all the memories.

Adeline lies toward the back of the grounds, shaded by a large oak. Her headstone rests beside her mother's—a quiet reminder of their bond. The path is familiar, and my boots know every bend and dip.

When I reach her, I take in her headstone. It's simple and elegant, like she was. I crouch, brushing away a few stray leaves and pine needles gathered on the stone.

"Hi, Adeline." My voice is barely more than a whisper. My fingers trace the engraved letters of her name. "It's been a while."

I sit back on my heels, letting the quiet stretch between us. I always feel like she can hear me here, as though the space between the living and the dead isn't so vast. Today, I need that to be true more than ever.

"You're probably laughing at me right now." I smile weakly. "I've been running in circles, trying to figure out what to do. How to move forward. It's been four years. Four long years of missing you, of feeling lost without you."

My throat tightens. I don't bother fighting the emotions rising—I just let them come.

"You were my best friend, you know? Before anything else. Before the love and our marriage, it was the friendship we shared that made me the man I am. You made everything in our lives feel so right. And when you left, the best part of me went with you."

The breeze picks up, rustling the oak tree's branches, and the first soft pinpricks of drizzle hit my face. I close my eyes, leaning into the sensation as though it carries some part of her.

"But now…" I continue, exhaling slowly. "I've changed." My chest tightens as I cross this threshold. "I've met someone. Her name is Maddie."

Saying her name out loud is like a confession, and my heart thuds hard against my ribs and lungs.

"She's… strong, kind, stubborn as hell," I say with a soft chuckle. "And when I'm with her, I feel… alive. For the first time in a long time, I feel like maybe there's something more for me. Something beyond the grief."

I rake my hand through my hair, eyes staring at the gravestone, looking for approval.

"But it scares me. I'm scared of what this means, of letting go. I don't want you to think I've forgotten. I could never forget you. You're a part of me. But I can't keep living like this—holding on so tightly to what I've lost that I can't hold on to what's in front of me."

Tears slide down my cheek, and I let them fall.

"I love you." I draw in a breath. "I always will. But I think… I'm ready to release the guilt and the fear. To let myself have this relationship with Maddie, even if it scares me."

The silence is heavy, as though the air around me understands my words.

I gently place the tiny bundle of wildflowers I picked this morning—her favorite—into the vase on her stone, brushing my fingers once more across her name.

"Thank you," I whisper. "For your love, the friendship, the lessons. For being my compass."

I stand, my legs unsteady beneath me.

"I'll always carry you with me," I promise, "and I know you want this chance at happiness for me."

As I turn to leave, the sun breaks through the clouds, casting a warm glow over my face, quietly affirming I'm on the right path and loved.

CHAPTER 20

MADDIE

I step out of my cottage into the cool early morning air and make my way toward the Inn, a notebook tucked under my arm. Dressed in an old T-shirt and cargo shorts, I expect the usual Monday morning dive team meeting.

Instead, I stop dead when I reach the dining room.

It's empty.

Where is everyone? It's Monday, and no one told me the meeting was canceled. Then I hear the voices outside the front door—excited chatter. Odd. Cautiously, I push the door open and gasp.

The front porch and grounds are alive with energy and cheerful chaos, far from the usual focused work and dive planning. Familiar faces buzz about, everyone wearing mismatched work clothes, their fervor contagious. Scott stands in the center of the porch. A tool belt slung low on his hips, with sawdust covering his snug blue T-shirt. Liam holds a mop, getting ready to go back inside. Jamie waves a paintbrush, and Margaret has a measuring tape clipped to her pocket. Even Ms. Connor is ready for action, her apron layered over an old shirt and faded jeans. They've been at this for a while already.

"What's going on?"

Scott turns toward me. He brushes some of the sawdust from his shirt. "Good morning, sweetheart." His expression is playful, mischievous. "No dive meeting today. We're giving this place some love."

I blink, trying to process. "Huh?"

"We're renovating," Scott declares, gesturing toward the inn. "Painting, fixing, sprucing up—whatever it needs. The Driftwood Inn deserves some TLC."

"You're kidding." It's clear he isn't.

"Nope," Jamie chimes in, attempting another twirl of his paintbrush and nearly dropping it. "Scott's idea, but we all jumped on board. This place is a local treasure, like Carter's Drop—except, you know, above the water."

Ms. Connor steps forward. "I've made extra coffee and cinnamon rolls." She hands me one. "We're fueled up and ready to go, honey."

"You're all completely insane. And you're wonderful. I love you." Emotion swells in my chest as I take them all in. "Thank you."

Ms. Connor claps her hands, her tone brisk but amused. "Enough talking. Eat your bun, and then let's get back to work."

The day unfolds in a whirlwind of sweat and friendship.

Scott tackles the porch railing, his hammer swinging in steady blows. Liam scrubs the weathered siding with an exaggerated effort, cracking jokes. Jamie and Margaret team up to paint the faded trim, the bright white transforming the inn's exterior into a fresh and inviting façade. Ms. Connor and I work in the garden, where we plant a riot of hibiscus and marigolds bursting with color under the afternoon sun and new herbs for the kitchen.

Midmorning, Hannah arrives with arms full of iced tea and bags of sandwiches. She surveys our work, her eyes twinkling. "I leave for a couple of hours, and suddenly, this place looks like it's being filmed for HGTV…" she teases, setting the refreshments on the porch table.

Scott glances up from his work. "I've got a hammer over here waiting for you, Hannah."

"I'm on it. Just let me get this passed out." She serves refreshments before jumping in to help Scott with the porch.

The hours fly by, the initial chaos turning into steady progress. By late afternoon, the Driftwood Inn has been completely transformed.

Standing back to admire our work in the garden, I brush a streak of dirt from my cheek and sigh contentedly. Scott appears beside me, wiping sweat from his brow with the back of his hand.

"Looks good." He gestures toward the flowers.

I turn to him. "You've all done so much. I don't even know how to thank you."

Scott shrugs. "Seeing you smile is thanks enough."

We all gather back on the porch, cold drinks in hand. Jamie leans back in his rocking chair. "Not bad for a hard day's work."

"We've practically rebuilt the place," Margaret says.

"I think this calls for a celebration dinner tomorrow," Ms. Connor announces. "My treat."

We all cheer. A lump rises in my throat as I take in my makeshift family, my heart full. We chat and relax for another hour or so before everyone begins turning in for the night.

Scott lingers, helping me tidy up.

I sit on the ground, stacking paint cans into a neat pile. Crouching down with me, he reaches for some stray trash near my hand. When his fingers brush against mine, warmth spreads through me, rising to a steady burn of anticipation.

"You know." His voice is low, his breath warm against the skin on my neck. "This place isn't the only thing getting a fresh start."

I pause, heart thudding. "What do you mean?"

His gaze searches mine, and for a moment, the air is heavier, charged.

"You." He rakes his fingers through his hair. "And me. Us, maybe?" He exhales. "Yeah. Us."

Fire rushes to my cheeks. "I like the sound of that."

He scoots closer, his touch slow and careful as his hands find my arms. "I'm glad you're here… so much."

He leans in—this time with no hesitation or caution. His lips claim mine, eager and insistent, pouring himself into the kiss. I grip his shirt, his warmth pressing against me, his desire undeniable. When his hips shift forward, he groans.

When we pull apart, his eyes search mine, and I laugh.

"What?" he asks, his voice rough, an eyebrow raised.

"Your face." I've covered Scott's face with dirt. "I think we both need a hot shower, stat."

"Is that an invitation?"

Heat floods my face. "Umm."

"Just kidding." He's lying. The hardness pressing into my stomach gives him away. "I could use a shower, though. Do you mind?" He clears his throat, standing and helping me up. He rubs my back and kisses the top of my head.

"Follow me," I tease, clasping his hands and pulling him to the cottage.

When we get inside, I pull out some night clothes for me and an old T-shirt and sweats from Nathan's dresser for Scott. I think they may be stretchy enough to fit him. Scott's eyes scan the room, and he sits on a chair by the table. The air is thick with anticipation. I think we both know what's about to happen and while exciting, it's scares me.

"You first, sweetheart." He motions to the bathroom. "I'll wait," he says hoarsely.

I wash quickly, making sure I'm ready for my close-up. Scott's reading a dive magazine when I get back. He looks up and his gaze turns heated as he looks me up and down.

"Reminds me of our swim."

"Your turn." He gets up and lingers near me for a moment, stopping himself from touching.

"Don't want to get you dirty." He winks. "Yet."

I watch him close the door behind him. Then I hear the shower. Changing quickly, I tuck into the blankets and try to look sexy as I lay my head on the soft pillow and stretch out. I think of Scott in the shower, the hot steam pouring around him. Then I think of our kisses and the fun day we just had… then I think of asking him to teach me to cave dive. Dang it. Oh no. I meant to ask him today. I'll have to do it tomorrow… then I think of what's about to happen tonight… and what will happen tomorrow… and how sleepy I am… and…

CHAPTER 21

SCOTT

I'm analyzing the dive plans spread before us. At the far end of the table, Maddie sits focused, tension tightening her shoulders. Her gaze flicks toward me every so often, hands clasped together, restless. What's on her mind?

What I'm thinking about are the moments we've shared over the last few days—those touches, kisses, and what's still to come. I take a deep breath, heat rising to my chest as I think about last night. I chuckle. When I got out of the shower, Maddie was sound asleep. Her little snores were so soft. Cute. I didn't have the heart to wake her. Not for our first time. So, I made sure she was tucked in properly and the cabin was secure, then I left. I'm eager to take her out again. Imagining our next date is a hell of a lot more fun than this conversation with Garrett. That's for damn sure.

"You're going to need to speed this up."

Garrett sets his pen down, clearing his throat. "I'm concerned about the team's progress charting the tunnels. It's been too slow." He places his fingers on the table, leaning in for emphasis. "Other dive teams are waiting in line to get in there… In fact, even Wes has expressed some interest. For the right price, he's open to it. His involvement could bring us good publicity."

"I don't play well with others, Garrett—I'll be damned if I suit up with Harrington."

"You may not have a choice," he counters, his tone turning testy. "My patience isn't unlimited."

I lean back in my chair, my expression flat. "I have a choice. And it's a hard pass on working with anyone else. Don't act like you don't need us. Without my crew, it'll take another team at least six months just to get up to speed." I glare at him, undeterred by his threats. They mean nothing to me. "That would put you almost a year behind, and you know it."

Garrett frowns but only shrugs, moving on. "Four months. That's what's left—not a day more. I expect to see faster results."

I tune him out for the rest of the briefing. When we finish, I catch him lingering near the stairs, intercepting Wes as he heads for the door with a dive bag slung over one shoulder. Wes doesn't slow down, pushing past him without a word. What are the two of them up to?

I'm getting ready to leave the table when Maddie approaches me. Her shoulders are squared, her expression set, as if she's made a decision.

"Can I talk to you?"

"Of course, baby." I motion toward the back door. "Let's go outside."

We step onto the wraparound porch. A warm breeze lifts some of the strands of Maddie's hair and blows them into her eyes. She squints, her lips pursed. So damn cute. I want to kiss her. She tucks a strand of hair behind her ear before meeting my gaze.

"I've been thinking a lot about Nathan's work and what I found when I went through his things." She's looking at the ground while she talks. "I have so many questions about what Nathan was doing in the Drop." She stops.

Worried, I put a hand on her back and gently tilt her chin up so I can meet her eyes. "Hey—what's on your mind?"

The shift in her mood worries me. It's a complete one-eighty from last night.

"Nathan didn't trust the people around him. He felt like he had to hide his findings. After the break-in…"

That's what this is. She doesn't feel safe. I jump in.

"You might feel safer with me close. Let me talk to Wes about having some of his men double up in the rooms they're renting. Liam and I can stay here at the inn for a while. We'll make the room. Unless you'd rather me…"

She shakes her head, jumping in. "I need you to teach me how to cave dive."

My throat tightens. I have to force myself to take in air.

"You need me to teach you to cave dive?" I repeat her words, hoping I misheard.

"Yes. When we dived the other day, everything came back to me in a rush. I know what I'm doing in the water, and I love it." She pauses a moment to look at my face, gauging my reaction. I fight to keep my face neutral.

"I'm already certified for advanced-level open water and have been researching what technical dives involve. I've already learned so much from watching you guys." She fiddles with her necklace as she speaks. Running her fingers over the jade.

"I'm a quick learner. It won't take me that long—you'll see." She squints, seeing the doubt in my eyes. "I have to explore the tunnels for myself and find the answers he was looking for—to figure out what was so important it cost him his life."

I exhale, running a hand through my hair. My protective instinct flares. I clutch her arms to still them. She looks at me hopefully.

"I think it's fantastic you want to dive. Seeing you in the water the other day was amazing. You're so good at it, sweetheart." Her eyes widen and her breathing picks up. She thinks I'm going to say yes. I need to get to the point.

"But."

Her face falls.

"You already know… penetration diving isn't the same as recreational. It has more dangers, even for highly trained divers. Things can go wrong in an instant."

"I know that." She's stubborn. "But you do it. Nathan did it. And I want to. I want to get in the water and see it for myself. He left clues—things only I might be able to piece together. I don't want to put this in someone else's hands."

Her determination tugs at my heart. I'm torn. "I know you want to find out what happened to Nathan. But this is about your safety. Cave diving is unpredictable. Even with the best training and skill, you're not going to be able to control everything. So much can go wrong."

"Please, Scott. Don't say no. I have to do this, and I know you can train me." She steps closer, face pinched, eyes wide with desperation. "I'll follow every instruction you give me to the letter and take every precaution. I'll do it right. I promise."

I grip her shoulders. Now I'm the one who's desperate.

"It's not just about training. Even expert divers struggle with an overhead environment. I've seen instructors—dive masters—who can't handle it. And when they can, I've still seen bad things happen. Tragedies happen every single day." I freeze. "You don't understand what you're asking of me, Maddie."

Her eyes widen, her face softening.

Then frustration flashes in her eyes. "So that's it? You're saying no without giving me a chance."

I sigh, my voice gentler. "You don't have anything to prove to me. I know you can do it. But this is about me protecting you, and I can't guarantee your safety down there. If something happened to you on my watch, it would kill me."

She looks away, her shoulders stiffening. The hurt on her face is like a gut punch. "I thought you'd at least hear me out." She looks to the floor.

"I'm sorry." I reach for her. She stiffens, but lets me pull her into a loose embrace. "You need to sit on this, think about what's motivating you. Is this something you want—or do you feel like you owe it to Nathan?" I take a deep breath and continue. "For me, this is about what I'd be risking," I add, my voice a whisper now. "You're asking me to risk too much."

She pulls back, her expression hardening. It startles me. "You're afraid."

Her words hit deep.

I am afraid.

But I won't let her put herself in danger. I need to convince her.

"…breaking news," a reporter announces, their voice urgent. "A tropical storm has formed overnight in the Gulf and is on track to arrive on Maverick Key within the next seventy-two hours."

We walk to the living room, the tension between us released, even though we both know we're at an impasse. On the screen, the reporter continues, outlining the storm's rapid development and potential to become a strong tropical storm or even a hurricane.

"Damn it," I mutter. "We'll need to secure the boats and equipment and make sure everyone's ready."

"What can I do?"

"Call Hannah and help Ms. Connor get the inn prepped," I run through a mental checklist. "Me and the crew will handle the watercraft."

Her expression is resolute. "Okay."

I lean in and kiss her, a simple goodbye. She lets me, but there's no passion in it, no fire.

As I head back inside to rally the team, I can't get the disappointment in her eyes out of my head.

I'm making the right call.

Like the storm, this will pass.

CHAPTER 22

MADDIE

After helping Ms. Connor get started on securing the inn, I step outside to take a breath of fresh air. The porch swing creaks beneath me as I rock, gazing out at the vast stretch of ocean. It's beautiful. Scott's refusal stings, not only because it creates a huge obstacle to my goals, but because I just wanted him to believe in me.

He didn't.

Nathan wouldn't have let fear or obstacles hold him back, and I won't either. If Scott won't teach me, I'll find another way.

Wes.

He's a wild card. His flair for theatrics is infamous. But he's good—the best. And most importantly, I know he won't tell me no.

This morning, Wes mentioned he'd be editing footage in his room. I walk to his door and knock.

Muffled music—Caspian's 'Sad Heart of Mine'—cuts off. "Come in," Wes calls.

I push the door open and step inside. He's perched over an organized desk, his laptop projecting a kaleidoscope of vibrant underwater footage. He swivels in his chair, headphones resting around his neck, his grin as charming as ever.

"Hi, Maddie, what's up?"

I close the door behind me, squaring my shoulders. "I need your help."

His eyebrows shoot up, amusement flickering in his green eyes. "Help? Oh, I like the sound of that. What kind of help are we talking about?"

I meet his gaze head-on. "I want you to teach me how to cave dive."

His grin falters, giving way to surprised concern. He leans forward, resting his hands on his knees. "Cave diving? That's… bold. Okay—I'm intrigued."

I step closer, sitting on the edge of his bed. My hands clasped in my lap to still their trembling. "I've been thinking about Nathan. About what he was doing before he disappeared. I need to understand it. I can't just sit back while other people piece together his work. I need to do this myself."

His eyes narrow. "Let me guess. Scott said no."

"He thinks it's too dangerous. Or maybe he's too afraid of what might happen."

He studies me for a long moment, his easygoing demeanor shifting to a serious expression. "Scott's not wrong. There's nothing simple about cave diving. It's one of the most dangerous activities you can engage in— period. If you screw up, you're dead. There are rarely any second chances." He pauses, then continues, "And more importantly, accept that you could do everything right—everything—and something you never anticipated could still kill you."

"I know the risks. Nathan took them because he believed in what he was doing. And I believe this is worth it. I'm not asking you to take me straight into the tunnels. I want to start slow and learn the right way."

A ghost of a smile tugs at his lips. "You've got guts, I'll give you that. Most people wouldn't even consider this, let alone fight for it."

The room falls silent. My heart races as I await his answer. Please say yes.

Wes stands up and walks to the window. He gazes at the ocean for a long moment before turning back to me.

"All right. I'll help you. But I have a nonnegotiable condition."

Relief surges through me. "What condition?"

His cockiness returns. "You follow my rules. No exceptions. If I say something's too dangerous, you listen. If I tell you to stop, you stop. Deal?"

I let out a loud breath I wasn't aware I was holding. "Deal."

"Good." He crosses his arms as he leans against the desk. "We'll start with the basics—gear, safety, and navigation. Once you've mastered your skills in open water, we'll discuss the overhead training."

"Thank you." My voice thickens. "I won't disappoint you."

Wes grabs a notebook from his desk and tosses it to me. "Let's hope not. Because if Scott finds out about this, I'm going to be the one who needs rescuing."

I flip through the notebook filled with detailed notes, diagrams, and observations. "I'll study this tonight," I promise.

"Do that," Wes says, giving me a stern look, then laughs. "Welcome to the world of cave diving. Let's see if you've got what it takes, rookie."

♥

The following morning, I stand at the edge of the dock, adjusting the straps of my dive gear. The snug wetsuit clings to me, and the heavy equipment presses on my shoulders. My heart pounds as I glance at Wes a few feet away, prepping his own gear. His face hints at mischief as if he's trying not to smile.

"All right, rookie," Wes says, securing a coil of dive line at his waist. His green eyes glint with a playful seriousness as he gestures animatedly, describing what's planned for today. "I hope you did some homework. The first lesson is simple. It's all about the fundamentals. It's about survival."

I swallow hard. "Got it."

He steps closer, his tone dropping. "Good. Because if you don't master the basics, we don't even think about cave diving. Clear?"

"Crystal," I reply, steadying my voice despite the nervous flutter in my chest.

I put on the full-face mask last. I'd practiced with it in the pool last night—getting used to the motions of putting it on and taking it off both over and under the water. Full-face masks allow underwater voice communication, which is valuable when visibility isn't guaranteed. But they are tricky to handle. Especially in caves. Wes walks over to me and double-checks my suit and equipment. He looks at me with approval.

"Good. Let's get in the water." He claps his hands before turning toward the edge of the dock. The weather is deceptively mild, with no hint of the approaching storm.

♥

We descend into the water by a reef near the coast. Sunlight filters from above, painting golden patterns on the sandy bottom.

I touch the spool and reel Wes gave me as we hover near a rocky outcrop.

"Lesson one is line following. This spool of nylon is your lifeline. Lose it in the caves of Carter's Drop, and you're as good as dead. Treat it like it's worth more than your life."

His voice crackles over our communication system.

"And never lose the line."

"Dramatic much?"

His firm stare wipes away any trace of levity. I grip the reel tighter. He starts to unspool a neon-yellow practice line, stretching it between two jagged rocks on the ocean floor.

"As important as it is to lay and follow the line, you also have to be aware of entanglement dangers," he continues. "Plenty of skilled divers have gotten tangled in their own lines, panicked, run out of air, and died. It's a pretty easy way to die. Doesn't matter how good you are. If you get stuck, you have to know how to react and have the right backups." He brushes his fingers across the many knives he's secured to his suit.

My stomach tightens.

My job now is to follow Wes's line, focusing on touch only. First, I need to get accustomed to the feel of the line and rely less on my other senses. My movements are careful, and my fingers brush against the cord as I keep myself steady.

"Good. Monitor your buoyancy. Mastering excellent buoyancy control is the most crucial diving skill. Keep your fins off the bottom. Avoid kicking up silt or colliding with the walls. Focus on your breathing."

I adjust my breathing, concentrating on slow, deliberate inhales and exhales. My body responds, rising and falling with each breath. Gliding along the line, pride shoots through me when Wes doesn't correct me.

"Not bad." He nods his approval. "You've got excellent buoyancy skills, Maddie, you've been holding out on me." Then his voice sharpens, carrying an edge of challenge. "Turn off your light."

My stomach clenches, but I don't hesitate. Reaching up, I switch off the light.

I'm plunged into near darkness.

Faint illumination from above penetrates the water. The line in my hand serves as my only anchor and guide. I tighten my grip, concentrating on the tension and direction.

"You're doing great," Wes says, his voice calm and reassuring. "Stay cool. Trust the line."

The knot of anxiety in my chest loosens. The line's presence gives me a tangible object to rely on. When Wes signals for me to turn the light back on, my fingers move, and a soft glow returns to the underwater world.

"See?" Wes asks, his voice brimming with pride. "That's how you maintain your composure. You'll need that if you ever lose visibility in the caves."

We move to a deeper area, where Wes demonstrates emergency drills—how to clear a flooded mask, transition to your own alternate or your buddy's air source, and hand signals when comms or slates aren't available or practical. His instructions are clear and methodical.

"These skills are designed to help you regain control in unpredictable situations." He pushes his emergency regulator toward me. "Your turn."

I hesitate for a split second before taking off my mask and taking Wes's octopus regulator. The freezing water on my face and the unfamiliarity of breathing from someone else's air source make my heart race. I focus, exhaling as a cloud of bubbles rises around me. I put on my backup mask. My anxiety wanes, replaced by steady concentration.

Wes motions for me to put my full-face mask back on.

"Good transition," Wes says, his voice calm. "Always be prepared to give your primary or octopus air source to your buddy. And be prepared to take it."

I repeat the drills until each step becomes second nature. Confidence replaces the nerves I've had since we started.

Now, I'm having serious fun.

"Ok, we've got one more test for the day. This one separates the winners from the losers." Wes's severe stare almost makes me laugh until it dawns on me. He's serious.

♥

"All right, rookie. It's time for the real test. We're going to simulate a lost line. Remember, if you panic, you're a goner."

He demonstrates the technique with methodical movements.

"Stop. Breathe. Think. Act. You must stay calm and trust your training over instinct. Panic kills."

Now it's my turn.

I close my eyes, letting the darkness swallow me. Wes puts a blindfold over my mask and guides me to a place where I don't know where I am or how close I am to the line.

He let's go.

At first, I'm calm, moving slowly. Searching, my fingers tracing the sandy terrain.

But the silence stretches. I'm underwater, blind. Where is Wes? Unease creeps into my head. I think of the ocean's expanse. The impossibility of finding one thin line in the millions of gallons of water and sand.

Images of Nathan flash through my thoughts. I picture his final moments. Lost, forever.

A surge of panic grips my chest. My breathing quickens and my hands falter.

"Hey." Wes's voice cuts through the fog in my mind. "Breathe. Slow down. You're okay."

I latch onto his words, forcing my breaths to steady.

His hand grips my arm firmly. He gently guides me back to the line and removes the blindfold. I open my eyes.

Relief floods me as I grip the neon cord.

Wes uses his thumb to motion up, ending the dive.

♥

We rise to the surface, emerging into the warm sunlight. I rip off my mask, gasping for air as water drips from my face.

Wes floats nearby, silent, watching me.

"I panicked," I spurt out, my voice shaking. "I thought I could manage it, but I just froze."

He tilts his head, studying me. "Yeah, you froze a moment, but you recovered and didn't give up. That's what matters." He takes my mask and clutches my shoulder. "Remember—Stop. Breathe. Think. Act."

I blink, surprised. "You're not mad at me?"

"Mad?" He huffs. "Most people don't even make it halfway through that drill without bolting to the surface the first time." He stares at me, pinching in his brows. "You've got the best buoyancy I've seen in a long time. You're an excellent diver, Maddie."

I relax my shoulders. "So… I passed?"

"You didn't fail." We swim to the boat ladder. He looks back over his shoulder. "But don't get too cocky. We have a lot more work to do before you're ready for the cavern, starting with training for closed-circuit diving equipment. Get ready for the rebreather."

He's a good teacher. Excitement rushes through all my muscles. For the first time—I know I have a chance at doing this. And I love it!

As we climb onto the boat, I turn to Wes.

"Thanks for today. Really. I know you didn't have to help me. You're a true friend."

He shrugs. "Don't thank me just yet. The next lesson is going to make this seem like a piece of cake. You'll probably hate me."

I raise an eyebrow. "That bad?"

"Oh, it's worse than you're thinking. I promise you that," he teases.

"Bring it on, Obi-wan," He laughs.

"Let's go home and get some rest, rookie. We'll pick this back up after the storm passes."

CHAPTER 23

MADDIE

The sky darkens throughout the afternoon until it becomes an ominous slate pressing down on Maverick Key. This morning's calm, turquoise waters are unrecognizable. They're now a churning, furious gray. I stand on the front porch with Ding planted by my side. Fat drops of rain spatter on the wooden planks beneath my feet, and the salty, static-laden air makes the hair on the back of my neck stand on end. The wind picks up, tugging at my loose hair as I stare at the horizon, the surf roaring against the beach with relentless force. Rows of palms along the shore beds lean unnaturally, their fronds straining against the wind as if they might snap at any moment.

Ms. Connor steps out from the inn, a towel draped over her arm.

"Come inside, honey," she urges, raising her voice over the howling wind. "This is just the beginning. It'll get worse before it gets better."

Ding runs inside, plopping down next to the couch. When I follow, a sharp gust slams the door shut behind me, making my pulse quicken.

I'd experienced my share of storms in Sarasota, but they're always different. Each is a unique monster, bringing its own brand of mayhem and destruction.

Ms. Connor moves with an efficiency honed by the countless storms she's weathered. She's already cleared all the outdoor furniture. Hannah's securing the shutters upstairs.

"How bad do you think this one will get?"

"It won't be a direct hit, thank the heavens." She's already turned on a battery-operated lantern in case we lose electricity. Extra batteries ready to go. The warm glow softens the edges of the dim room. But it's close enough to give us a beating. "Best to prepare for the worst and hope for the best."

Scott had promised to check on us before the storm hit, but hours have passed without a word. I tell myself he's okay. He can handle himself, but a knot of unease in my stomach tightens with every crash of thunder.

The inn is quiet. Garrett and Elaine are staying at a hotel on the mainland, and Wes and his crew are securing his boat.

I head upstairs to assist Hannah in fastening the last of the shutters, their old wooden frames creaking under the relentless pressure of the wind. Rain lashes against the windows.

Hannah flops onto the edge of the bed, pushing damp hair out of her face. "I hate this part," she mutters. "The waiting. It's like the storm is taunting us until it slams us."

I sit beside her, and the coiled tension in my chest threatens to snap with each passing moment. "At least we're not alone." I'm unsure whether I'm trying to reassure her or myself. We lay and chat, catching each other up on recent events.

"Did you ask Scott about cave diving?" Her face gives her away. She's hoping I'm going to give this up.

"Yes. He said no."

Hannah frowns. "I'm sorry. I know you had your heart set on it… maybe he'll come around after he has a little time to process. You can still be an important part of the work… share the maps with Scott… he'll help you."

"I'm not giving up on this. I've found someone else who's willing to help me."

She bolts up. "Who?" Her face flushes with anger. "That asshole—he wouldn't."

"Please don't tell Scott." I swallow, ashamed of asking her to be a part of this. "He doesn't need to know. I'm in good hands with Wes."

"I'm going to kill him."

"No, you're not… because you love me."

She huffs, then pulls me in a hug. "I do. Please be careful… and tell Scott. It won't be good to wait. He's falling for you. Hard. Tell him."

I swallow the guilt and tell her I will.

By evening, the storm is in full swing.

The wind screams through every gap in the shutters. We're watching the progress of the storm on the television. The power flickers twice before shutting off completely, plunging the inn into darkness. The glow from the lantern is our only light. After a few minutes of sitting in the dark, Hannah jumps up. "All right, it's time to play. I'll get the wine."

Ms. Connor pulls some old board games from under the coffee table, and we all gather around the dining room table.

"Go straight to jail. Don't pass go," Hannah commands.

I frown. I'm terrible at this game. We're on our third round, and while it's kept the boredom at bay, I'm a nervous wreck.

Still no Scott.

A thunderclap rattles the walls.

Ding jumps up, rushing to the window, barking his lungs out.

"It's ok—it's just more thunder." He doesn't stop and instead barks more insistently.

"What is it?" I mutter. I walk over and pull away the curtain, peering outside.

Movement.

A man wearing a raincoat stands near some bushes along the driveway. I yelp and drop the curtain. The darkness of the night hid his features, but it has to be him. With my heart in my throat, I open the curtain. Nothing.

"Honey, what is it?"

"Someone's out there."

Ms. Connor walks to the pantry and retrieves a shotgun. She walks to the door to put on her raincoat.

"Stop. You can't go out there. It could be dangerous… what if it's…"

What if it's my stalker?

"It's okay. I'll be careful. Call the police if anything happens." She walks out the door, leaving Hannah and me unsure what to do.

"We can't let her go out there alone. Let's go." We brace ourselves and step outside into the storm. The wind slams into me like a wall. Rain pelts us in stinging sheets, and I nearly lose my footing in the mud. Ding walks beside us, barking defiantly into the gale, trying to chase it away. We catch up to Ms. Connor as she's assessing the ground around the bushes where I spotted the man.

"It's a man's footprints. But no man." Ms. Connor's voice shakes, and her brows knit tightly together.

"Listen up if you're out there. If you get near us, I'll blow you away." She waves her shotgun. Once we're satisfied there isn't anyone still lurking around, we go back inside.

Soaked and shivering, we peel off our raincoats in the kitchen. My fingers are numb, trembling, cold, and my body's full of adrenaline. We call the police to report the stranger.

There isn't anything they can do.

Where's Scott?

We all jump when we hear someone opening the front door.

Wes walks in with his crew. His brows raise and the corner of his mouth turns down after taking one look at us. We're all huddled together on the couch around the lantern. Our eyes stare back, wide from fear. All three of us exhale in relief.

"What's going on?"

We fill him in on the Peeping Tom and the evidence we found near the bushes. He goes outside with his men to investigate. A few minutes later, the lights flicker and come back on.

Wes is back. "We got the generator running. It should be okay." He walks over to the alarm on the wall. "Let's get this back on." He fiddles with the alarm and turns back to me.

"I don't like this. We'll have to step up the vigilance and monitor this place twenty-four-seven." He looks around.

"Where's Scott?"

"We haven't seen him all day. He said he'd come by, but hasn't. He's not answering his phone."

"I saw him at the marina. He left with Liam about an hour and a half ago. I'm sure he'll be by soon."

A sudden knock at the door startles us.

Wes peers through the peephole and opens the door.

"Speak of the devil."

Scott stands there, drenched to the bone. His hazel eyes lock onto mine before he steps inside. Water drips from his jacket, but he shrugs it off and runs a hand through his soaked hair.

"Do you forgive me?"

I rush over to him and give him a huge hug.

"We're fine." I mask my relief with a hint of exasperation. "But you look like you took a swim out there." I cross my arms. "And then there's this thing called a cell phone."

"Yeah, I'm sorry about that. My phone died, and Liam needed a ride home after we secured *Adeline*. When we got there, he needed help with some windows that had blown out." He puts his arms back around me.

"You worried me." I squeeze him tighter.

Then he notices everyone standing around, looking spooked.

"What?"

♥

After the others settle into their rooms for the night, Scott and I sit alone on the couch. The wind is still howling outside but losing its strength, and the rain is virtually gone. The storm is moving off the island.

Scott spent the last hour and a half worrying about me and strategizing on our next steps to find out the identity of the stalker.

I rub his shoulders. "You're too tense. Let's do something about that… get you more relaxed." I smile at him coyly, kissing his neck as I move my hands down his back.

"Yeah, I like that idea." He lets out a soft groan. "Mmmm… that feels good." I continue the massage and keep chatting. Before long, his shoulders soften, and he moans deeply. I sigh, a warm jolt of pleasure shooting to my core.

"That's it." He pulls me over his lap and takes my mouth, his tongue searching mine. I kiss him back. We move our hands all over each other. He fondles me under my shirt and groans. I'm not wearing a bra. He pushes his hip into my thigh to show me how turned on he is, then sits up and pulls off my shirt and his own. Now we're just daring someone to catch us.

We keep roaming—a hair's length from fully giving in to temptation. When we stop to catch our breath, it occurs to us what we look like. We're almost completely naked in the middle of the living room, with an inn full of visitors, including Ms. Connor, who could walk in any minute.

"Damn."

"Take me to the cottage."

Scott scoops me up to go, then his face drops. We forgot he has to check on the boat. Disappointed, we put on our clothes and try not to make too much noise as we stifle our laughter.

"I have the worst timing. Ever."

"Thanks for coming," I whisper.

He smirks. "Oh. I wish."

I smack his arm.

Scott pulls me into his arms, squeezing me in a playful bear hug and kissing me deeply. "You're mine to protect now. Can I… come back after I check on the boat?" He inhales against my neck.

"Please, I'll be in the cottage."

He brushes his fingers through my hair, his eyes lingering on my face.

"I can't wait. And I've got something fun planned for us tomorrow," he murmurs and gives me one last kiss before he lets go and steps out into the rain.

That's when we hear a loud call over the wind.

CHAPTER 24

SCOTT

Margaret's voice cuts through the howling wind, her silhouette brightened by a flash of lightning. "We've got an emergency."

I stride toward her without hesitation, pushing the chaos of the lingering storm to the edges of my mind. Maddie starts toward me, and I gesture for her to stay on the porch, reassuring her that I'll be fine.

"What's going on?"

Margaret pushes her drenched hair away from her face, her expression grim. "The Coast Guard called. We have two divers, Miguel Rivera and Josh Lanning, who didn't leave Coral Fang Reef before the storm hit. Miguel sent a distress call. Josh is trapped. The connection was garbled, so the details were unclear. Neither has surfaced."

The news hit me like a punch to the gut. I know both men. And they're young. I grit my teeth against the mounting tension in my chest. "Where's the Coast Guard now?"

"They're coordinating the rescue effort. We need to get to the docks and join them."

The front door creaks open and Wes steps outside. He greets Maddie before walking over to Margaret and me.

"I got the call," Wes says, his voice steady and grave.

"Let's go. There's not much time." I glance back at Maddie, her frightened eyes locked on us, and wave goodbye.

The docks are in chaos, with the storm's aftermath amplifying every frantic movement and shouted command. Coast Guard officers call out orders over the wind, their voices barely audible above the engine. Men hurry to load gear onto the boat, their faces tense with focus.

Margaret and I board the boat and join a cluster of people huddled around a folding table where the rescue commander outlines the plan. A map of Coral Fang Reef lies pinned beneath waterlogged clipboards, its jagged edges illuminated by a swinging overhead light. The boat takes off.

"The storm has created some dangerous currents," the commander says, pointing to a mark on the map. "Miguel's distress call places him approximately at this location. Josh was trapped near this location. We need two teams—one for Miguel and the other to search for Josh. Visibility is near zero. This won't be easy."

I step forward, scanning the map. Miguel's location is a particularly treacherous spot on the reef. "I'll take Miguel's location. My team will get him out." I look at Wes. "Do you have enough men to get to Josh?"

He tightens his gear, his jaw set with determination. "We'll find him."

"If you find them alive, signal us right away. We'll send backup if it's needed," the commander says. We get ready to dive.

Sliding into the inky, chaotic void, I push down the dread I've allowed to sink into my thoughts. The conditions are bad. Ocean water churns around me, debris of all kinds swirling through the unpredictable currents. My flashlight casts a narrow beam through the darkness, illuminating jagged coral formations.

"Stay sharp." The steady hiss of my regulator is loud in my ears. "Miguel's somewhere in this mess."

"Copy that," Liam's voice crackles back—his dive light bobs ahead, carving a path through the murk.

Minutes stretch before Jamie's voice breaks the silence. "Movement. Nine o'clock, low."

I swing my light, and relief floods me as I spot Miguel. He's tangled in debris, his movements sluggish. But he's alive. Panic flickers in his wide eyes as I approach.

"Liam, secure the tether line. Jamie, clear the coral."

Miguel's breathing is frantic as I offer him my emergency octopus regulator. "Breathe slow." I keep my voice steady. "We've got you, Miguel. You're safe."

His gasps begin to even out as Jamie dislodges the last of the coral. "He's free," Jamie announces.

Together, we stabilize Miguel and begin the ascent. Every second is like an eternity, the weight of the unforgiving waters pressing down on us. When we break through the surface, the Coast Guard boat awaits us. Hands pull Miguel aboard, wrapping him in a thermal blanket as he shivers, his wide eyes darting between the divers.

Back at the docks, the storm's chaos has subdued. Miguel holds onto his wife, her sobs muffled against his shoulder, but the dark expressions of Wes's returning crew bring sad news for Josh's loved ones.

I stand silently as the stretcher is brought ashore, the draped blanket concealing the form beneath it. Josh's father breaks away from the gathered crowd, his anguished cry piercing through the rain as he collapses beside the body. My throat tightens, his pain burrowing deep into my chest. I catch Wes's gaze. He looks down.

Maddie waits for me at the edge of the dock with her arms wrapped tightly around herself. Her eyes shine with unshed tears, and her face crumples with relief when I approach.

"You're okay," she whispers, her voice trembling as she steps closer.

"Yeah." I exhale, exhausted. "We got Miguel out."

She wraps her arms around me, holding me tightly. I sink into her warmth.

When she pulls back, her desert brown eyes search mine. "And Josh?"

I'm unable to find the words.

Her expression turns to sorrow. "You did everything you could."

I want to tell her it doesn't feel like enough, but the conviction in her eyes stops me. She rests a hand gently on my cheek. I lean into her touch, drawing strength from her.

"Come on." She takes my hand. "Let's get you cleaned up."

CHAPTER 25

MADDIE

A cool breeze carries the subtle sweetness of wilting flowers. We stand at the edge of the crowd gathered beneath the sprawling oak tree. We're here to say goodbye to Josh Lanning.

My fingers fidget against each other as my gaze sweeps over the gathered faces. Josh's mother stands closest to the casket, her shoulders trembling under the weight of her grief. Her husband's arms are the only things supporting her. Beside them, Josh's younger sister clutches a single white rose, her knuckles pale against the stem. She doesn't cry. I weep for her.

To my right, Scott stands rigid. His broad shoulders slack with grief. His hazel eyes remain fixed on the casket, his jaw clenched. There's turmoil simmering beneath his calm exterior. It's been a few days since the storm ended. He hasn't said much since the rescue.

The minister's reverent voice cuts through the breeze. "Today, we honor and remember Josh Lanning." He turns his attention to each family member. "A man whose passion for the sea is cherished by those who loved him. He courageously embraced its beauty and challenges, inspiring those who knew him. He was a son, a brother, and a friend, and he will be deeply missed."

Soft sobs rise from Josh's family, slicing through the minister's words. I swallow hard, my chest tightening as guilt and sorrow twist together within me. Training with Wes without telling Scott feels hypocritical. I'm risking more than my own safety.

Josh's sister steps forward and places her white rose on the casket. Her voice trembles as she speaks. I have to strain to hear her. "Josh loved the ocean. It meant freedom and passion to him. He always said it was where he felt the most alive. We'll keep that part of him with us forever."

Her words carry through the air, leaving a deep ache in their wake. I clench my hands tighter. My eyes flick to Wes.

He stares near the casket, his expression unreadable. There's tension in his face, and his posture is rigid. Defiant. He's unaccustomed to failure. He believed he could save Josh. It doesn't matter to him that Josh was already dead when he found him.

After the service ends, people step forward to pay their respects. Scott moves ahead of me, resting his hand on the polished wood of the casket. His lips move, but whatever he says is meant for Josh alone. When he returns, his eyes meet mine, and I reach for his hand, intertwining my fingers with his.

As we linger, a man approaches the Lanning family. He carries himself with grace, extending a firm handshake to Josh's parents and sharing a few kind words with his sister. He seems familiar, though I can't quite place him. His face softens when he turns and spots Scott, and he walks toward us with determination.

"Scott," the man says warmly, his voice filled with affection. "It's good to see you, son." Scott straightens up, his expression softening. "Charles." He takes the older man's outstretched hand, and they shake.

This must be Charles Hayes, Adeline's father. I hadn't met him before. He's not what I expected. He looks very young for his fifty-five years. But he's sad. His eyes suggest he has experienced his share of tragedies.

Mr. Hayes holds onto Scott's hand. "You've done right by Adeline, by all of us. I'm happy to see you finding your way forward."

Scott's throat bobs as he swallows. "Thank you, sir. That means a lot."

Mr. Hayes's gaze shifts to me, and his expression softens further. "You must be Maddie. I've heard a lot about you. Nathan was a good man."

"It's nice to meet you, Mr. Hayes."

He smiles at me and chats with Scott for a few minutes longer before turning to leave. "Take care of each other." He pats Scott on the shoulder before stepping away to greet someone else.

Scott stares after him for a moment, his jaw working silently. When he turns back to me, there's a flicker of peace in his eyes. "He's a good man."

I tighten my grip on his hand. "You, okay?"

He doesn't answer right away. His eyes drop to the ground, and he exhales slowly. "I'm getting there."

Scott and I linger at the cemetery's edge, the last mourners drifting away.

"I hate this."

I squeeze his hand.

His eyes turn to me, dark with guilt and frustration. "I keep thinking about Josh's family."

"You brought them closure." I force some confidence into my voice. "That matters more than you think."

His gaze drops. "It doesn't feel like enough."

We head back to the inn along the sandy path. Scott's hand remains clasped in mine, providing comfort to us both. The ocean continues its steady and unyielding course, a reminder to us of its beauty and its capacity to take.

♥

The streets are alive with the energy of the 45th Annual Maverick Key Seafood Festival. Booths line the beachside road, and colorful banners and string lights sway in the breeze. Tables overflow with conch fritters, shrimp tacos, and other island specialties. My stomach rumbles. This is our first date since the funeral.

I've been on the island for almost two months and life has settled into a comfortable routine. The police haven't found out who broke into my cottage, but there haven't been any other incidents since we saw the man through the window at the inn. Scott and I haven't been able to spend much time together since the funeral because of his schedule with the dives. And I've been diving nearly every other day with Wes. A knot of guilt twists in my stomach. I know it's wrong. But I'm too afraid to tell him.

Scott snaps me out of my thoughts, holding my hand and pulling me close. He nuzzles his face into my neck. His hazel eyes are beautiful as they glimmer in the sunlight. He points at a booth where a man handles a tray of oysters, a crowd gathering to watch.

"Let's see if we can win." He points to the *World's Spiciest Oyster Challenge sign.*

I wrinkle my nose. "Hard pass. I'd rather enjoy my food than set my mouth on fire."

Scott leans in closer so I can hear him over the noise. "Smart move. Me, though? I might give it a try later. Setting my mouth on fire sounds kind of fun."

"You're braver than me," I tease, my shoulder brushing against his as we make our way to a booth selling fresh crab cakes.

Scott takes my order slip to the vendor, returning with a perfectly golden crab cake wrapped in paper. "Try this. It's the best on the island."

The first bite explodes with flavor, and my eyes widen in surprise. "Oh my God. You weren't kidding. This is incredible."

"Told you."

We wander deeper into the festival, stopping at a game booth where stuffed animals hang in neat rows, the brightly colored prizes beckoning challengers. A booming voice calls out from behind the counter. "Step right up. Knock all of them down and win a prize for the lady."

Scott glances at me with a raised brow. "Think I've got what it takes?"

I cross my arms, pretending to size him up. "I don't know. Those bottles look pretty tough."

With determination, Scott hands the vendor a few dollars and picks up a softball. His first throw clips the pyramid's edge, making the bottles wobble but not fall. I stifle a laugh as Scott rubs the back of his neck.

"All right, now I'm serious. Watch this." He narrows his eyes at the target. On this throw, all the bottles crash to the ground in one clean hit.

I cheer when the vendor hands Scott a large plush octopus. "For the lucky lady."

Scott turns to me, his triumphant smile brighter than the festival lights. "For you. An octopus. Never go diving without it."

I take the stuffed toy, laughing. "I'll cherish it forever."

Further down, we stop at a photo booth decked out with silly props. Scott grabs a pirate hat and a plastic sword while I put on oversized sunglasses.

"I look ridiculous." I adjust the enormous glasses as Scott strikes a swashbuckling pose beside me.

"Ridiculously cute," he quips, pulling me into the frame as the camera clicks.

A moment later, the photo strip pops out with the captured images: Scott's exaggerated pirate scowl and my mid-laugh expression, the sunglasses hang lopsided across my face.

"I'm framing this." He tucks the strip into his back pocket.

As the sun dips lower, painting the sky with soft oranges and pinks, we find a spot near the stage where a local band plays lively island music. Couples dance barefoot in the sand, their soft voices carried on the breeze. The festive energy is infectious. Scott and I sway to the music, our shoulders brushing as we hold each other close.

I catch myself stealing glances at him, drawn to his smile, which reaches his eyes.

"You've got some sand in your hair." He brushes a strand of my hair away.

Warmth rises in my cheeks. "A hazard of dancing on the beach."

His hand lingers, tucking the strand behind my ear and rubbing his thumb across my cheek. The tenderness of the gesture makes my breath hitch.

As the night wears on, we wander toward the festival's quieter edge. The noise from the crowd is replaced by the gentle lapping of waves against the shore. The scent of the sea wraps around us.

Scott strides ahead with his hands in his pockets. "Did you have a good time?"

I hug the stuffed octopus to my chest. "Amazing."

Scott's gaze drops before meeting mine again. "I enjoy seeing you like this. Happy."

My heart skips a beat.

The festival lights twinkle in the distance like stars.

I break the silence. "Will you show me where you live?"

Scott blinks. "I haven't taken you to my place yet?"

"You know so much about me already. I want to know more about you."

His lips curve into a slow smile, and he gestures toward the parking lot. "All right. Let's go."

I walk with him, when suddenly he turns and picks me up and carries me the rest of the way to his truck. Laughing, I feel as light as a feather when he puts me down on the leather seat and kisses me with all he has.

"I can't wait to make you mine."

CHAPTER 26

MADDIE

Scott rests his hand on the gearshift, his eyes flicking toward me like he's trying to be sure I'm still here. We turn onto a sandy drive, and the headlights sweep over his house. I gasp.

Tucked behind a canopy of palms and sea grape trees, the house belongs on a postcard. It's simple and understated, perched by a private stretch of beach. A wraparound porch hugs the structure, and in front of it, there's a fire pit surrounded by several Adirondack chairs facing the ocean.

"This is incredible." I get out of the truck and the cool, soft sand covers my bare feet. Endless swaths of water open beyond the beach.

Scott rubs the back of his neck. "It's nothing fancy, but it's home." He grabs a blanket from the backseat.

We walk toward the shoreline hand in hand. "It's beautiful."

"*You're beautiful.*" He pulls me close, wrapping an arm around me as we walk.

As we stroll along the shoreline, the moonlight sprinkles the sand with shimmering dust. Waves roll in and try to keep pace to match the beat of our hearts. Scott leads me to a weathered driftwood log that washed ashore long ago. He motions for me to sit, but before I can, he picks me up and cradles me in his arms, spinning me around until we're both dizzy with laughter. He gently puts me on the log and sits next to me, holding me tight so I don't fall over.

"You're too good to me." I snuggle in to his chest and squeeze his waist.

Scott lifts my chin to turn my face to his and clears his throat. "I just want to make you happy." He takes a deep breath and looks at the sand. "I want…" He meets my eyes, suddenly he looks so much younger.

"What?" I brush my fingers along his jawline.

"You. I want you. I really thought this part of my life was over. I never expected to find someone again, someone I can trust…"

A pang of guilt shoots through me. I should tell him what I'm doing with Wes, but I can't.

"…with my heart. Do you see us together for the long term? Just us?" He takes another deep breath. "I want you badly."

He takes my hand and kisses it. "This chapter in my life. It's one I can't wait to begin—with you." He waits for my answer.

My gaze drops to the ground, and I trace small patterns in the sand with my fingers. My heart is pounding in my ears. I'll tell him everything soon. But right now, this moment is for the two of us.

"What are you thinking, Maddie? What are you feeling?"

My muscles tighten. "This is my home. And you're the one I want." I swallow. "I want us."

He pulls me toward him. A warm shiver rushes over my skin and I catch my breath when he lets his hands linger at my waist and gently, but firmly, squeezes his fingers into my skin. He gazes at my lips.

Then he kisses me. It's a tender kiss but deepens quickly. The spark in my stomach spreads like wildfire through my entire body. I place my hands against his chest and the rapid thrum of his heart pounds against them.

He rests his forehead against mine. "I don't want to stop this time." His smoky, sweet, masculine scent surrounds me, intensified by the rising temperature of his skin.

"Don't." My fingers trace his jawline and move down across the valley of his neck, pausing at his scar. I kiss him there. "I can't wait any longer," I whisper, huskily.

He smiles and lays the blanket across the sand. Gently, he lifts me and puts me onto it, careful not to get me dirty. Resting beside me, he leans over my body, trailing his fingers down my neck, grazing over my collarbone and softly cups my breasts, caressing and circling them through the fabric of my shirt.

"My sweet girl." He covers me with his body and pushes his hips into mine—I can feel his hardness. "God. I need to kiss you, every inch of you." His voice pitches. "Right now." After unbuttoning and pulling down my blouse, he nuzzles his face into the soft spot between my shoulder and arm, then moves slowly back up my neck. He breathes in deeply as he caresses my skin.

"So soft… you smell so good."

I tug at his shirt. He pulls it over his head and tosses it aside, lying back down on top of me.

"Tell me what you want. Let me make you feel good." We continue our kiss as he moves his hands over my bare breasts and squeezes my nipples.

I gasp, pulling away. "Here," I pant into his ear, gently easing his head down, begging him to move his mouth to my breasts. He moves his hot tongue over my nipples in playful circles as he takes his time with them while he moves his hands beneath my underwear.

"Mmm. Your taste is driving me crazy. Vanilla, jasmine… so sweet."

He helps me remove the rest of my clothes. Kneeling, he reaches for me. Hot puffs of air warm the soft skin of my thigh. He pauses for a moment, breathing hard. I can't bear the stillness.

"Please…" I whimper needily and push my thighs together, pressing him in.

He curses and lets out a choppy groan into my thigh. Moving to my center, he grips me tightly, playfully squeezing.

Anticipation laps at me, and I try not to show my frustration, but he sees it and laughs.

"Okay sweetheart… I won't make you wait any longer."

Then he puts his mouth on my aching skin. His kisses are sweet and hungry. He's murmuring words I can't understand while he moves his tongue and lips over me and teases me with his teeth. I plea helplessly.

He lifts his head. His hair's a mess and his face strains with desire. "That's it. Let me hear those sweet sounds. Give them all to me." His voice is so deep it's gravel.

I pant and beg, twisting under his touch. Delicious and unbearable at the same time. I cry out so loud the ships offshore can probably hear me. Encouraged by my cries, he quickens his pace. I clutch desperately at his shoulders, lifting my hips, trying to hold back the swell pushing to break the surface. Then I let go.

"Scott!"

Pleasure surges through me as he continues with his kisses and touches, helping me ride through it. After the last bubbles of sensation burst, I lay stunned. So happy, I just laugh. I'm flushed from head to toe and my arms and legs no longer work. Once I catch my breath, Scott moves back to my mouth and kisses me with all the passion we've been kindling for months.

Without a word, he cradles me in his arms and gently pulls my head to his chest, kissing me sweetly on my forehead. I can hear the rapid beating of his heart. He carries me into the house and to his bed. This time, when he kisses me, he doesn't hold back. He wants to make me his.

"I can't wait to be inside you," he murmurs. "I need to be inside you right now."

I slide my hands into his soft, thick hair, and the world blurs. He reaches for the nightstand, his hands shaking, searching for a condom.

"It's okay. I'm on the pill." Placing my hand softly on his chest, I look into his eyes.

"Are you sure?"

"Yes." My chest flutters.

He groans, squeezes me, and pushes me down. I'm lying on my back, and he's on top of me in an instant. Burying his face into my neck, he whispers breathlessly.

"I love you."

Then he's overtaken by desire. His hands, mouth, and body are all over me, and urgency rushes through me, too, as I wrap my legs around him, begging him to go as deep as he can.

He moans in pleasure as he pushes into me. "Oh yes—you feel too good."

I encourage him as he moves.

"You're made for me Maddie—you're mine. Mine." I reach out with both hands and caress his face. He turns his head and kisses my hand.

Scott's gentle. A generous and a greedy lover, moving from one place on my body to another like there's not enough of me.

He pulls me up and takes me from behind, as he runs the palms of his hands down my back and grasps my hips. Caressing my skin slowly so he can tease me and I can feel how much he wants to please me. His breaths are rapid and choppy. He's at the edge of his control.

"So tight…" He leans in and I feel drops of his sweat hit my back. I yelp when he reaches a spot that sends sparks shooting up my spine. I can't control my whimpers anymore.

"That's it… let me hear you, baby."

He slows a moment and fondles my breasts and kisses my back before returning to his thrusts, still maddeningly slow.

"I need all of you," I pant, clutching the sheet.

He shouts a curse. Breathless now, he loses his grip on my hips and tries not to fall over as he continues to move, clasping my waist. He lets out another loud string of curses.

His filthy words send more pleasure through my core. I look over my shoulder. His eyes lock on mine. I gently touch his thigh. Catching his breath, he holds himself as he rolls me over. I put my arms around his neck, holding onto his shoulders as he pushes into me again. He kisses me fiercely, gazing into my eyes a moment longer before closing his tightly.

"Maddie—" He rolls his hips once more, his legs trembling, and releases a long groan, his face softening into bliss.

Drained, he collapses beside me, pulling me into an embrace against his chest, still kissing me as he catches his breath.

"*You're beautiful,*" he whispers.

Then we're silent. Overwhelmed in a good way.

Only a few minutes pass before his soft breathing and murmurs break the silence. He's dreaming. I smile. My fingers trace lazy patterns across his chest while I take him in. He looks so different in sleep—younger and at peace.

I love you too, Scott.

I listen to his heart's steady beat and close my eyes, letting myself sink into sleep with him.

♥

The ceiling fan spins above us, cooling our bodies after our latest round. Scott's insatiable. A contrast to the constraint he's shown for months. The afternoon sun streams through the windows. I giggle.

"What?" he laughs. "Should I be worried?" His face is dreamy. We're both crazy drunk with exhaustion.

"Just thinking," I whisper. "About how happy I am right now." He starts to open his mouth. The phone on his nightstand buzzes again.

"Can't a man get some rest?" He grumbles and picks it up, streaming through the missed messages. He shakes his head. "Well… I know who we heard drive up earlier."

"Who?" I ask.

"I think we've scandalized Margaret." We both glance up at the open window and laugh.

He calls his team to let them know they have a few days off.

We lay in bed chatting for a little while, sharing funny stories and even some of the boring things about our lives. Comfortable, my eyes grow heavy. I start to drift off. Scott shifts, pulling me closer, his voice rough with sleep.

"Don't get shy on me now."

I tilt my head to meet his gaze, catching his half-smile and his hazel eyes gleaming at me. "I'm so happy, Scott."

His smile deepens, and his irresistible dimples make my heart flutter. "That makes two of us." He kisses my forehead tenderly, and a warm flush spreads through me, leaving me weightless.

Last night is still a dream. The festival, the beach, the sex. I don't want this to end.

Scott's hand strokes my back, slowing down each time he reaches my ass. His touch is both soothing and electrifying. "I have an idea."

"Oh yeah?" I raise an eyebrow.

"Let's stay here the whole day. No phones, no interruptions. Just you and me—maybe some food. Although I'm going to be honest that I don't want to get out of bed."

"Don't you have something you need to do today?"

He shrugs. "It can wait. I'm on vacation."

"You too?" I tease and sit up.

He jumps on me and rolls us over in one smooth motion, pinning me beneath him. Mischief dances in his eyes. "Hey, I deserve a break and some fun, too." He raises his brows. "Especially when I have you."

His words make my heart skip, and my breath catches as he kisses my cheek. He leans down to capture my lips in a languid kiss. "I've fallen for you. I want to do this right."

My breath hitches. "Me too."

He gives me a naughty look, then lifts his palms in the air, counting the fingers on both hands.

"Six." He flicks my nose mischievously.

"What?"

"That's how many times we've done it so far," he says, howling with laughter. "I knew you were trying to do the math."

I smack his chest and push him back to his pillow. Slowly, I crawl toward him, lowering my head between his legs. I blow out a teasing kiss. He squirms as I hold him down.

"Let's make it seven."

His face lights up, making it impossible for me not to smile back.

♥

Our vacation has been a sanctuary. Mornings are soft kisses and tangled sheets, followed by lazy breakfasts we prepare together in his small kitchen. In the afternoons, we stroll along the beach and explore the island hand-in-hand, our laughter carried by the ocean breeze. Each night, we end up in bed, making love and exchanging promises. Word travels fast on the island, but neither of us minds.

Today is Scott's thirty-sixth birthday, and I've got a special surprise planned for him. I'm in the kitchen cooking his favorite breakfast as he takes his shower. I touch the chain around my neck and caress the jade elephant pendant. After we made love the first time, I took it off. He insisted that I put it back on. That he loved to see it against my skin.

When the water shuts off, I take my place at Scott's piano. The piano was built in the eighteen hundreds, a birthday gift from his father, who was an old west enthusiast. The professional restoration makes it possible to play, and while not perfect, its sound is unique.

"I smell something delicious…" Scott's cheerful voice carries down the hallway toward the living room. When he enters the room, he stops dead in his tracks. His hair and skin are still damp from the shower, and he's wearing a towel around his waist. His eyes widen, and his mouth opens, but no words come out.

I curl my fingers, motioning him to come to me.

He doesn't move at first, then takes a deep breath, clears his throat, and walks toward me. When he reaches the piano, I meet his heated gaze.

"I tried to think of a gift that you'd like." I bite down on my lip. He swallows. I can feel him through the towel. I'm tempted to pull it down, but refrain.

"What I finally decided on was this." I lower my gaze and gesture to myself. "And a song of your choosing." I look back up, locking my gaze on his.

He takes a sharp breath and reaches out to brush his fingers across my face.

"What do you think about my gift? Do you like it?"

"Oh yeah."

"What song?"

Crouching down, he whispers huskily into my ear. "Play the song you played that night at the bar. The one I can't get out of my head."

He sits next to me, gently clasping the chain around my neck before letting it go.

"Play it for me while I touch you." He brushes the back of his hand beneath my chin.

I gasp. My fingers run across the keys, creating the first notes as Scott slowly slides his fingertips down my back, murmuring as he savors the softness of my skin. He moves his hands back up to the back of my neck and removes the blue silk ribbon tied around it. The pretty bow falls to the floor. Revealing his birthday present. My nipples are hard, and I whimper when he squeezes them. He curses and removes the towel, moving behind me and putting me on his lap. I pause, which prompts him to command.

"Keep playing. Please, baby." I focus on my place in the music and keep going until Scott moves his hands around me to my center and he plays music of his own.

This is impossible. His hot breath moves along my neck as he tilts my head and takes my lips. The piano is forgotten as he kisses me urgently and moves himself inside me. Grasping my hips, he guides me up and down. I try to take over, but he isn't having that. He takes my breasts into his hands and squeezes them hard in warning, playing with my nipples as he rolls his hips.

"Do you feel that?" He groans into my back. "Tell me. Do you feel that?" he repeats, louder this time.

I let out a needy whimper.

Pounding into me now, our movements become so frantic we tumble off the bench.

Laying in a cluster of limbs, we laugh.

After we catch our breath, Scott picks me up and gently puts me on the rug, taking one of my legs and wrapping it around his neck. I follow his lead. He hisses in pleasure and thrusts. Gradually, he picks up speed and urgency. I pull him closer, then gasp in surprise when I clench around him. I cry out as Scott finishes with a deep groan.

We lay there, silent and content in each other's arms, breakfast forgotten.

"Happy birthday."

Scott kisses me tenderly. "I love you."

He looks down at me with his beautiful eyes, open wide with his love for me. My heart skips.

"I love you." Tears stream down my face, their soft trace pulsing off my skin.

We both believe what we're feeling right now will never change.

CHAPTER 27

MADDIE

I'm beneath the water's surface, double-checking my dive computer monitor and adjusting my face mask. My heart rate picks up as we get closer to the entrance to Carter's Drop. Hovering a few feet away, Wes gives me the **OK** sign, his green eyes bright behind his mask. We're using hand signals for me to get the practice and will only use our comms if there's an emergency. He gestures toward the opening. I take a deep breath through my regulator, my pulse quickening. This is the moment I've been training for.

For weeks, Wes has pushed me through endless drills. I've trained in the dry suit and rebreather, completed countless line-following exercises, and performed emergency maneuvers to address all kinds of failure scenarios. His relentless yet patient teaching method has brought me to this point. I trust him completely, but now I need to trust myself. I can do this.

Scott weighs heavily on my mind. It's like I'm living a double life. At home, I'm 100 percent committed to him and our little canine family. We've each fallen into the roles that make our household hum, and we're so happy… and in love. But then there's this training behind his back. It's wrong. The truth will hit him hard. But I still can't stop. I'm compelled to finish Nathan's work and to bring him justice. Just this one cavern dive. After I do this, I'll be prepared for deep cave diving and I'll come clean to Scott. I have to believe he'll forgive me after these weeks we've been together and how much we love each other.

Wes and I enter the cavern, and it's like we're in another world. The water cools significantly. I follow Wes, and my movements are controlled. Just as we had practiced.

The deeper we go, the dimmer the light becomes. However, it's not complete darkness. In the cavern, sunbeams still sneak through cracks in the rock, creating shifting, ghostly patterns. The walls widen, rough and jagged, with patches of algae giving them an alien texture.

Wes signals for me to stop near a cluster of limestone. He unspools a dive line and secures it to a pointed rock edge. His hand signals are clear: Watch. Learn.

He'd drilled the mantra into me during my training: "The line is your life. Never lose the line." I repeat the words silently, holding myself still for a moment. My line reel hangs at my side, its presence quiet reassurance that I'm in control of what happens next.

As we move deeper into the cavern, it opens into a large chamber with multiple tunnels branching into darkness. My heart races as I recognize one feature from Nathan's maps. A distinct arch. I motion for Wes's attention and point toward it. When I move closer, he clutches my arm.

His other hand points to the sign bolted near the tunnel entrance. It's the grim reaper sign. Its deathly image and words are stark and sobering. A chill runs through me as I read the words. **STOP! Prevent your death! Go no further. There's nothing in this cave worth dying for.** Below the grave warning, a bulleted list of cave dangers is printed. Wes shared a history of how various professional dive organizations collaborated to craft the signs in the late 1980s to reduce the rising number of deaths associated with cave dives. I respect the danger, but it won't stop me. I look back at Wes, who shakes his head firmly. Not yet. We're going to take one step at a time.

We continue the cavern dive without incident, focusing on my buoyancy, breathing, and the drills we'd practiced endlessly. Wes gives me an **OK** sign every once in a while, the approval in his eyes boosting my confidence. He's proud of me. For a moment, I allow myself to believe I belong here. And that I know what I'm doing. But the darker tunnels pull at my curiosity, Nathan's clues murmuring in the back of my mind. Where do they lead? Go see.

When Wes signals that it's time to ascend, I hesitate. My gaze drifts to a small opening visible in the rock wall. It's nothing more than a shadowed crack, but I can't help myself. I gesture toward it, asking silently.

Wes signals a firm—No. His body language leaves no room for debate.

Still, as he turns to prepare for our ascent, I edge closer to the opening. Just a peek. I'll only go in a couple of feet. That will be okay, I tell myself. I slip inside, my heart pounding as curiosity overtakes caution.

The walls close in, and the dim light from the main cavern instantly disappears, leaving only faint illumination from my diving lamp. The sudden shift in lighting startles me, causing my fin to scrape along the bottom. Instantly, a silt plume engulfs me.

Panic takes hold. My visibility has vanished. There is nothing but thick, swirling gray clouds, spinning around me. My chest tightens, and I almost lose my grip on my regulator. Wes's words from our training ring in my mind. Stop. Breathe. Think. Act. I grip the dive line like a lifeline and try to steady my breaths. Yet, the silt obscuring my vision won't settle, and my head spins as my heart threatens to beat itself right out of my chest.

Although it seems like forever, Wes is by me in seconds. His grip on my arm is steady.

"Stop. Don't move," Wes says through the comms.

I freeze as he unhooks his backup light and scans the area. His usual easygoing demeanor is gone, replaced by tense focus.

"Calm down—we're safe here. We have plenty of air. But you need to slow your breathing. Don't hold your breath." He pauses, watching me as I try to calm my breaths. "We'll wait a little while for the silt to settle, then we'll go home." He holds my hand and gives it a tight squeeze. I try very hard to focus on his words and calm down, but it's a struggle. What I've done is very dangerous, and I've put both of us at risk.

Once the silt settles, Wes turns to me. His expression behind his mask is a mix of exasperation and concern. He taps his mask. Pay attention.

Embarrassment prickles my skin. After he guides me back into the main cavern, I lean against the limestone wall and just breathe in relief.

He signals to prepare our ascent, but as I reach to move forward, there's a sharp tug at the back of my head. My heart leaps into my throat. My hair is caught on a jagged piece of limestone. I scream through the regulator.

Green eyes lock on mine.

"Don't move." He signals vehemently with his hands while also speaking into the comms.

I stay as still as possible, fighting back another surge of panic as I almost spit out the regulator. A sharp headache and wave of dizziness hits me. I'm going to pass out. Wes swiftly removes a dive knife from his suit vest.

I focus on my breathing, on Wes's presence.

With one slice, I'm free. Wes grabs my arm, and together, we ascend immediately. I'm vaguely aware of the ascent, like I'm in the middle of a dream.

Breaking the surface, Wes tears off my mask, and I gasp for air as sunlight blazes overhead. Wes climbs to the boat first and pulls me up with steady hands, pulling me the rest of the way up the ladder. His face is pale, but his grip is firm.

"Are you okay?" He crouches before me and holds my shoulders. After a moment, he lifts my chin. A flash of fear crosses his face. Then he takes a deep breath. "You're okay."

Tears roll down my eyes. "I'm sorry. I didn't think—"

"Ssh… It's okay." He puts his arms around me.

"…so stupid. I'm sorry, I—"

"You kept your head when it mattered. That's what's most important." He's rubbing my back, trying to get me to calm down. "But dammit, this place doesn't forgive mistakes. Never do that again. Ever."

I nod, his words sinking into my chest like stones. I'm still trying to catch my breath and stop crying. My breathing becomes more raspy and uneven, and then I can't breathe at all.

An anxiety attack. But this is worse.

Panicked, my eyes lock on Wes's. All blood leaves his face.

And then nothing.

CHAPTER 28

SCOTT

"Scott—I can't breathe."

Maddie squirms as I tease her. Bringing her just to that point, then stopping. I've learned her body well over the past few weeks, and now she's at my mercy. I laugh when she bats her little fists on my chest. I'm not going to let her have her way that easily.

"That's it." Frustrated, she wiggles out from underneath me and pushes me down, getting on top.

Not that I mind one bit. She smiles and starts to move. I gaze at her beautiful body. The way her firm breasts bounce and her long hair cascades over her shoulder. Beautiful. Touching her breasts first, I squeeze, feeling a jolt of pleasure when she yelps and tightens around me. I move one of my hands over her stomach and pause. Then a thought, an emotion so intense. I freeze.

"What is it?" she asks breathlessly. I press my hand to her stomach more firmly and make eye contact, begging her to see me. Surprise flashes across her face. Then I see a longing that matches my own. Pulling myself up, I kiss her there once, then circle my arms around her and kiss her mouth. I hold her as tight as I can.

After, as we lay side by side, she takes my hand and puts it back on her stomach.

"That's what I want too, Scott."

♥

"Scott… Scott!" I'm jolted out of my daydream by Liam, who stands next to me.

His brows pull together in concern. "What's on your mind, man?"

"Nothing."

He stares at me, then smiles. "My advice. Don't wait." He walks back to the locker and unloads the equipment.

I shouldn't let my thoughts wander on the job, but Maddie's always on my mind. Maddie and Ding are staying at my house, but I haven't officially asked her to move in yet. I think of the small satin box hidden in my dresser. And last night when she put my hand on her stomach. It changed everything. Why wait?

I look up at the sky. Bright and sunny a few minutes ago, it's now overcast with dark, angry clouds. A shiver runs up my spine.

But it's not bad enough to call the dive. Jamie and I suit up and get ready to descend.

♥

My dive lamp cuts through the murk, illuminating the jagged limestone wall. Behind me, Jamie reels out some replacement line, his movements smooth and practiced. The line between us reminds me of where we are. My mind wonders to Maddie again. There's a desperate tug at my thoughts today, like I need to be near her.

Margaret's voice crackles through my comms. "Any progress down there?"

"Not yet," I reply, scanning the uneven walls, ignoring Jamie's stare. "We're finishing cavern inspection. Then we'll head back."

A cut line near a tunnel entrance catches my eye. Looking closer, I bend down and pick it up. It's not a line. What is this? Hair. How did hair get down here? The only others authorized to dive into Carter's Drop are Wes's crew and the Coast Guard. Wes was scheduled to dive earlier today. It's hard to distinguish the color of the hair, but it's a few inches long. None of the guys have long hair.

Liam's voice slices through the silence, sharp and urgent. "Scott. You need to get to the surface now, man. We've got an emergency."

My pulse spikes. I signal Jamie to come over, and my voice comes out steady despite the fear building inside me. "What's going on, Liam?"

"Just get back up here," he says, his voice tense. "It's bad. You need to hurry."

I don't ask any more questions, signaling Jamie to ascend. I follow him.

When I surface, I take a deep breath. The sun, which has reemerged from the clouds, blinds me. Hauling myself onto the deck of *Adeline*, I spot Liam pacing with a radio clenched in his hand. Jamie's already onboard, talking to Margaret.

"Shit." Liam's dark skin washes out. "Is she… is she going to make it?"

"What the fuck is going on?" I demand. The urgency in his voice has set every nerve in my body on edge.

Liam turns to face me, his expression solemn, his eyes wide with dread. He takes a breath and hurries toward me. "The Coast Guard just sent out a relay. Two divers got in trouble a couple of hours ago. They're asking for a temporary pause on dives today in case they need to investigate the Drop."

My stomach turns to liquid, and my limbs go weak. I can't breathe.

"Who?" But I already know. Jamie and Margaret have gathered around me, and they are preparing to hold me down.

Liam hesitates for a beat, then spits it out. "It's Wes and Maddie."

The words punch the air from my lungs. "What?" I step closer, my voice hoarse. "Is she alive?" My head spins as I brace myself for my world to shatter.

"They were diving in the caverns and had to ascend quickly because of some kind of emergency," Liam explains, his voice strained. "Wes made the call for Maddie. She was in respiratory distress and lost consciousness. He performed rescue measures. I'm sorry. It doesn't sound good. The Coast Guard already took them to the hospital. They don't know her condition."

"God, no." I collapse to my knees, my hands the only things keeping me from completely falling against the deck. Margaret rushes forward to help me catch my fall and wraps her arms around me. Jamie and Liam are silent as they jump into action to get us back to the shore. Margaret squeezes my shoulder, trying in vain to reassure me.

"We'll get to her as quickly as we can. We have to believe she's going to be okay."

I can't respond. I just sit and stare at the horizon. Then, I put my head in my hands and weep. I don't care who sees me. Instead of the usual prayer I say when we dock, I pray Maddie will be spared. Please, just let her live.

And then the bargaining begins. I'll do anything. Make any promise to anyone. Give up everything I have.

All the same—just like I bargained for Adeline.

♥

The hospital's fluorescent lights are too bright, buzzing overhead as I push through the doors to Maddie's wing of the hospital. Wes called me on the way in and assured me she was alive, but I had to see it for myself. The sharp scent of antiseptic floods my senses—I feel numb.

I find Hannah sitting near the reception desk, her eyes swollen with tears and her arms crossed tightly over her chest. She's staring straight ahead, slouched in her chair. I approach her. She glances up and straightens, her expression a mixture of relief and worry.

"Room?"

"Two-oh-four," she answers quickly. "She's stable. It was touch and go at first, but she's going to be okay." I let out an audible gasp.

"Scott, Maddie didn't—"

I give her a terse nod and continue down the hallway, my boots thudding against the tile floor. Each step is heavier than the last. The knot in my chest tightens as I imagine what I might find when I open the door.

When I push it open, the sight of Maddie stops me in my tracks. She's pale against the white hospital sheets, her damp hair clinging to her forehead. She's been wearing an oxygen mask, which has since been removed. They're treating her for mild decompression sickness. She's small and fragile, nothing like the woman in my bed just this morning, full of determination and fire. Her eyes flutter open and her lips curve into a weak smile.

"Hello," she rasps, her voice barely audible.

I stay by the door for a moment, taking her in and reassuring myself she's alive. It should be enough. But the anger and fear swirling inside me won't settle down. I step closer, my voice tight and controlled. "You're okay." I'm reassuring myself rather than her.

She nods weakly. "I'm fine. Just… shaken up. I—"

"What happened?" My words are clipped as I interrupt her. My tone is harsher than I mean it to be.

Her gaze drops, guilt flickering across her face. "My hair… got caught," she explains, trembling. "I panicked. Wes helped me. I didn't mean to hurt anyone. On the boat, I couldn't breathe."

My heart clenches. I want to wrap her in my arms and comfort her, but the anger is too fierce. I don't trust myself.

"You could've died," I choke out, the words snapping out before I stop them—the thought of losing her, burying her, crashes over me hard and fast.

"I know," she whimpers, her voice breaking. "I'm sorry… Please forgive me."

The weight of her apology settles over us, heavy and suffocating. I take a deep breath, forcing myself to calm down. She's weak. I don't want to beat her down any further. "You're alive. That's what matters right now. Get some rest. You'll need it."

Her fingers twitch like she wants to reach for me but, she doesn't. Clutching the sheet, she opens her mouth to say more. Her eyes stare into mine, pleading.

I cut her off. "Take care of yourself. Focus on that. We'll talk more about this later."

Before the storm inside me spills over, I turn and leave the room, ignoring her tiny voice call for me to stay and resisting the urge to turn back.

♥

The late afternoon air is stale as I step outside the hospital and make my way through the parking lot. I lean against the hood of my truck, replaying the last few minutes. Her pale face and the guilt in her eyes. She lied to me. What has she done to us? She could have died. The thought of her dying today twists something primal inside me. I close my eyes, exhaling slowly. What do I do now? Just this morning, I was planning to get on my fucking knees and ask her to marry me. I'm a fool. Letting her go is the logical thing to do. I can't trust her. She's been sneaking behind my back, trusting that asshole with her life while she makes love to me every night. I can do the math. I know she did this because I told her no and the fucker said yes. How could she do that? She's not the woman I thought she was. I slam my fists down on the hood.

"Damn it!" I let all my anger out on the truck. Before I smash the windows, I get in and start the engine instead.

♥

My boots slam against the weathered planks of the dock. I focus on the man leaning against a piling near his sleek boat. He's been waiting for me. His arms crossed, his face as infuriating as ever, although he's not smiling.

I stop a few feet from him, keeping my voice low. "We need to talk."

Wes pushes off the piling and steps closer. "I figured after you called." He gestures toward his boat, his tone cautious. "How about we take this onboard? Grab a beer, talk it out like we're civilized men?"

I don't move. "This isn't a friendly chat, Harrington."

He straightens. "All right. Let's have it."

I step closer, inches from his face. "You had no business taking Maddie into the caverns. You know the risks, and you took her anyway. Now she's hurt. That's on you."

His face sinks, but he recovers quickly, crossing his arms. "She came to me. She wants to learn. And guess what? She's damn good at it. She deserves the respect of letting her make her own choices and know the truth about Nathan's work. And you made it clear to her you weren't going to help her."

"I wasn't going to risk her life," I snap, my voice rising enough to draw a few glances from dockhands. Let them look. I don't give a fuck. "You think dragging her into that hole makes you a hero?" I scoff. "It makes you a reckless asshole who doesn't give a damn about anyone but himself."

His green eyes flash with anger and defiance. "And you think coddling her is any better? She's not a porcelain doll. She's capable, and she made a choice. You're pissed because you can't control her."

My fists clench at my sides, heat rising in my chest. The urge to punch in his face is intense. "This isn't about control. It's about responsibility. You're supposed to know better, Wes. You've been down there enough times to know how quickly it can all go to hell. And you let her go. You fucking took her there." I move in closer to his face, hoping he feels my spit. "You arrogant piece of shit."

Wes's voice becomes lower but charged. He leans in. "You're right. I do know better. That's why I stayed with her every step of the way and made sure she didn't get lost, or worse. I never left her. I was there for her when things got complicated." His eyes narrow. "Were you?"

His words cut deeper than I want to admit, but I'm not about to let him off the hook. "Don't you dare lecture me." I ball my fists. "Until you hold the woman you love in your arms and watch her die, you don't get to do that." I'm trembling, a hair's breadth from killing him. He has the decency to look ashamed.

A gentle lapping of water against the dock and the faint cry of a gull overhead are the only sounds as we stand there.

Wes exhales. "Scott, look. I'm sorry. You care about her, probably more than you're willing to admit. And for what it's worth, we shouldn't have kept you in the dark. You're right about that. I am an asshole. But she's not going to stop. She'll see this through, no matter what you or I tell her. If that means diving headfirst into hell, she'll do it. With or without us."

The truth of his words settles uneasily in my chest. Maddie's stubborn determination mirrors her brothers in ways that terrify me. "So, what?" My voice is quieter now, but no less pained. "You think letting her risk her life is the best way to help her?"

"I think being there to catch her when she falls is better than leaving her to fail alone."

I glance past him toward the horizon, where the sun gives way to dusk. The fiery colors are fading fast into muted blues and grays. "She's not just a project to you, is she?"

Wes's posture shifts, his usual confidence replaced by vulnerability. "No," he admits. "She's not. But I'm not the one she wants. That's you."

His eyes stare through me, waiting, daring me to argue. But I can't. Instead, I meet his gaze.

"If anything like this happens again, and you're a part of it… you're dead."

"Noted."

I turn on my heel, the planks creaking underfoot as I walk back toward my truck. I'm going to go home and have a whiskey. I'll try to drown my dreams about our future and instead focus on my job and how I can keep her safe at a distance. There's no going back.

CHAPTER 29

MADDIE

Ding and I are heading home to the Driftwood Inn. Even though I've been keeping myself busy, during the quiet times, it hurts. I really screwed up. It's been more than a month since my diving accident. Even though life has settled back into a routine, I'm untethered, like a compass spinning endlessly without ever finding north. I want to take away the pain I've caused and just start over. But that's not the way life works.

Scott is a storm cloud hovering in the room at the dive meetings. His eyes only meet mine once in a while. And when they do, their coldness cuts deep. He speaks with clipped words in a formal tone. Like I'm nothing more to him now than another person he has to manage. The tenderness and love we shared is buried, smothered by my betrayal.

"Cheer up." Hannah's voice jolts me from my thoughts as I walk into the dining room. She links her arm through mine. "Scott's just being a grumpy old soldier nursing his broken heart. He'll come around soon. I promise." She gives me a peck on my cheek.

I try to smile, but it feels thin and forced. "I'm not so sure."

"He will," Wes says, sliding into the conversation as he appears at my other side. "The guy just needs time. He's scared. He thought he lost you. Until he comes to his senses, you've got Hannah and me to keep you company." I give him a nudge and grab a water bottle from the side table.

The dive crew is gathering, their voices carrying across the inn as Garrett and Dr. Fischer prepare to speak at today's meeting. Members of the Coast Guard are also present. They've started attending the meetings and taking part in the dives. Considering the increased public interest and scrutiny of the recent incidents, they are closely monitoring all activity at the Drop. Everyone is on edge, with the thinly veiled threat of shutting down the project looming over us.

I take the opportunity to finally introduce myself to Mark.

"Mark?"

"Hello, Maddie." His kindness softens his rigid demeanor. He looks like he's in his thirties, which is about right since he and Nathan went to college together. "I'm sorry I never got back to you. It's been so busy I let the time get away from me. Are you feeling better?" He gives me a look of concern.

"Yes, that's okay. And I know you're working now, but I hope we can have lunch one day to talk about Nathan. Hannah told me you knew each other well. There's so much I don't know about his last years."

"We were best friends." His eyes seem to shroud, like he's remembering something he had forgotten. "Did everything in college together, but when we moved to the Key—life got in the way." A sad expression crosses his face. "We grew apart. He was a good man." He pats me on the back. It seems like he's eager to finish the conversation. "My wife Crystal and I will have to have you over for dinner one night. I'll share some of those college stories." He winks. "I'll have her call you." He excuses himself and walks to the table to start the meeting.

I catch Scott watching our conversation. He turns away, like he's uninterested.

"We've logged three unauthorized dive attempts this week alone," Mark announces as he gestures at the map pinned to the wall. He speaks in a measured tone. "We're lucky no one else has been hurt, but until this madness dies down, only pre-approved authorized dives are allowed."

Scott adjusts the dive schedule. Even as I bristle at his coldness toward me, I have to admire how he commands this space. When the meeting ends, I linger on the Driftwood Inn's porch, watching the waves crash against the shore.

"Maddie," Elaine's voice startles me. She approaches, the streaks of silver in her hair gleaming in the late afternoon sun. "Do you have a moment to talk?"

"Of course." I step aside to make room at the railing.

"Somewhere private."

We walk to my cottage, where I invite her to sit, then fix us both some tea. After sharing a few pleasantries, Elaine talks.

"There's something about your brother you should know."

A nervous knot tightens in my stomach. Another secret. "What is it?"

She hesitates for a moment before speaking. "Did you know Nathan was in love?"

I'm surprised, this wasn't the topic I expected. "Yes. But I know nothing about her."

She frowns. "Well, I'm sorry I haven't come to you sooner. Nathan and I were working in the university offices one day when I noticed a picture lying on his desk—a beautiful young woman. I teased him, and he shared something with me. It was like he wanted to get it off his chest with someone he could trust. He told me she was his fiancée. I, of course, was thrilled for him and asked who she was. He said he couldn't tell me or anyone who she was yet. He was hiding something, but I didn't want to pry. Later, he left the photo on the desk and… never had the chance to pick it up. It was clear how much she meant to him." She pauses, giving me a moment to soak in the information. "I thought you should know. I've been looking into it, hoping to find her and share this with her. There's a lead. I'm meeting a man tomorrow who claims he knew about the relationship. He's asked I keep his identity secret for now. But he's someone we can trust. I'll let you know what I find out afterward. He was close friends with them both."

She slips me a small photo.

I turn it over, and a shock jolts through me. It's the pretty blond woman from the general store and the airshow. The one with a hidden bruise and a little girl. The little girl who had to have been born just months after Nathan disappeared.

Should I tell Elaine about her? No. I'll wait until she meets with her contact. I want to trust her, but I have to be careful.

"Thanks, Elaine."

Elaine squeezes my arm gently. "You remind me of him. In all the best ways."

"I have something to share with you, too." I lay Nathan's maps across the table. "These are the entrances he explored," I explain, tracing a line with my finger. "And here, these were areas he thought were worth investigating further," I tell her what I found in Nathan's stolen notes and the warning.

Elaine studies the maps, her gaze sharp and focused. "This is remarkable. Nathan's work on these maps may help us find what he was searching for."

"I've been careful about who I share this with. It's hard to know who I can trust."

"You're right to be cautious," Elaine says. "After hearing about what you've found in Nathan's notes and these maps—what he was hiding." She hesitates. "I'm worried that someone may have harmed him, and they don't want us to find out who they are."

A creak at the cottage's front door makes us both freeze. My heart pounds as I slowly look.

"Did you hear that?" I ask.

She pales. We walk over, and I carefully open the door and peek outside. There's dirt on the front step and fresh footprints on the ground below the stairs, large footprints—a man's size. We can see the footsteps trail around the corner of the inn. A chill runs up my spine.

"Someone was here," I whisper hoarsely, dread coiling in my chest.

Elaine, fearful herself, places a steady hand on my shoulder. "Lock your doors. Have someone stay with you at the cottage. Be careful. I'll call you tomorrow."

Unease clings to me. Whoever was listening at the door heard everything we said.

♥

I approach the marina slowly—Scott's boat rocks gently in its berth. My heart is pounding hard and fast as my gaze lands on him, wiping down *Adeline*'s railing. The sunlight frames his figure, painting his broad shoulders in amber and shadow.

Ding trots beside me, his tail wagging like this is an ordinary walk. I envy his blissful ignorance as I stop at the edge of the dock. Ding barks, once, eager to get Scott's attention. I draw shaky breaths, forcing myself to steady my nerves before calling, "Scott?"

He bristles and straightens his back, turning to face me. His beautiful eyes are guarded, and his expression is unreadable. He grips the cloth before speaking.

He clears his throat. "What are you doing here?" My heart sinks. He doesn't want me to be here. My chest tightens as I approach the boat. I take a deep breath. Stumbling, I catch myself and push forward.

"Can we talk? It won't take long."

Scott sets the cloth aside and jumps off the boat's ladder to stand beside me. His posture is relaxed, but there's tension in his face. "I'm listening."

Clasping my hands in front of me, I force myself to hold his gaze. "You deserve an apology," I begin, my voice trembling. "A real one. No excuses. What I did. It was wrong. I should've been honest with you from the start."

His face remains unreadable, but the silence between us presses down like a weight, urging me to keep going. I move my gaze from him to the dock, unable to fix on him for too long.

"I was scared—scared that if I told you, you'd try to stop me… or walk away. I know I wasn't fair to you. I hate what I did." My voice trembles, but I push forward. "You're everything to me. I know I ruined it." I look up, hoping he'll tell me it isn't over. He doesn't move. He's listening. "I'm so sorry, and… I love you."

My confession hangs in the air, raw and exposed. Heat floods my face, but I don't back down. He needs to know how bad I feel, even if it changes nothing.

Scott tightens his jaw and swallows. I think he's going to turn away. Then he sighs, running a hand through his hair as he approaches me.

"Maddie…" His voice is softer than I expect, and the ache in my chest deepens. "I won't lie. What you did… it hurt. It's hurt like hell." Anger flashes across his features. "But I understand why you did it. You're searching for answers. I know how much Nathan means to you. I share the blame for what happened between us." He takes a breath and looks back at me, his eyes filled with sadness. "I shouldn't have dismissed you so quickly. I should have listened. We could have met in the middle."

His hazel eyes shine. "We didn't ruin everything. Not completely. But this…" He gestures between us, his hand dropping back to his side without touching me, his eyes dimming. "I won't go there again. What I can give you is friendship and protection."

The tears I'm holding back are stinging my eyes. "I understand." I take a deep breath, my voice shaky. "It's just, I… I hope that maybe someday we might be able to…" I stop, unable to say anymore. I'm too scared.

"No. I'm sorry. I just can't." He stares at me with unyielding eyes, destroying any hope that we can get back what we had.

His expression softens, yet the distance remains. "I still care and will help you find those answers you're looking for."

The blend of relief and heartache is overwhelming. "Thank you," I whisper, my voice shaking.

Scott reaches out, his hand brushing against my face. It's fleeting. Not the embrace I long for. The softness of his touch only makes me want more. "No more secrets, okay? If we're going to work together, you need to trust me as much as you trust yourself."

"No more secrets. I promise." I force my voice to remain steady even as a few tears fall. He pretends he doesn't see them. I pull the maps from my purse. "I want to give you these. They're Nathan's. He charted the tunnels he explored. I think he was close to finding what he was looking for. Please use them."

He takes the papers from my hands, careful not to touch me. "Thank you for trusting me. I'll take good care of them. See you tomorrow." He glances down at Ding, sprawled out on the dock. Scott crouches to scratch behind his ears. Ding eagerly licks his hands and when Scott stands, Ding circles his feet. He misses Scott and wants him to stay.

Taking one last look at us, Scott waves goodbye before returning to the boat.

I try to find hope in what he's offered me, even if it's not what I want. I turn and walk away, my steps heavy.

Scott's gaze burns through my shirt to the skin on my back. I imagine him standing at the railing, his grip tight as he watches me leave.

CHAPTER 30

SCOTT

"We're all set," Jamie calls from the aft deck, adjusting the straps on his gear. He's full of nervous energy. "You ready to make history, boss?"

My mind is on the dive ahead. "Let's aim for the kind of history we walk away from." Jamie tries to laugh, but it's hollow. He hastens away to grab his reel without a quip or joke. The whole crew dynamic has changed these last few weeks without Maddie in my life. We're all walking around like shells of the people we were, and we miss her sweet face. After Maddie's visit yesterday, I went home and tried to make peace with it. My love for her is still strong, but it's tainted. I wanted to tell her I don't want to be her friend and I want to marry her, but I forced myself to tell her the truth. It wasn't possible to go back. I can't get past the distrust. To heal this wound, I'd have to open my heart enough to give her everything she needs. I can't do that. It's better this way.

The sharp trill of the satellite phone cuts through the morning stillness. Margaret picks it up, rolling her eyes as she hands it to me.

"Garrett," she mutters.

I sigh, pressing the phone to my ear. "Rickter."

"Update," Garrett snaps.

"We're at the descent point. Jamie and I are about to go in. Margaret and Liam are topside."

"You're running out of time, Rickter. Don't waste it."

I tighten my grip on the phone. "You'll get results when we have them. We're not cutting corners." I pause, considering whether it's worth stirring the pot. Yeah. If I can piss Garrett off, it's a good thing.

"Talk to your partner, Dr. Fischer. I think she'll be happy to share she's negotiated more time with the university."

I don't wait for his reply. Hanging up, I hand the phone back to Margaret. "Let's get this done," I say.

I turn to Jamie. "Stay sharp. We're going down the tunnel that Nathan marked. And it's going to be a wicked trip."

"Got it, man."

I'd stayed up late last night with the crew, studying the maps Maddie had given me. Nathan had been doing extensive solo cave dives deep into the system for weeks. It looks like dozens of dives. If this wasn't Dr. Nathan Carter, I'd say he was insane—and just plain stupid. The stakes had to be high to drive him to push forward with solo cave diving, especially in a system as challenging as Carter's Drop. But this makes me think of the obvious. What he was doing wasn't exactly solo. He had to have a boat captain. Who the hell were they? I couldn't remember all the details of Nathan's disappearance or who may have been questioned. The captain had to be someone he trusted. I'll look into it when we get back.

From the main cavern, we trace Nathan's old dive line, following the path on the map that seems to be the one Nathan took last. He's still down there. Dread seeps through me from the thought of what we may find today. All our movements are careful. At the first junction, I pause to check my slate that has the copy of Nathan's map. His notations point us toward an even tighter passage.

"We're taking the left." I shine my light into the tunnel.

Jamie lets out a low whistle. "Whoa. That's a tight squeeze. You sure about this?"

"Positive. Watch your equipment. Let's go."

The tunnel narrows to where the rock brushes against my shoulders. The walls are alive as they squeeze. They're trying to strangle us. Halfway through, my light catches another line. To follow, it will require a squeeze through an even tighter pinch point. This one is vertical. Shit.

Jamie's the thinner man, so he goes first. He doesn't say a word as he concentrates. I follow.

Turning sideways, I'm able to push through. Thankfully, this tunnel opens into another chamber with some breathing room, the ceiling rising two feet above us. There are over a dozen more passages. My light sweeps the space, and faint imprints of disturbed sediment trail into the distance, proof that someone's been here before.

"Incredible," Jamie whispers. "I've never seen anything like this. There's the next tunnel over there. Are we going to take it?"

I'm drawn to a cluster of objects buried in the silt. Kneeling, I brush away the debris and uncover dive weights, a rusted carabiner, a cracked flashlight, and a waterproof video camera—evidence of an emergency ascent.

"Jamie, over here." I hold up the camera.

Jamie's eyes widen behind his mask. "That's got to be Nathan's."

As I examine it, a knot forms in my stomach. The casing is scratched, but the seals are intact. If this is Nathan's, it might hold answers—answers I'm not sure Maddie is ready for. But where is Nathan's body? My dive monitor beeps. We're at 45 percent gas. We need to get back.

"Let's go." I give the thumbs-up to signal we're ending the dive. Jamie's surprised by the gauge. We should have calculated the effort it was going to take to get through restrictions better. It took a lot out of us and used up more oxygen. We need to plan better next time.

The return journey is grueling. Our hands grip the dive line, and we take each meter forward cautiously.

"We're almost there."

When we break into open water, it's like I'm surfacing after holding my breath too long. Margaret and Liam help us onto the boat, their faces tight with concern. We pushed too far this time.

"That was the hardest shit I've ever done." Jamie shakes the water out of his hair.

"What'd you find?" Margaret asks, her gaze flicking to the camera in my hand.

I hesitate, my mind racing. "Debris from Nathan's dive."

Margaret frowns but doesn't push.

"Let's get the fuck out of here."

CHAPTER 31

MADDIE

I sit on the edge of the couch in the inn's living room, my hands clasped in my lap. The camera rests on the coffee table. The low hum of the air conditioner reverberates through the room. Scott sits beside me, his jaw tight, his hazel eyes fixed on the camera like he's trying to will it not to be cruel. Ms. Connor and the rest of the guests are giving us privacy and have left the inn or are in the kitchen.

"Are you ready?" He caresses the small of my back. I try to ignore the worry in his eyes.

My insides churn with doubt. "I need to know."

Scott plugs the camera cord into his laptop and clicks on the first file. The screen flickers, then steadies, and there's Nathan. I catch my breath. There's his handsome face, as alive and vibrant as the last time we were together.

But the place on the screen isn't what I expect. Nathan stands in a secluded tropical cove, with waves cresting against the shore in the background and palm trees swaying in the wind. I don't recognize the place at all. He's relaxed, his hair tousled, and his face unguarded in a way I'd never seen him. Was he on vacation? Was this Belize?

"I'll get to that in a second." Nathan glances off-camera, his tone playful. "Can't a guy have a moment to think?"

"You always overthink, Nate," the woman teases. Her voice is light, carefree. My stomach clenches. I recognize the accent. It's the mystery woman.

Nathan turns toward her voice, his playful expression softening. The light in his eyes is unmistakable. It's pure, unfiltered love.

"I'm not thinking." He gazes into the camera wistfully. "I'm dreaming."

"What about?"

Nathan glances at the camera, his face shifting from soft to serious. "About you." His gaze lowers. "I'm thinking about both of you. About what comes next for us."

The words hit me like a wave, my breath catching in my throat. Both of you. What does he mean? Is he talking about…? I think of the little girl again, and I know this time. She's his. I wish I could remember the details of her face, but I'd only seen her for an instant. Does she look like him?

The screen dissolves into static.

Abruptly, the serene cove is replaced by the muted depths of the ocean. Nathan's professional voice comes through as he narrates the dive.

"Entering a primary chamber. Walls are made of smooth limestone. I estimate over ten thousand years of erosion. Visibility is excellent. Depth— eighty feet."

His dive light sweeps across the cavern, the beam catching jagged stalactites and a silty floor glittering in the light. A cluster of bubbles cascade across the camera's lenses.

"It's true." Awe fills his voice with boyhood enthusiasm for just a moment before he moves back to professional archaeologist mode. He continues to narrate his observations.

"Artifact one." The camera zooms in on a ceramic shard, its surface carved with intricate patterns. They resemble those on the mysterious stone I found.

Nathan moves on, cataloging more. Then he wraps up, saying he's ending the dive.

The screen flickers again. This time, he's in another chamber. His movements are frantic. He had turned the camera back on. "This isn't an accident." He's panicked. Pain stabs my heart. I'd never once in my life seen fear on my brother's face. The camera falls to the ground, and there's nothing else.

I stare at the blank screen as my ears roar. Tears flow down my face. The air is heavy, charged. He's dead. As irrational as it was, I'd held hope it was all a mistake, but now I've seen his last moments with my own eyes. Scott puts his arms around me and rubs my back.

"I'm sorry, sweetheart." He lifts my face and wipes away my tears.

"He said it's not an accident. Does that mean that someone did this to him?"

"Yes. Someone tampered with his equipment. I believe whoever took him out to the Drop that day will know more. We'll find out who did this, Maddie. I'll call in a favor. The Coast Guard will tell us who they interviewed after Nathan's disappearance."

"Nathan found evidence of the lost civilization he was looking for. It's down there," I mumble through sobs.

"I think Jamie and I were close to it. We'll need to be careful with our gas management, but we'll be able to make it there on our next dive."

"Please don't do it if it's dangerous."

He cups my face. "We'll be careful, and we'll have backups for our backups."

Scott holds me with the patience and tenderness I remember. We talk about Nathan. I share my thoughts about the little girl. Nathan has a daughter. Now I have even more questions to answer, and I need to find her and her mom. After a while, we sit in silence, and he just holds me. I rest my head on his chest and drift off.

A muffled cry from the kitchen cuts through the stillness.

Scott and I exchange glances before rising in unison. We move and find Ms. Connor hunched over the table, her shoulders shaking as she sobs. The inn phone lies in pieces on the floor. Garrett stands nearby, pale and shaken, his hands gripping the back of a chair.

"What happened?" I rush to comfort Ms. Connor. Putting an arm around her, I lead her to the closest chair.

Ms. Connor's face is streaked with tears, and she just shakes her head, unable to speak. Garrett turns toward us.

"There's been an accident."

Dread coils in my cold, heavy stomach as my mind races with the possibilities.

Elaine, alive only hours ago, is gone.

I'm back at my cottage, trying to reconcile all my emotions. Nathan's video, the little girl, and now Elaine's death.

An auto accident. The explanation is sterile, clinical, and just wrong. None of this makes sense. No one drives much faster than thirty-five miles an hour on the island. How could Elaine have died in an auto accident? The police said she hit a pole and broke her neck.

A knock at the door jolts me from my spiraling thoughts. "It's me," Scott calls from the other side.

I stand, my legs shaky beneath me. When I open the door, Scott's gaze meets mine. He puts his arms around me and nuzzles me to his chest. "I'm so sorry. It's been a hard day for you, baby." I'm unable to speak past the lump in my throat. I step back to let him in. Closing the door, I sit on the couch.

"I don't think Elaine's death was an accident."

His brows knit together.

I sink back into the cushions of the couch. "Elaine and I were talking here at the inn just yesterday." My voice falters as I replay the conversation. "She mentioned Nathan was in love with someone before he disappeared. She said it was important, but she didn't have a name. She was going to meet with someone to learn more today…" My throat tightens.

Scott crouches in front of me, his hands steady on my knees. "Go on."

"We heard someone listening to our conversation outside the front door," I whisper, my voice barely audible. "We were right here in my cottage. I opened the door, and they ran behind the corner of the inn."

Scott's eyes darken. "You think someone killed her because of what she knew?"

A tear rolls down my cheek. "I'm scared. If they would go that far to silence her, what if?"

"Stop." His hands rest on my knees with a comforting pressure. "We're going to get answers. Let's start with the police."

I gaze at him, my voice trembling and uncertain. "Do you think they'll take us seriously?"

"They have to." He extends his hand to me.

♥

The fluorescent lights in the police station cast a harsh glow. The walls are cold. I sit next to Scott as he shares our suspicions with Detective Daniels, who listens intently.

"Are you saying that Dr. Fischer's accident was a murder?" Daniels asks, leaning back in his chair. His expression remains neutral.

"I'm saying it's suspicious," Scott replies calmly. "Do you know for sure it was the car accident that broke her neck?"

I add "Elaine was meeting with someone who wanted to keep themselves hidden. Now she's dead."

Daniels taps his pen against the desk, his gaze shifting between us. "The coroner signed off. There wasn't an autopsy. Do you have any proof? Any idea who might've been eavesdropping? A description?"

Frustration twists in my chest. "No."

Scott throws his hands in the air. "Garrett and Wes were at the inn for both intruder incidents. They both stand to gain from Nathan's work and they've been up to something for months. Now we have proof Nathan was murdered. You need to start with them to find out what they know."

Wes doesn't deserve this. I start to jump in.

Scott looks at me with sadness in his eyes. "Don't defend him. You don't really know him."

Daniels scribbles in his notebook, his expression unreadable. "I'll look into it. But without hard evidence, there's not much I can do about Elaine. But we do have enough to reopen Nathan's case immediately."

Scott leans forward, his voice sharper now. "People are dying, Daniels. How much more evidence do you need?"

The detective raises a hand, his tone steady yet authoritative. "I understand. It's frustrating for me too. But I can't file a report based on your gut. Let me know if you uncover anything concrete, and I'll put some questions out there in the meantime."

As we leave the station, the cool evening air wraps around us. My hands tremble as I adjust the strap of my bag.

Scott turns to face me, his eyes determined. "You're staying with me."

"What?"

"You're not going back to the inn or sleeping alone. Not until this is resolved. You're staying at my place."

"But I…"

"No arguments. You'll be safe there. I'll make sure of it."

I agree to go. My fear gives way to a fragile sense of security.

"Okay, let me call Hannah and ask her to watch Ding at her place tonight."

After I get off the phone with Hannah, Scott places a hand on my back as we walk to his truck. "Let's go. We'll figure the rest out in the morning."

As the truck rumbles down the quiet streets, I lean my head against the window. The fear lingers, but I'm not alone. Scott will keep me safe.

CHAPTER 32

MADDIE

After I put away my things in the extra room, I curl up on the worn leather couch, staring out the window. His house is quiet except for the occasional clink of a spoon and mug in the kitchen. He's brewing us some tea.

Like Scott, this room is sturdy, reliable, and cozy. It's covered with bookshelves filled with titles about diving and marine exploration, along with framed photos of Scott with his dive team and family. Every object serves as a reminder of why I trust him. My eyes turn to the piano, and my chest clenches. A beautiful vase of fresh flowers rests next to it. While we were together, Scott created a morning routine of picking fresh flowers from his backyard and putting them on the piano for me. He hasn't stopped.

Scott walks in, holding two steaming mugs, his hazel eyes soft as they meet mine. "Chamomile." He sets one down on the table before me. "Thought it might help you relax."

"My favorite. Thank you."

He sits beside me, the couch dipping under his weight, and for a while, we drink our tea in silence. It isn't awkward anymore. It's comfortable. This place is home, and my heart aches with longing. I want my home back. We don't turn on the television, but Scott takes out some cards and shuffles them. I pick mine up and we play. After he beats me a few times, I feel an urge to clear the air. I need to know where we stand.

"Hey," I say, setting my cards down. I pull my hair back and straighten. He turns to me, his expression open yet cautious.

"I'm sorry," I begin, my voice trembling. "For everything. For Wes, the secrets, all of it. I didn't mean to hurt you. I know what I did to you, to us. I was so focused on finding answers about Nathan that I didn't think about the risks or you. I'm grateful for your help."

Scott leans forward, his elbows resting on his knees. He wipes his face with his hands, his gaze dropping to the floor a moment before returning to mine. "I was angry. But more than that, I was scared. Scared of losing you. After everyone I've lost…" He pauses, drawing in a deep breath, the raw emotion in his voice cutting through me. "I didn't know how to handle it."

Tears fill my eyes as I whisper, "I didn't mean to hurt you."

"I know you didn't. Maddie… I've been in love with you since the day we met. Even though I tried to let go, I can't. I don't want to…"

The corners of his mouth rise as he speaks, then they fall. He's so handsome, every part of him. I'm falling in love with him all over again.

"…and then, when I thought I may have lost you." Darkness crosses over his face. "I couldn't bear it."

His words pierce my heart, causing my tears to spill over. "I…"

"Never apologize to me again," he murmurs. "Just tell me we're done hurting each other."

My lips tremble. "No more secrets. I love you."

He leans in, his lips meeting mine in an urgent kiss, dissolving the remaining walls between us. Scooping me up into his arms like he did our first night on his beach, he carries me to his bed and lays me down, hovering over me.

"We have all night to make up for lost time, sweet girl. I'm going to make sure you feel how much I love you."

♥

Light from the dawn filters through the windows. I stir, waking to the warmth of Scott's arms around me. When I turn, I find him awake, watching me.

"Morning." His voice is rough from sleep.

"Good morning." My cheeks flush as memories of the night before washes over me. We made up, indeed.

He leans in, pressing a soft kiss to my forehead, his hand brushing a stray strand of hair from my face. "Last night meant everything to me."

My heart is full. "Me too." My fingers trace his scar, and I kiss his chest. I want him to touch me again.

Scott glances toward his dresser and sits up. "Maddie, there's something I want to…"

The rude trill of Scott's phone breaks the moment. He curses as he pulls away from me to answer it.

"Rickter." His brows furrow in concern and confusion, his jaw clenching as he listens. "Yeah. I'll be there in less than thirty."

"What is it?" I ask as he ends the call, a knot of unease forming in my stomach.

"The Coast Guard," he explains, swinging his legs over the side of the bed. "They said they need me to come by to help with something urgent happening at the Drop."

"Is something wrong?" I sit up, clutching the sheet to my chest.

"It might be nothing, but I need to handle it." He's putting on his pants and grabbing a shirt. "I'll call to check on you in an hour at the most." I put on my nightgown and follow him into the kitchen.

"Denver. Here, boy." Denver rushes to meet Scott. "Protect." He nods in my direction. Denver barks once, signaling he understands.

"Call Hannah, have her pick you up, and take you back to the inn. Don't let anyone else in and call me if anything concerns you or if anyone other than Hannah shows up."

Scott leans down, pressing a lingering kiss to my lips before pulling back. "Until she gets here, stay. Rest. I'll see you soon. I love you." He slides his hands down my waist, palming my hip with a playful squeeze. Then he turns to leave.

He sets the alarm and the door clicks shut behind him.

CHAPTER 33

MADDIE

Watching from the window, Scott's truck disappears down the road. I try not to worry about being alone. I have Denver, and he's pacing dutifully nearby. I left a voicemail message for Hannah, asking her to leave Ding at the inn and come by and get me as soon as she can. My emotions are all over the place. It's like nothing bad ever happened between Scott and me. He loves me and I love him. The only difference is me. I'm never going to take what we have for granted again. A pleasant shiver runs up my spine. Last night was amazing. He hasn't lost his touch, that's for sure. I'm excited to see him again. But as the minutes stretch by, a strange feeling of dread presses against my chest.

Still in my robe and needing a shower, I head toward the bathroom. My heart sinks when I hear the doorbell ring.

Who could it be? I rush to the door but hesitate with my hand on the knob. It's too soon to be Hannah. My heart's beating so hard, it's about to give out. I force myself to look at the screen on Scott's front door monitor.

Mark Glassier.

Relieved, I start to open the door, but pause. Wasn't Scott meeting the Coast Guard? Did something happen to him on the way? Oh God. My palms are sweating. I press on the intercom.

"Mark?"

"Something's happened. It's Scott. Can you let me in?"

I gasp and clutch my chest tightly. In tears, I turn off the alarm and open the door for Mark. His crisp uniform makes him approachable.

"You're scaring me. What's happened to Scott?"

"I'm sorry." He coughs and holds up his hands, urging me to calm down. "I didn't mean to scare you. I was just on my way to check in with Scott, but it looks like I missed him." His eyes are tracing the room methodically, looking for something. He's speaking, but he's not focused on what he's saying to me. What is going on?

"He just left for the Coast Guard station."

Mark turns his eyes back to me and glares, his pupils blown.

"I thought he was meeting you guys at the blue hole," I squeak. He doesn't even look like the same person anymore.

Mark's forced smile stays locked in place, his gaze lingering on me for far too long. Looking straight through me. I tighten my robe.

"Are you staying here with Scott?"

"For now," I answer slowly. "I'm visiting. He let me know he'll be back in just a minute."

The corners of his mouth turn down and a dark vein along his neck throbs. "You and Scott seem pretty close." He turns away, walking around the room.

I box my shoulders and shrug, keeping my response neutral. "He's helping me investigate my brother's disappearance. Scott's… a good friend."

Mark freezes and turns back to me then. His smile is completely gone, though he laughs wryly.

"Friendship like that doesn't come cheap, I bet."

His nostrils twitch and his eyebrows draw together.

"Tell me—*Is he paying you to fuck him?* I smell him all over you."

He grabs Scott's boat keys off the wall rack.

"Here they are." A dark smile flashes across his face as he pockets the keys.

Terror jolts through my entire body. Mark is going to hurt me. I rush across the room, trying to get as far away from him as I can.

He moves toward me.

I'm still trying to process what's happening. His fake kindness is gone, like a mask that has slipped off, revealing the monster hiding beneath. "You've been sticking your nose where it doesn't belong… and now you're going to come with me. Nice and quiet."

My pulse spikes, panic clawing at my chest. "I'm not going anywhere. Stay away from me." I'm backed against the wall and there's nowhere else to go. Mark grabs my arm, pulling me toward him with a rough jerk. I can smell him. While the rest of his appearance is immaculate, his sweat is feral and rancid.

Out of nowhere, Denver howls and jumps toward Mark, biting his arm with a vicious tear, the sound wet and jagged.

Mark shouts in pain, his expression hardening into a deadly scowl. In a swift motion, he pulls the gun from his belt and shoots Denver.

"No!" I scream. Denver cries in pain and slumps to the floor.

Mark pivots the gun to my heart. "Don't make me use this on you. It'll get messy." His words are cold and final. He grabs a kitchen towel and wraps it around his arm. "Damn dog. We're leaving now."

My breath comes in shallow gasps as my mind races for a way out. I'm hovering over poor Denver. I try to stop his bleeding with a throw from the couch, praying it will be enough until Scott gets back. I do my best to ensure the right pressure, but not too much. "Please live, boy. You're strong. Scott needs you." I stroke his back. He mewls.

Mark gathers my personal things, including my phone, which he smashes. "Why?" I lift my eyes from Denver to Mark. "Why are you doing this? You're Nathan's friend."

Mark remains silent but stares at me with pure hatred. Why?

"Mark, please, don't do this," I beg, my desperation rising.

His glossy eyes clear, and he moves toward me. "Move." He grabs my arm with a grip like a vise. I wince. The fear bubbling within me erupts into terror as he drags me toward the door.

I struggle against him, my instincts screaming at me to fight back, but he's way too strong. His grip tightens, and his movements are swift and unyielding as he pushes me outside. He throws my purse and smashed phone on the porch. The dark SUV parked off the driveway looms. Its tinted windows glint in the sunlight, the sight sending a fresh wave of terror through me. I open my mouth to scream.

"No one's going to hear you out here," Mark says darkly, his voice dripping with menace. The scream rips from my throat and echoes down the empty road. It infuriates him. With a harsh shove, he pushes me toward the open back door of the SUV. My hip hits hard. I yelp in pain.

"Let me go!" I cry, my voice breaking as I twist and try in vain to pull away from him. I scratch at his eyes.

"Shut up and stop moving or I'll kill you sooner than I intended." He drills his cold eyes into mine as he forces me inside. The door slams shut, trapping me in the confined space.

My heart stops at his words.

He's going to kill me, just like he killed Nathan.

CHAPTER 34

SCOTT

Mark Glassier's call. It was cryptic and rushed with terrible news. Now, I'm sitting at a small desk in the front office waiting for Michaels, a grizzled Coast Guard veteran. My gut tells me something is off.

"Rickter," Michaels says, sitting down at the desk. "I didn't expect to see you today. What's up?"

"I got a call from Mark Glassier. He told me to come in."

"Oh yeah? What did he want from you?"

"He told me you found a body in the Drop—Nathan's."

Michaels exchanges a glance with another officer before turning back to me. "Glassier? He's out of town, had a family emergency. He won't be back until next week."

A cold knot tightens in my chest.

"And no one has found a body at the Drop. What's going on, Scott?"

"What the?" I mutter. "Okay. This is important." I take out an old business card from my wallet that has my number on it and hand it to him. "I need you to tell me who reported Nathan's disappearance. Find out who took Nathan out to the Drop that day."

"What's this all about?"

"Talk to Daniels. He's reopened Nathan's case."

Without another word to Michaels, I bolt from the office and jump into my truck, adrenaline surging as I tear down the road toward my house. Worst-case scenarios race through my mind, each more gut-wrenching than the last. When I pull into the driveway, my stomach drops.

I dial Mark's number. It rings before going to voicemail. "This doesn't make any sense," I mutter, trying Maddie next, straight to voicemail. My heart pounds as I scroll through my contacts, dialing Hannah. No answer. Wes. Nothing.

My unease twists into full-fledged fear.

The front door is ajar and swaying in the breeze.

I run to the porch. Maddie's bag lies on the deck, her phone smashed beside it. I shove the door open, my heart pounding. Inside, it's worse. Much worse. There's blood all over the floor. It doesn't take long for me to assess the source.

Denver. He's on his side and he's not moving.

"Oh, no. No boy." My throat closes in. Looking him over, I determine he has a faint pulse. His wound has been wrapped in a tight blanket.

Maddie.

Like a madman, I search through every nook and cranny in the house. She's nowhere.

The crunch of gravel snaps me out of my panic. I spin around. Wes's Jaguar pulls into the drive, followed by Hannah's compact car. They jump out, their faces etched with worry.

"What's going on? Maddie called but didn't tell me anything. She sounded spooked." Hannah's frantic as she storms through the door, her voice trembling.

She takes one look at Denver and screams, throwing her hands over her mouth.

"Maddie's gone." I gesture toward the chaos on the porch and inside. "She's been taken."

Hannah gasps. "No…" She picks up her phone and dials 911. "We've got to get him help. It doesn't look like he's got much time."

Wes runs a hand through his hair, his face pale. "Who did this?"

I round on him, fury boiling over. "Don't you have an answer, Harrington? What the hell have you been doing, creeping around Maddie for months like a spider? You know something."

Wes's eyes flicker to the ground. "I… I don't know where she is. I swear it."

"Bullshit." I take a step closer, anger surging within me. "Spill it. Now."

Wes raises his hands in a mix of guilt and desperation. "All right. I think Garrett might be involved."

"Garrett? What the hell does he have to do with this?"

Wes exhales, his shoulders slumped. "He's been pressuring me to bring him information about Nathan's research. He's been blackmailing me."

"Explain."

"He's got a video, one that implicates me in a caver's death in the Yucatán."

"Where did he get a video like that—are you guilty?"

"It's doctored. Actual footage, altered."

"I don't really give a shit about your problems. What's this got to do with Maddie?"

Hannah's eyes widen. She starts to get up to confront Wes, but stays crouched by Denver, holding his wound. "Wes! How could you? Did you steal Nathan's things?"

"No. I'd never do that to her. She's my friend," Wes snaps, his voice hoarse and cracking. "I strung Garrett along, trying to buy time. But I never gave him anything real. I swear on my life that I'd never let anyone hurt Maddie."

My fist connects with his jaw. He stumbles back, clutching his face, but he doesn't retaliate.

"You son of a bitch. I'm going to kill you."

"I deserve that. I know I do," Wes says, his voice thick with guilt. "But I didn't take her and don't know what's going on." His chin drops. "Garrett might be behind this, but I swear I've been trying to protect her."

I pace, running my hands through my hair, barely holding my fury in check. Stopping, I glare at him. "How the hell does Mark Glassier fit into this?"

Wes frowns, confused. "Mark? The Coast Guard guy? I've got no idea."

My thoughts are scattered, pieces of a fragmented puzzle refusing to fit together. I turn to Hannah, my voice sharp but steady. "Stay here with Denver until help gets here. Talk to the police and tell them everything. Don't stop until they listen."

Hannah nods, her hands shaking as she comforts Denver, still applying pressure to his wound and talking to the emergency operator. She looks up. "They're sending a vet from Naples, so we don't have to move him. They're on their way. It should be less than thirty minutes."

I crouch, running my fingers through his fur. "Thank you, boy. I know you tried to save her. You're going to be okay. Help is coming." He lets out a soft sound and licks my hand. I take a deep breath and take off my tags. I put them around his neck and pet him once more.

My eyes are stinging when I turn back to Wes. "You're coming with me. We're going to Garrett's. If he knows anything, I'll make him talk."

"Let's go."

♥

The air between Wes and me is thick as we approach Garrett's room at the inn. We haven't said a word since we left my house. My fists clench, fury radiating off me in waves. I sense Maddie doesn't have much time. Wes follows a step behind, his jaw already turning an ugly shade of blue.

I don't knock. Instead, I slam the door open, rattling the frame. Garrett springs to his feet, his desk stacked with papers with a tumbler of whiskey now teetering on the edge.

"What is this?" Garrett demands, his eyes darting between Wes and me.

"Where is she?" My voice is low but sharp enough to cut through steel.

Garrett blinks, confusion flashing across his face. "Who?"

"Maddie." I step closer. "She's missing. Taken. Start talking now."

Garrett's confusion twists into irritation. "I don't know what you're talking about." He acts like he's going to dismiss me as he flicks his wrist. Fuck that.

I grab him by the collar, slamming him back against the wall. Papers flutter to the floor and the whiskey tumbles, flooding the room with the sharp smell of oak.

"Don't lie to me. You've been sniffing around Maddie for months, trying to get your claws on Nathan's research. You're out of time, Garrett. Don't play games."

He struggles in my grip, his voice strained. "I don't have a clue what you're talking about." He tries in vain to get loose. After I put one hand around his neck and squeeze, all his bravado disappears, replaced by cold fear.

"All right. Stop, please." I ease off the pressure. "I used Wes to get close to Maddie so I could find out what she knows about Nathan's research." I release his neck. "I didn't take her. Let me go."

"Why should we believe you?" Wes steps closer.

Garrett's eyes narrow at him. "You've got a lot of nerve showing up here, Harrington. You're the one who screwed this all up. I told you to use your charm to get me Nathan's maps and notes. But no, you couldn't do it before someone else jumped in and took them. So much for a ladies' man. I guess Rickter has the bigger dick."

Dropping him, I punch his face, holding back only enough to avoid killing him before I get the information I need from him.

Grabbing his collar, I pull him back up off the floor. His smug face grates against every nerve I have left. "So you've been after Nathan's things all along?"

"Of course," Garrett snaps, his arrogance cracking under the weight of his fear. His nose and lips are bleeding.

Good.

"Do you know what's down there? What those caves could hold? But I didn't take Maddie. I need her alive, cooperating. Not… whatever this is."

His words ring hollow, but my gut tells me he's not lying. "If you're telling the truth…" I drop him and step back. "Then Mark has her. If I find out you're lying…" My words hang in the air, heavy with promise.

Garrett straightens his collar. "I have no idea what Mark wants from Maddie. I like her. She's a sweet girl." Glaring at Wes, he scoffs at him.

"You're done, Harrington. Pack your bags. They're going to love you in prison."

Wes bristles.

Without another word, I leave.

Mark has to have Maddie. It's the worst kind of threat. We've got no idea why he'd do it, and if he also killed Elaine, what's the connection? Did he want what Nathan was looking for in the caves? He's shown no interest in it before. None of this makes any damn sense. My phone buzzes. It's Michaels.

"Yeah," I bark into the phone.

"Scott—we have the name of the boat captain who was with Nathan when he disappeared." Michael's voice is strained, like he can't believe what he's about to tell me.

"Yes? Who?"

"It was Mark. Mark Glassier." All the blood leaves my body. Wes is staring at me as I pocket my phone.

"What is it?"

"Mark Glassier killed Nathan," I state numbly, frozen, as I feel my world cave in.

Wes inhales sharply and closes his eyes.

In the living room, Ding is wandering around, looking for Maddie. He rushes to me, jumping on my leg.

"It's okay, boy. We'll get her back."

Ms. Connor is on the couch. Her eyes are red. Hannah must have called her. Beside her sits a young blond woman. At first, I don't recognize her, but then I do. It's Mark's wife.

"Scott. This is Crystal Glassier. She has information about Maddie."

CHAPTER 35

MADDIE

I sit on the bench of the boat, my hands bound in front of me, trying to keep my breathing steady. I can't afford to have another panic attack now. We're on Scott's boat. That drives the knife deeper. I should feel safe on the *Adeline*.

Mark has said little since we left the dock, but the tension hangs like a noose in the air.

"You're as dumb as your brother," Mark says, his voice slicing through the silence like a knife. He doesn't even look at me as he stands at the helm. I flinch at the words, each one sharp and calculated to hurt me, but I stay silent. My throat is too tight.

"We were best friends. Do you know all the things I did for him?" I look over at him, but I'm too afraid to say a word.

"At least that was what I thought until he took what was mine." He straightens. "Do you know why he's dead?" he presses on, his grip on the wheel tightening.

"He was so arrogant. Pretty boy, he thought he could run all those caves, chasing some grand discovery and outsmarting everyone else. Keeping secrets. I didn't give a flying fuck about his stupid caves and secrets. Except for one."

The venom in his tone makes my stomach churn. I find my voice, though it shakes. "Nathan was good. He was brave. He…"

Mark's bitter laugh cuts me off. "Good? Brave? Don't kid yourself. He was a fool. Just like you."

I swallow hard, mustering the courage to meet his stare. His words sting and there's a deeper personal hatred behind them.

Mark pulls out his phone, his entire demeanor shifting. He dials a number and waits, his hand relaxing on the wheel. He's very pale, and a thin film of sweat covers his skin.

What's wrong with him?

When the call connects, he changes into another person. "Hi, baby. I just wanted to tell you goodnight."

A woman's voice responds, tinged with concern. "Mark? Is everything all right? What are you doing? Where are you?"

"Don't worry, I'm fine." His voice trembles. "It's just been a long day. I love you. Please tell Natalie I love her too."

"Mark, you're frightening me. What's happening? We can talk about this. It's not too late. Come home." He's staring in the distance, not all here. Her voice is muffled, but familiar.

"Goodbye, love."

He cuts off the call, ignoring her questions. The tenderness evaporates as he slips back into his cold, detached facade. My heart races.

And then it clicks. That voice, it's Nathan's fiancée—the woman I met at the general store. All the pieces fall into place, at least enough to understand why Mark might have killed Nathan and why he's trying so hard to keep Nathan's fate hidden. Nathan was in love with Mark's wife.

My breath catches. I swallow. "My God," I whisper.

Mark turns to me, his expression darkening. "What am I going to do with you?" he mutters to himself.

The boat slows, the engine shifting to a low idle as we approach the Carter's Drop descent point. The swirling ocean waters above the blue hole glimmer under the moonlight. I can't see it, but I know it's there.

Mark snatches a random dive kit from the locker and tosses it to me. He cuts the bindings on my wrists. "Suit up," he barks, his tone allowing no room for argument.

My hands tremble as I gaze at the gear, bile creeping up my throat. "Mark, please—"

"Now," he snaps, his voice as sharp as a whip.

My fingers are clumsy and slow as I fumble with the suit. Every part of me screams to fight, to run, but there's nowhere to go. The endless ocean is all around us, and Mark is watching my every move.

"Cheer up. You're going to see your brother today." His eyes are dull and emotionless. "A joyful reunion. And you'll both be right where you belong." He suits up. "If they find you, it will look like an accident. Poor Maddie, searching for her brother, she just couldn't quit. She wouldn't listen to all the warnings we kept giving her."

His words crash over me like a suffocating wave of dread. He's not planning to bring me back. Like he did to Nathan, he'll leave me down there in the depths of the caves. I'm going to drown in the blue hole. He's just keeping me alive long enough to make it look like another dive accident and hide one more murder.

"Scott will come for me. He'll find you," I choke out.

He laughs.

"Oh, I have plans for him, too. Poor crazy Scott. That's what they'll say after they find out he made all this up after murdering Wes Harrington and killing himself. Nasty love triangle. Seems I have a busy night ahead of me."

"But you shot Denver," I snap.

He freezes. Maybe he's not as smart as he thinks he is. Then he tightens the straps on his rebreather, not even sparing me another glance. "You shouldn't have been digging into things that weren't yours to find. Just like Nathan." He looks to the sky. "I hope you can see this, old friend. And I hope it hurts like hell."

He's delusional. And I'm not sure if he really cares if he lives or dies anymore.

Panic claws at my chest, threatening to consume me. There must be a way out, some way to stall him, to escape. My mind races, but every thought is drowned out by the sheer terror coursing through me. I finish suiting up, trying to be as prepared as possible for what awaits me below. But I don't have all the gear I'll need to survive long enough.

Mark yanks me to my feet, his grip iron, as he pulls me toward the edge of the boat. "Let's go." His voice is devoid of emotion.

I look down.

The blue hole is waiting for me.

Scott, please find me.

CHAPTER 36

SCOTT

Ms. Connor puts a throw over Crystal's shoulder and sits beside her with her hand on her back.

"Scott, Crystal believes Mark has taken Maddie to Carter's Drop to harm her." Her forehead wrinkles with worry.

My first reaction is to storm to the docks. It's Wes's too because he pulls out his phone and walks into the kitchen, making calls. But, we need to know as much as possible before we go. I take a breath and crouch in front of Crystal.

"This is my fault. I didn't know what Mark did to Nathan. If I had, I would have never…" Her voice cracks.

"It's okay. None of us knew. Just breathe and start from the beginning. Anything might help."

"Mark, Nathan, and I were college friends. We did everything together. Nathan was like a beacon, so brilliant. When he moved to Maverick Key, we followed him. Mark got a job with the Coast Guard, and I landed one at City Hall." She takes a breath. "Mark and I dated for a little while. We were friends and he was so attentive. I thought I'd try."

She takes the tissue she'd been holding and dabs her eyes. "But I never felt more than friendship with Mark. It was Nathan and I who grew closer. And we admitted to ourselves we were in love." Her chin quivers. She takes a sip of water from the glass Ms. Connor offers her. "We told Mark right away. At first, he took it in stride. We hadn't been intimate or agreed to a commitment, so it seemed we could still be friends. But then he distanced himself from me, saying it was too painful to be near me." She squeezes her eyes. "He stayed friends with Nathan and helped him with the trips to the blue hole." She grimaces and puts her hands on her stomach. "Nathan asked me to marry him, we…" She turns her gaze away as if she's saying too much. "Then, I got pregnant. We kept that to ourselves. Nathan wanted to wait to share our relationship because he was concerned that someone dangerous was trying to sabotage his work. He didn't want anyone to know I was important to him. No one knew, but Mark. Less than four weeks after I found out I was pregnant, Nathan was gone." She stops. Quiet tears pour down her face. Taking another tissue from Ms. Connor, she blows her nose.

Ms. Connor rubs her back. "Crystal, dear, when you're ready, please go on."

"I was so lost, I couldn't pay my bills, and I was heartbroken. There were complications with the pregnancy. Mark offered to marry me and take care of us. To be a father to another man's baby. I said yes and thought we could make it work for Natalie. After Mark realized I would never love him in the way he wanted me to, he changed. He became controlling, and sometimes he would—" She sobs, the tears now falling in heavy streams down her face. Ms. Connor hugs her.

She takes a few moments to compose herself, then she continues. "When Maddie came to the island, I wanted to meet her and have that connection with Nathan's sister. But then I noticed how much Mark was keeping an eye on what Maddie was up to. It seemed so strange since he also kept avoiding her when she tried to see him. He was furious when he found out I approached her at the general store and—" She touches her cheek. "It clicked. I just knew. Mark had hurt Nathan. My guess is he sabotaged his dive equipment. Mark was Nathan's boat captain. He must have killed him and hid his body. Nathan would have never left us." She cries harder. "A few days ago, I told Mark I was going to leave him. He called me about an hour ago. He was on a boat. I think he's taking her to Carter's Drop to hurt her. I'm so sorry I didn't say something sooner."

I hold her and rub her back. "It's okay. None of this is your fault. We're going to get her back and we'll try to get him help."

I stand. "Thank you, Crystal." I look at Ms. Connor. "Take care of her."

I nod to Wes. "Let's get to the pier."

My cell rings. It's Margaret.

"Scott, the *Adeline* is gone."

♥

Waves beat against Wes's boat like the second hand of a clock, counting down the time Maddie has left. We're pushing the boat to the limits of how fast it can go. We don't know how long they've been in the water, only that it's been too long to feel good about her chances. Maddie's life depends on us. On me. Wes and I already have our gear on and we're just minutes away from the Drop.

Jamie hunches over the boat's tracking equipment, his face illuminated by the faint glow of the screen. "*Adeline* is anchored right over Carter's

Drop. The Coast Guard's en route right now, ready to assist us with surface rescue."

"Jamie, Liam, board and take back the *Adeline*. Margaret will stay on Wes's boat here for underwater and Coast Guard communication. Wes and I dive."

Margaret adjusts her headset. "We've got eyes on everything up here. Just get her back. When you find her, let her know we love her and we're waiting for her."

I scan their faces, reading the same determination mirrored in my own. "Let's move."

♥

Wes and I swim into Carter's Drop. We're staying off the comms for stealth and will communicate using hand signals until it's safe to go back online. We find the dive marker Mark laid. It's shoddy work. Has Mark even been in a cave before? Doubtful. The acid in my stomach rushes to my throat. He's following Nathan's line. I grip the old line, propelling myself forward with measured kicks. Wes follows closely behind.

The dive line continues into a narrow tunnel on the far side of the chamber. I signal to Wes with my hands. **Stay Close. I know this trek. It's gnarly.**

He signals he understands and is ready.

We press on.

The tunnel narrows, forcing me to adjust my movements. The walls are closing in, like claws scraping our tanks. I adjust my BCD and my fins kick in short, controlled bursts. I try not to think about Maddie down here, navigating this. This is bad for an experienced cave diver. My heart drops. I glance at Wes. How well did he teach her?

Why didn't I?

We make it to the nearly impassable squeeze that gave Jamie and me so much shit the last time. I have to remove my tanks this time to get through it. Wes is just behind me when my loose tank grates hard against the limestone, the sound jarring in the silence.

Wes taps my shoulder and signs, **OK**?

I respond, signing, **OK**.

As the passage widens again, my light catches a green glint in the sand. I freeze, my heart lurching as I pick up Maddie's necklace. Her little elephant isn't there to help her through this.

I squeeze my eyes shut.

I hold it up to Wes. **Maddie's**?

Yes.

I clutch the chain and put it in my thigh pocket.

Tightening my grip on the line, I move. She's close. She made it this far. I know she's still alive.

The tunnel leads us to the vertical shaft. The chamber below is about as far as Jamie and I got the last time. I pause at the edge, shining my light downward. The dive line disappears into the black void below.

Descending. Follow me. Watch your angles.

The shaft is tight, and the walls press in as we swim. The water is so murky, the light can't penetrate it. My breathing echoes in my ears, and the regulator's steady hum keeps my rising panic at bay. Maddie has been dragged into this hell. I try to calm my rapid breaths. Even though the passage is tight, there are several offshoot openings that can easily cause a wrong turn.

My hand slips.

The dive line drifts out of my reach, and my light swings as I force myself not to hold my breath. Stop and think. Training takes over, and I sweep my light in wide arcs until the faint glint of the line catches my eye again. Relief floods through me as I grab it.

Wes signs again. **OK**? He doesn't have a clear line of sight into what is happening.

Got it. Let's move.

We keep going, pushing through fatigue.

Then, my light catches on a figure in the distance—a faint movement.

My heart lurches.

It has to be Maddie.

Found her.

CHAPTER 37

MADDIE

Mark pulls me roughly as we enter the cavern. Icy water has seeped into every layer of my wetsuit, chilling me and leaving my breaths shallow and shaky. Instead of using a dry suit and rebreather, I'm diving open circuit with no extra tanks. But we are wearing full-face masks equipped with comms. Mark's shadow looms ahead, his flashlight beam cutting through the darkness like a predator's glare.

"Move," he orders, pushing me toward the tunnel.

I'd tried to reason with him before this dive, but Mark's intentions never wavered. He remains cold, unyielding, and terrifyingly resolute. He lays a marker and follows an old line. Now, as I grip the dive line with trembling hands, my chest tightens. The Grim Reaper stands at the tunnel entrance with his death sentence. **STOP! Prevent your death! Go no further.** Scott's face flashes in my mind. Will he find my body? What will that do to him? Stop it, Maddie, you can't afford to lose it down here.

In front of me, Mark's flashlight swings erratically, illuminating jagged rock edges. He's not an experienced cave diver and it shows in his poor buoyancy control. But he's stronger than me and has a very short fuse. I'm not only fighting to survive the overhead environment. I'm going to need to fight him if I want to live. My breath fogs the edges of my mask, and I slow them down. Focus, Maddie. You've trained for this.

The tunnel walls press against me as I move deeper, every twist and turn forcing me to angle my body. The limestone scrapes against my right arm and my tank, threatening to destroy my air source. I keep Scott's face in my thoughts to try to fight back the panic. If I don't stay calm, I'll die.

Ahead, my light catches a branching tunnel, its entrance a distinct shape. It's one of the passages Nathan had marked on his map. My heart pounds as I adjust course, veering toward it. The dive line is covered with algae, but still intact. I grip it and pull myself forward, determined.

"What the hell are you doing?" Mark looks back over his shoulder, his distorted voice crackling through the comms, sharp and angry. "You crazy bitch. You're determined to kill yourself before I get the chance to do it."

I don't respond. Gritting my teeth against my regulator, I push forward, entering the narrow passage. The walls close in almost immediately, the limestone squeezing against my suit and gear. I don't look back. The passage is too tight for Mark to follow easily. If I get far enough ahead, I might have a chance to hide from him. For a little while.

The small space narrows further, forcing me to exhale sharply and deflate my chest to squeeze through a vertical shaft. My tank scrapes the rock, and the grating sounds like the screams of a horror movie's final girl. Every movement is agonizingly slow. This is the first time I'm doing this. I have to focus on all the potential scenarios I was taught. My fingers tremble, but I force them to keep gripping the line. Stay calm. Breathe slow. One careful move at a time.

Never lose the line.

After pausing in a small chamber with some breathing room, I follow the line through another tunnel.

This tunnel opens into a large chamber, and I gasp as a rush of relief floods over me. My flashlight sweeps across the space, revealing massive stalactites and stalagmites glimmering in the water. It's breathtaking, like stepping into another world. An auditorium with sub chambers blocked off by huge limestone walls. I sense Nathan's presence. His essence is infused into every inch of this place. And the water is warm.

On the cavern floor, artifacts lie scattered in the silt. There are fragments of ceramic pottery and metallic fragments glinting in the beam of my light. My chest tightens. This is Nathan's discovery, his dream. Thousands of years old.

You did it, Nathan.

I check my gauge, and my stomach twists in fear. My gas is at 32 percent. I'm way past the rule of thirds. My breathing quickens despite my attempts to calm down. I'm consuming even greater amounts of the precious air I need to live. If I stay much longer, I won't make it back, regardless of Mark. This is what happened to Nathan.

Mark's voice cuts through the comms. "Maddie, where are you?" His tone is icy, carrying through the water. "You're making this harder than it needs to be." I hide behind a limestone wall dividing the chamber, hoping it will provide me some shelter from Mark's view. My only hope now is if someone is looking for me and finds me soon.

"Maddie… Maddie. I know you're in here. There's nowhere else to go."

I freeze, every muscle tightening as Mark's silhouette appears at the chamber entrance. His flashlight slices through the water, illuminating the artifacts. His face has distorted into a wide grimace, his eyes wide with exhilaration.

He laughs, the sound hollow and warped. "Well, look at this. Nathan wasn't making it up. He found it. Now, where are the little green men?" He flashes his light around the room.

Anger erupts within me, briefly overshadowing my fear. I rush to confront him, my chest rising and falling with emotion. "This isn't yours, Mark. It never was."

He swims closer, slowly, his flashlight beam blinding as he moves it to my face. "There you are. You don't get it," he sneers. "I don't care about this old junk. Nathan took everything from me."

"What are you talking about?" I know exactly what he's talking about, but I hope the question stalls him.

"Crystal was mine. My future, my family." Mark's voice grows more agitated, his words tumbling out. "Nathan poisoned her with his dreams and all his stupid obsessions. I was his friend. His best friend. He knew I loved her and he stole her from me."

Crying, he continues. "He thought he could just explain to me that they were in love and I'd forgive him… got her pregnant as soon as he could so he could keep her from me. She would have come back to me. She always does." His eyes are wild. "She will this time, too."

My stomach twists as I continue to listen to Mark rant. I need to get out of here.

Mark continues, his voice dripping with bitterness. "I made it right. Nathan was stupid, and he trusted me. Thought all was forgiven. He was so worried about that jerk Garrett that he failed to see the real danger was the man he'd stabbed in the back."

As Mark continues, I start to unspool line from my reel. Carefully, I wrap it into a lasso.

"The stupid fuck had me take him to the Drop, over and over for weeks. He was diving solo. Well, that last time, I ensured his backup system was hosed, and he wouldn't have the gas he needed in his rebreather. Easy as sin. I left his ass at the Drop."

I gasp. A vision of Nathan—deep in the Drop, struggling to breathe—flashes through my mind.

"I promised Crystal I'd take care of her and the baby that he put inside her. It wasn't her fault or Natalie's. I married her. I gave her a real family. I became Natalie's dad and their breadwinner. All I asked for was for her to love me, but she never did. Do you know she still dreams of him? She used to call out his name when I made love to her. Now she's stopped letting me touch her at all. He hasn't let go of what is mine even after death."

"You're insane!" I yell, my voice trembling. "You killed my brother!"

Mark's eyes narrow. "You look just like him." His grin through the mask widens. "I'm going to enjoy killing you, too. Two Carters—in one hole. The island will never forget either of you. One day, they'll find both of your little skeletons floating in the tunnels. You'll make someone famous."

My grip tightens on the spooled line as my panic surges. I can't out swim him, not here—my mind races. I'm going to die. I try to swim away from him, moving back behind the limestone wall in the cavern's center.

Mark pulls out a knife, the blade catching the light. "There's nowhere left to go. I'm going to kill you now. It's time." He rushes toward me, clumsily kicking up silt along the way. The room is saturated with dark clouds, bringing our visibility so low I can barely see what's in front of me. I can sense his approach and let him get as close as I can before I move.

I wrap the lasso of line around his hand that's holding the knife. Before he reacts, I dive below him to wrap more line around his left fin. He slings his arms wildly in every direction at me. After I've tied as many places as I can on his body, I pull with all my strength to tighten the binds. He swats at it frantically, trying to cut it, but this causes him to drop the knife. Both his arms and legs are now impossibly entangled in the yards of line and are forming their own knots like a bunch of necklaces carelessly tossed together. The more he pulls at the line to loosen it, the tighter the knots become. Entanglement 101. I pick up the knife.

"What the—" His voice is frantic as he becomes impossibly entwined. I have so much hatred for this man who took the closest person in my life away from me. He stole a lover and a father and a genius from the world.

"Cut the fucking line, bitch," he snaps. My fingers tighten around the dive knife. I strap it to my suit. There's no way in hell I'm going to free him. An urge for revenge consumes me, and I almost pull off his mask and regulator to end this quickly. I could take his tanks. But I don't. Instead, I head back toward the opening we came from. I tell myself leaving him alive is a small mercy, but I know it's not.

I leave Mark to meet his fate alone.

CHAPTER 38

SCOTT

I move quickly, not caring about safety. She's fighting for her life. The line tugs in my hand. I signal to Wes, and together, we focus our beams. There she is.

Maddie clings to Nathan's dive line, her body trembling, barely holding herself upright. She's exhausted. There's terror in her eyes. She points to another line, signaling Mark is that way. She's alive. Relief crashes over me, but it's fleeting. Her gas has to be critically low. She only has one tank.

I push forward. When I reach her, her wide, desperate eyes search mine. Through the mask, I see her fear and hope. She's shaking, her breaths coming too fast, fogging the mask. I clutch her arm to steady her as Wes swims to us.

Maddie's strength is fading fast.

"Don't use the comms. You need to reserve your gas as much as possible. Stay calm. Take slow breaths. I love you, sweetheart." I turn to Wes, who has moved next to us. "Wes, get her out now."

He darts his eyes to the darkness ahead, to Mark.

"Take her back now. I'll finish this," I say.

He looks me in the eye and puts his hand on my shoulder.

"I've got her. She'll get out alive." Gripping her arm, he guides her back the way we came. I watch them go, the light of their dive lights fading into the distance. My chest tightens as I force myself to let her go. She's safe now.

Nathan's secondary line stretches deeper into the cave, leading toward the next section of the cavern. I follow it, each tug of the line pulling me closer to Mark. This ends here. Whatever it takes. When I enter it, I'm shocked. It's the largest chamber I've ever been in and it's almost unnaturally intricate in wall formations. It's also warmer in here. Like a heated pool. This is the room we saw on Nathan's video. I use my lamp to look for movement.

There he is. Mark thrashes near a jagged outcrop of rock, entangled in a large net of dive line. His jerky, erratic movements in the entanglement make him look like a spider caught in his own web. Bursts of bubbles escape his regulator as he struggles against the line.

"Stupid bitch! She killed me!"

I slow my approach, instincts on high alert. I signal to him, gesturing for him to stop struggling. For a moment, his wild eyes soften when we make eye contact. Recognition flickers, but vanishes just as fast, swallowed by fear. I pull out my dive knife and show it to him. Letting him know I'm going to cut him free.

He sees the knife and his hands slash wildly through the water. I yank back, narrowly avoiding his mindless grasp. He's not thinking, only reacting.

I try again, edging closer with measured movements.

"Let me help you, Mark. It doesn't have to end this way. Think of Crystal and Natalie. You can get out alive."

But his struggles only intensify, and the web tightens around him with every wild twist. His panic is worsening his situation, pulling the web of line tighter and binding him more firmly.

My dive computer flashes a warning. My gas is running low. Frustration and anger swell within me, but Mark isn't giving me a choice. I dart forward, grabbing his arm to incapacitate him until I can cut him loose. He lashes out with all his strength. His kicks stir up a thick cloud of silt. The chamber dissolves into a murky blur, leaving me with no visibility. My flashlight catches glimpses of his kicks, but his face is obscured.

Then, his regulator slips from his mouth, his body jerks violently, and his mask floods. He rips it off. I shove my octopus toward him, but he bats it away, his eyes wide and wild. He's spiraling, caught in the grip of terror. My chest tightens as the realization crashes over me like a wave. I'm not going to save him. Mark is too far gone, his fear and rage sealing his fate. I back away, my flashlight lingering on him.

His struggles slow, the silt swirling around him as the tangled web of line holds him tight. Then he stops moving.

I thought he was a good man.

What happened to him? There's nothing else I can do now. I'll need to come back with others to retrieve his body.

I follow the dive line back to the main cavern. The water clears, but my thoughts remain clouded, and my chest tightens with regret.

I push those thoughts aside, focusing on the one thing that matters. Maddie. I say a prayer and move.

CHAPTER 39

MADDIE

I cling to the line like it's my tether to life because it is. The trembling of my fingers makes my hold on the nylon precarious. Exhaustion overwhelms me, threatening to pull me under. Wes's flashlight cuts through the darkness ahead, my sole focus point in this endless maze of limestone and shadow.

I force myself to concentrate on my breathing, but the clicks from my tank sound ominous.

Wes swivels, and his beam slices across the surrounding rock before settling on my face. He checks my gauge, and his expression hardens into a grim line. When his eyes meet mine again, I know I'm going to die.

I'm out of air.

My chest tightens, and panic scratches the edges of my control. Wes reaches for my arm, his grip firm.

"Stay calm. I'm going to help you." He meets my eyes directly with the confidence of a man who doesn't believe in failure. "You're doing so good, rookie. Well, I guess I can't call you that anymore now, can I? How about apprentice? Let's focus. We're going to go off comms and get out of here together. That means we'll have to move a little faster than we should, but it's going to be okay. We only need a couple of decompression stops. You can do this."

It feels like we're training again. I focus on his instructions.

"Maddie. I need to remove your mask so we can get you some air. Ready?"

I signal to him I understand and swallow hard, remaining silent even as my body screams. With steady, efficient movements, Wes swiftly removes my mask, and my face is instantly flooded with the icy cold water. Blind, I feel his octopus mouthpiece in my hand as he guides it to my mouth. My hands shake violently as I inhale from the regulator, and the first breath reaches my lungs. Relief washes over me, but it's fleeting. I'm blind and no longer have a mask. I can't possibly open my eyes. Then Wes secures his back up scuba mask to my face, and helps me purge the water. My eyes open, and I'm breathing. But without the full-face mask, our voice communications are gone. We'll have to rely solely on signals.

Wes doesn't let go of my arm. His presence is steady as he propels us forward with powerful strokes and kicks. I follow along with him as best as I can, gripping the dive line and swimming with all my strength.

Time stretches endlessly in the darkness of the underwater cave. Each motion is excruciating and slow, the passages ahead twisting and narrowing. The limestone walls press close, scraping against our tanks, each graze of rock amplifying the fear coursing through me. The water is a heavy, living force pressing in from every side, intent on swallowing me whole.

Wes moves us along as quick as he can, pausing only to check on me and to coach me on. His flashlight illuminates his face, the lines of exhaustion mirroring my own. He signals. **Keep going. Don't stop.**

The shared gas line tugs between us with every motion, binding us in this fight for survival. Each inhale is tenuous, as if there might not be enough air left for either of us. I force myself to match Wes's slower, measured breaths, even as my instincts scream to gulp the air greedily.

As we continue, the water clouds with silt once more, shrinking my world to the tension of the dive line in my hand and the pull of Wes ahead. My limbs grow heavier with each kick. My strength is fading. It's like I'm dragging the weight of the ocean behind me. We stop twice to wait out time for decompression and then move forward.

Then a soft glow breaks through the water ahead. Disbelief floods through me. Moonlight.

We've reached the main cavern exit.

His signals grow increasingly insistent, his grip tightening as my legs grow weaker. He's determined. My heart swells with hope, but my body betrays me. My breaths become shallow, and my vision blurs, a headache threatens to burst my skull open. As close as we are, I might not make it.

Wes doesn't let go. He kicks harder as he pulls me forward with all his strength. I cling to him, to the glimmer of light above.

We're in open water now, and the world expands around me. Relief washes over me, but there's no time to savor it. The surface looms above, still so far away, the moonlight shimmering like a mirage.

My limbs tremble violently as Wes pulls me upward. His strength is the only thing keeping me moving. I fight to stay conscious and breathe. My head spins.

"You're so close, Mads. You've got this. Don't give up." It's Nathan's voice, calling to me from the distance.

The water is getting brighter, the surface closer with each kick—the boat's shadow forms above us. Muffled shouts reach me. They're enough to push me one last time. I stretch my arms upward with all my strength. We break the surface, and my mask and regulator are pulled from me.

My fingers brush the ladder as Wes pushes me up, and several hands pull me up the rest of the way. I collapse, gasping, my chest heaving as the night air rushes into my lungs. My body shakes uncontrollably, but I'm alive. Tears blur my vision.

I close my eyes, Nathan's voice fading into the back of my mind like a whisper. "You did it, Maddie."

CHAPTER 40

SCOTT

As I climb up the ladder to Wes's boat, every muscle in my body screams from the strain of the dive. My movements are mechanical, like a wooden marionette who wants his legs back. Where's Maddie?

I see her sitting on the deck, wrapped in a thermal blanket. Her damp hair is plastered against her pale face. Her chest rises and falls in slow, even breaths, the rhythm comforting and maddening. I say a prayer of gratitude as I gaze at her tiny frame. She made it.

I take off my rebreather and set my gear on the bench. Years of training make the motions instinctive, but my hands shake. I walk over to her, kneel, and take her hand, kissing the back as I use my other hand to pull her close. I put my forehead against hers.

"Mark?" she asks. I shake my head. Sadness and guilt wash across her face. I don't need to know the details of what happened in the cave.

Maddie did what she had to do to save her own life, making her a hero in my book. Her eyes widen.

"What is it, sweetheart? Calm down, it's going to be okay."

"Denver, is he—"

"Denver was alive when I left him, thanks to you. Hannah got him help. He's strong. He'll pull through."

"As soon as Mark threatened me."

I clench my fists.

"Denver attacked and tried to save me."

"Everything is going to be all right now. You're safe, and we're going home."

"Thank you for finding me Scott… I love you." Her eyes close.

"I'm here. Get some rest." I hug her tighter and then rub her back until she falls asleep. I hold her like that for a while, grateful to have her in my arms, alive and safe. When I spot Wes standing near the stern, I lie her down and cover her with a few blankets, kissing her on the cheek.

Wes's gaze is locked on the water. His hands fidget with the strap of his gear bag, tightening and loosening it in a loop. I walk over and stand next to him. We stand in silence for a while.

"We made it."

Ahead, the faint glow of the island grows brighter, its familiar silhouette taking shape in the night. We're almost home.

"I'm glad she's going to be okay, and she has you to watch over her." I say nothing. "She was so brave. That cave was a fucking nightmare. She never panicked. She pushed through it like a pro. I've never seen anything like it in my life." He looks to the horizon. "You're a lucky man."

He looks lost, like he's searching for something. "They'll be coming for me soon. This is it for me." He turns to face me. His words hang in the air, heavy. He knows Garrett will make good on his threat. There's a good chance he's already released the video. Not only will it destroy Wes's reputation, but it may put him in jail. Wes says it's bogus, but perception is reality. He knows that better than anyone. Whatever lies ahead in Wes Harrington's life, it's going to be different.

After a long moment, I exhale through my nose and glance over my shoulder.

"They won't know you're here."

Wes meets my eyes, his expression unreadable. "How's that?"

"The authorities will find out you didn't make it out of the cave… It's a tragedy."

Wes nods, his mouth twitching into a faint smile. "You finally got your chance to kill me." His face is solemn. "I appreciate it."

"Me too." I pat him on the back.

Wes motions toward the dinghy, his bag slung over his shoulder. He looks at Maddie for a long moment, something unreadable moving across his face before turning to me.

"This is where I disappear."

I extend my hand, and he takes it without hesitation. His grip is firm. Our goodbye is filled with unspoken words neither of us will say out loud.

"Stay out of trouble, Harrington."

"Trouble finds me, Rickter. You know that. Tell Maddie I said goodbye."

He gets into the dinghy and steers it away into the night. I'm glad the asshole made it and will live another day. I glance at Maddie, who's just waking. I owe him my life.

The boat glides into the dock, and we work to tie up Wes's boat. The tension in my shoulders ease. Maddie steps down with Margaret's help.

The sky lightens, and the first streaks of dawn chase the night away. I slip an arm around her shoulders and we walk home.

CHAPTER 41

MADDIE

I look at the bright new sign above the door—*Maverick Key Dive Club*. A swell of pride rises in my chest. This is real. This is mine. Ours. Nathan would have been proud.

The small group of friends who made this possible are gathered around me, chatting and having fun. Margaret, Jamie, and Liam congratulate us, each holding a gift for me and shop supplies. Ms. Connor brings her world-famous island lemon bars. Hannah hugs me, squeezing the breath out of me.

"You did it." She's bouncing on her toes.

"We all did it."

"I saw the posting for swim lessons. Is it for kids only, or are you opening it to adults?"

"It's open for all ages. We'll divide up the lessons."

"Well, sign me up. You've got your first customer." I give her a big hug. I'm so proud of her for taking this step to learn to swim.

Scott's hovering on the outskirts of the crowd with his buddies. His hazel eyes fixed on me with quiet intensity. My heart flutters. When I meet his gaze, he winks. Denver stands at his side. He's healing. It'll be a long road, but the large cast around his middle doesn't stop him from standing at attention by Scott. And Ding stands by Denver. He's taken on the role of his protector.

The shop is filled with infectious joy, and we all take a tour. The smell of neoprene is heavy. Suits, tanks, and all other kinds of scuba gear line the walls and fill the shelves. To add a personal touch, the walls are covered with cheerful artwork donated by local artists.

I'm smiling, but a tug of sadness pulls beneath the surface. As I look through the window toward the water, my thoughts move to those who aren't here today. Wes, Elaine, my parents, and Nathan.

Wes. I'm the only one in the world who knows where he is.

For now.

When Scott and Wes were looking for me in the Drop, Ms. Connor convinced Garrett to not release the video. Scott also threatened him with bodily harm. Garrett didn't believe us when we told him Wes didn't make it and promised he'd release it if Wes ever had the gall to show his face in public again.

Wes's reputation isn't ruined. If anything, he's now an urban legend. Thousands of tribute videos posted in the weeks following his "death." For those of us who followed him, his older posts keep popping up in our streams. Eerily keeping his memory alive for millions for just a while longer.

Unfortunately, Garrett's still in charge of the Carter's Drop project, but the university has hired a new hotshot scientist who's expected in Maverick

Key in the coming weeks. He's a replacement for Elaine. The investors have paused the project until he gets here.

And then there's Nathan. The question of where his body is remains unanswered. I keep thinking of one day, in one of those unexplored tunnels, we'll find what's left of him. I blink away tears. When we do find him, we'll bring him home. The Coast Guard found his notes and the mysterious stone in Mark's belongings at the station. I was surprised he didn't destroy them. They haven't given them back to me yet, but have promised to after the investigation is over.

The party's almost over and I'm about to head to Scott when Crystal arrives. She's holding her little girl's hand. They approach with wide, curious eyes.

"Maddie?"

I hug her. Her eyes glisten with unshed tears. Crystal and I have talked over the phone, but this is the first time we've been face-to-face after Mark's death. She's been dealing with the fallout.

"Thank you for inviting us. I was so excited to hear about the shop and your swim school. I'm happy for you and Scott." She beams.

We're kindred spirits, and it's time we put all the darkness and sadness behind us and live for the future. Crystal kneels, whispering to her little girl, who walks up to me shyly.

"I'm Natalie." Her voice is sweet and bright. "I'm your niece."

My heart swells as my entire world is filled with the little girl gazing up at me. She looks so much like her father, with glasses which cover her light brown eyes. Eyes that are like mirrors to both Nathan's and mine.

"Hi, Natalie. I'm so happy to meet you." I kneel in front of her.

She pauses for a moment, studying me. Then she wraps her arms around my neck. Tears flow down my cheeks, and I hold her close.

"Here." She takes my hand. I feel something cold. "It's for you."

"She wants you to have it. It's one of the few things we have left of Nathan," Crystal says.

Lying in my hand is a pretty shell pendant attached to a silver chain. Examining it closer, I recognize the heart shape—Nathan's sketch.

Crystal wipes tears away. "Nathan found the shell on the beach in Belize. He gave one-half of it to me the first time he told me he loved me." She takes in a deep breath. "I promise Natalie will know her father. As much as it's possible, she'll know how much he loved her." Neither one of us can stop the flood of tears now.

"I want to give you something, too." I take Nathan's poem from my purse. I've kept it there all these months. Until now, it was the most special thing I owned.

"Nathan wrote this for you." I give her the poem.

Her eyes sweep over it. "I just wish—"

"It's okay. He's still alive… in here." I place my hand over my heart.

Crystal and I sit together the rest of the afternoon, sharing stories about Nathan's nerdy quirks, dreams, and boundless love for the ocean. We promise each other we'll raise his little family together.

After Crystal and Natalie leave, Scott grabs my hand. His grip is warm and firm.

"Come on." A secretive smile plays across his lips.

"Where are we going?"

"You'll see."

♥

Scott takes the *Adeline* into the open water. The waves shimmer beneath the afternoon sunlight as we cruise from the shore, and golden reflections dance across the surface. The wind smells of evergreen, like the air after a lightning storm, as if we're the first and last to experience it. We stop and anchor above Carter's Drop. The polished water reflects the sun, sky, and our hearts like a mirror. He cuts the engine, turns to face me with a serious expression, and sits beside me on the deck couch. I refrain from asking questions, content to let the moment's beauty wash over me.

We left the dogs at home and are enjoying companionable silence. Scott pulls me close, his familiar scent washing over me. As the sun warms our skin, he turns to me with a mischievous grin.

"Maddie." He clears his throat. "I've been through a lot in my life, have seen and done things I thought would define me." He pauses and wipes his eye. "Sweetheart, none of those things compares to you. I'm crazy about you."

I take his hand, and he continues. "Remember that first day we met at the inn? You stood before me in that sexy bikini, blazing like the sun over the desert. A goddess. Stunning and stubborn as hell. It was like boom. Surprise. All my prayers were answered. Here she is, the woman for you." I giggle at the memory. I'd had a different experience, standing there, wearing next to nothing. I was mortified, with three hot strangers and Margaret and Denver staring at me. But my future also changed that day.

"I want to share the rest of my life with you. If you'll have me." I catch my breath, and my heart thunders in my chest. He slips a ring on my finger and leans in and kisses my lips. Maverick Key, Carter's Drop, and everything else falls away.

"It looks like I'm the one that's surprised you speechless this time." He tickles my nose. His grin widens as he waits for my answer.

I look at the beautiful ring—a simple round diamond.

"God—" I put my arms around him. "I love you… yes! yes!"

He leans down and kisses me deeply. The day couldn't be more perfect. We sit there chatting about the dive shop and our wedding plans when it dawns on us that we don't want to wait.

"Let's call Daniels. He'll get someone lined up, and we'll be married before the night is over."

After calling all our friends to tell them the news and have them haul their butts up to the courthouse, my stomach drops. In all the excitement, I almost forgot to tell him.

"Uh, Scott?"

"Sweetheart?"

"Before we get married, I've got some news."

His eyes flash with concern.

"Oh?"

I'm about to give him a lengthy explanation—my missed period, feeling crappy every morning this week, the test, and how the antibiotics I've been taking for an infection after the cave dive screwed up my birth control. But instead, I just spit it out.

"I'm pregnant."

He's staring at me, shocked. After a few seconds, he composes himself, then puts me back on his lap, and pushes his hands through my hair, tilting my face upward to his. His beautiful eyes are filled with hope and love.

"You're telling me we're—"

"We're pregnant."

"Well, damn." He chuckles and shakes his head in disbelief, nuzzling his face into my neck. "Best day ever."

He nods to the boat locker. "Let's get in."

"But we're getting married tonight… all our friends are coming."

"Tomorrow?" he asks sheepishly and motions toward the sunny sky and the deep blue ocean below, both beckoning us. We've got a couple hours of daylight left.

"Okay. Let's suit up then." I laugh.

At the edge of the *Adeline*, we're holding hands. We take one more look at each other before we let go and jump, taking our giant strides into the water.

EPILOGUE

ELLIOT

The faint hum of fluorescent lights filled the dimly lit hospital hallway. It's a sound that goes unnoticed until everything else falls silent. Elliot pushed the mop across the linoleum floor, his movements conscientious but automatic. His shoulders hunched forward as he worked, carrying an invisible weight. The name on his ID badge read Elliot. The name he answered to, even though he knew it wasn't his.

"Hey, Elliot." Karen's cheerful voice sliced through the hum.

His grip on the mop loosened. Karen approached, waving a newspaper. She always found fun things to chat about during her rounds and treated him like more than a shadow lurking in the hospital corridors.

"Hi, Karen." Karen was easy to like.

"You see this yet?" she asked, stopping beside him and tapping the paper with her manicured nails. "Big news out of Maverick Key. Some guy, Bob Clark, found that billionaire's treasure everyone's been hunting for months. It's all anyone in the break room can talk about."

Elliot frowned. The name Maverick Key sent a faint ripple of recognition through him, a stirring deep in his chest. "What treasure?" he asked, leaning the mop against the wall.

Karen unfolded the paper and shoved it into his hands. The bold headline jumped off the page. *Treasure Found! Billionaire's Secret Cache Hidden in Plain View at a Local Café.*

"Turns out it was right under everyone's noses the whole time at this 'Coconut Café.' Can you believe that? All those adventurers and treasure hunters were combing through the sand and underwater caves, spending months and millions of dollars in travel and lodging, and the crate was sitting as a centerpiece in the café in plain view all along. Turns out the owners were redecorating and wanted a pirate theme that included large crates. Brilliant."

Elliot's gaze locked on the photo accompanying the article. Maverick Key's coastline was vast and lush beneath a bright blue sky. It was a simple picture, yet it struck him with the force of a shockwave. The fragment of a recollection stirred in the back of his mind, but he couldn't recall any specific detail. It was the same thing when he watched the Discovery Channel. He knew all the intellectual information shared on the National Geographic and science shows, but he couldn't remember a damn thing from his own life. He knew Maverick Key.

Karen tilted her head and furrowed her brow as she studied him. "Hey, you look like you've seen a ghost. You, ok?"

He blinked. "Maverick Key?"

She crossed her arms, leaning against the wall. "It's a beautiful place. I've been to the beaches myself a few times. It's too expensive for me to stay there, though. Have you ever been?"

Elliot hesitated. "I can't remember."

"Still nothing, huh?" She looked at him with the sympathy he was used to receiving. He didn't like it, he didn't want anyone's sympathy, he wanted to remember who he was.

He shook his head, the ache in his chest deepening. "I felt something when you said Maverick Key, but I can't remember anything."

Karen nodded thoughtfully, then grinned. "Maybe that's your brain's way of saying it's time for a change of scenery. Who knows? Maybe Maverick Key is the key. Pun fully intended." Her eyes flicked briefly to the pendant hung around his neck with a leather band, then opened the newspaper to another page. "Look here, Elliot. There are classified ads for jobs in Maverick Key. This one is for a cleaning company that services several rentals and bed and breakfasts across the island. Lodging is included."

He liked Karen's enthusiasm. He dropped his gaze back to the newspaper. The image of the island tugged at emotions buried deep inside. He knew there was some connection.

Karen gave his shoulder a gentle squeeze. "Hey, don't you work too hard tonight, okay? You're more than just the best-looking janitor this hospital has ever had. You're my friend." She gave him a quick peck on the cheek.

"Thanks, Karen."

As she walked away, he folded the newspaper she'd left behind and slipped it into his back pocket. He returned to his work, but his thoughts wandered. Maverick Key echoed in his mind like a siren's call, growing louder every minute.

By the end of his shift, the yearning had burrowed deep, scratching at his core. There was something or someone important from his past on that island.

The early morning light painted the hospital parking lot in pale gold as he stood by his car, gripping the newspaper. He didn't know what awaited him, but he was confident about this decision. He got in the car and headed northwest.

Elliot was going to Maverick Key.

Thank you for reading Maverick Key: Hearts on the Line! I'd be incredibly grateful if you left a review. Your feedback helps other readers discover the book—and means the world to me.

<u>Leave a review:</u>

www.amazon.com/review/create-review?asin=B0F5S2TJKY

<u>Want more from Maverick Key?</u>

Join my newsletter @ <u>margotkeene.com</u> for exclusive content, behind-the-scenes updates and access to ***Clint & Sandy***, available exclusively to subscribers. Follow me on <u>Instagram</u>!

ACKNOWLEDGMENTS

This book will always be the most special to me because it's my first. It's been a labor of love for the past seven months and is the culmination of my lifelong dream to write a book. I always believed I would, but as life, family, and career got busier, that dream began to feel out of reach. But I have no regrets. I couldn't have done this at any other point in my life. This was the right time.

And I didn't do it alone. To my wonderful husband, who sat down with me and said, "Yes, you can retire and focus on your dream—I've got your back." You are my hero and my inspiration. To my family and friends who believed in me and pushed me over the finish line—I wouldn't be here without your unconditional love and support.

To my editor, Jenn, thank you for helping me shape that bumpy first draft into something closer to my vision. Working with you has been a pleasure. Kristen, thank you for guiding me through the business side.

Your advice has been invaluable. To Ashley, who created a beautiful cover and interior that captures the essence and characters of the story—your artistry is amazing.

Thank you to the book community, both online and offline, for your friendship, advice and encouragement. To my early readers and ARC team, I deeply appreciate your willingness to take a chance on a new author and share your time and thoughts.

And most importantly, thank you, dear reader, for choosing this book. I hope you've enjoyed Maverick Key and love the characters as much as I do. I'm at work on the next book in the series and feel incredibly fortunate to be doing what I love. It's my sincere wish you stay with me on this journey, and I hope Maverick Key brings you joy for many years to come.

With gratitude,

Margot Keene

DISCUSSION QUESTIONS

1. What was your initial impression of Maverick Key and how did it change as the story unfolded? Can you relate the experience of this location to any memories you have about a place from your past?

2. Were there moments in the story that surprised you? Which scenes or revelations were the most impactful to you?

3. How did Maddie's journey through grief and self-discovery resonate with you personally?

4. Describe the relationship dynamics between Maddie, Scott and Wes. How did their interactions drive the plot and shape your reading experience?

5. What do you think motivated each main character? Were the decisions they made good or bad?

6. Who was right? Scott or Wes? Why? If the outcome had been different, would that have changed your mind?

7. Which character did you relate to the most, and why?

8. Discuss the significance of "found family" in the story. How do you see this theme playing out through the characters?

9. What other themes did you take away from the story?

ABOUT THE AUTHOR

After a successful career in finance, Margot Keene turned her lifelong passion for storytelling into a full-time pursuit. A Florida native with a deep love for the sun, the sea and small-town life, she writes romantic suspense set in coastal communities where love, danger and second chances intertwine.